UNLIMITED

2

Impossible Projects

By

Kevin Cox

FORWARD

I highly recommend that you read book one first. This is not a stand-alone book; it picks up where the first book left off. To my large family of siblings, cousins and in-laws, first, thank you for the feedback on book one, and second, I think you'll like the few Easter Eggs I put in here!

Kevin

TABLE OF CONTENT

CHAPTER 1

July 1999: Net worth $900 Billion

"Dad. I'm telling you this will work." said 14-year-old Alex Moore.

"I've come to trust you when you say that. But I don't see how this will work without an energy source. And it is too large to fit on a skateboard." His dad Greg replied. "We'll have to build a larger skateboard."

Alex's sister Marie and his mother Jean had come out to the garage to watch the experiment.

"Or go buy a surfboard," Jean suggested.

Both guys looked over. "Brilliant!" exclaimed Greg.

"What are you inventing today?" asked Marie.

"Anti-gravity board," Alex stated.

"Are you going to apply for another patent?" Marie asked.

"No," Alex replied. A guy named Viktor Grebennikov already applied for a patent in Russia, but it was rejected. So, he wrote a book. But it was never officially published because the technology was so advanced that the Russian government wouldn't allow the full book to be published."

"I'm curious how you got a copy of his book." asked his mother, Jean.

"THE LIBRARIAN helped me find it," replied Alex.

"You mean the ethereal or universal library you see in your dreams?" asked Jean.

"Yes. I asked THE LIBRARIAN for anti-gravity information and was given Viktor's work on the Cavernous Structure Effect," said Alex. "And today, we are building the device to attach to a skateboard but the size to lift a human body looks like it will be too large to fit."

Several months earlier, Alex had described a series of strange dreams in which he found himself wandering through an immense library composed of interconnected hexagonal rooms. He was guided by an enigmatic figure he called *THE LIBRARIAN*. This vast, otherworldly archive was said to contain every piece of knowledge ever written or that ever could be written, and it could be searched in any human language. However, there was a catch: only one section of a book could be accessed at a time. To navigate and retrieve the scattered fragments, Alex relied on the guidance of THE LIBRARIAN.

Jean asked. "Well, if this works, how are you going to control it so that it doesn't crash?" She was a lawyer and, of course, was always concerned about safety.

"If we can get the levitation to work, then we'll add a gyroscope and other control mechanisms," replied Greg.

"OK. As long as I get to do a final safety inspection," stated Jean.

Greg agreed and he and Alex went back to work building the device. "Dad, according to Viktor's book, this design was based on different insects that should be too heavy to fly, but the way their shells were constructed with these beehive-like structures we are building here, the insects actually levitate. They also have a second set of wings to control direction and speed."

"I find it hard to believe that this has existed in nature, but nobody has ever discovered it before," Greg said. "And NASA is still using big rockets to send astronauts to the space station. I wonder if this will be a better way. We'll have to experiment to see how much one device will lift."

They worked on building something that resembled a beehive for another hour. They used the dimensions from Viktor's book. After covering it with a board they could place metallic things on the board and watch them flip off, like the way magnets reacted when placed end to end.

"So, the theory is that if you put sufficient weight on top of the board covering the hive structure, the anti-gravity properties will push against the earth and lift the whole board and hive structure up," Alex explained.

"How much weight will it lift?" Greg asked.

"Don't know. We'll have to experiment. The book didn't say. But it did say that his board had multiple hives underneath." Alex explained. Then he sketched the diagram of the device Viktor built that showed a large square board with a pole and handle with some controls on it. "He didn't give any detail on the controls, and there are no pictures in the book, but I assume it would be to adjust the lift and the direction. " The pole was long enough that the handles were about chest-high to an average adult. Instead of using a skateboard that Alex originally proposed or a surfboard that Jean recommended, they created a platform using some wood that was left over from the prior summer when they had built a nice deck in the backyard. They went to the local hardware store for the other parts. They went to a Radio Shack to pick up a gyroscope because Greg thought they might need something to stabilize the contraption.

It was nearing dinner time when they finished. Jean and Marie came out to the garage to announce that dinner was almost ready just at the time Alex put a large wrench on top of the device. The wrench levitated a few inches, spun a few times, and then quickly flipped off the board. Everyone gasped as it was almost too quick to see. Alex retrieved the wrench and repeated it several times. Then, he got other nearby items to add to the test. Same result. Almost all the items ended up on the floor after getting rejected from the platform. Only the small wooden items remained inert.

Alex wandered to the open garage door and stood staring into space. The family recognized this as his 'thinking' position. He soon returned and said, "The hive structures underneath are generating a magnetic-like force upward. It's probably also generating a downward force that would lift the whole platform if there was enough weight on it. If the weight on the platform was greater than the upward force, it wouldn't get tossed off, but instead, the downward force would lift the entire platform."

"Should I stand on it?" Greg asked.

"NO!" Alex said quickly. "As fast as the tools were tossed off, this may rise too fast, and you would hit your head on the roof of the garage. "

"How about we take it down to the park?" Jean asked. "With helmet and knee and elbow pads."

Greg thought for a second, then said, "Too many people might witness this. Let's call Grandma and Grandpa Moore to see if we can go out to their house."

Jean gasped, "Dinner," and rushed inside.

"I thought we were going out to celebrate your return," Greg asked Marie. She and her best friend, Aimee Satrat, were home for the summer after visiting Aimee's grandparents in France. Aimee was the daughter of the French Ambassador to the United States. They had met years before and instantly became best friends. They had been on the same soccer team for years. Of course, Aimee called it football since she was from France.

"That was the original plan," Marie replied. "But we saw how involved you were with your project, so we decided to make dinner here."

While Greg and Alex were washing up for dinner, Marie called Greg's parents, who were delighted to hear that their grandkids were coming to visit. Ginny, their grandmother, said she was anxious to hear about her acceptance to the Sorbonne and her trip to Paris.

The discussion at dinner was back-and-forth between Marie's stories of Paris and the invention. Next door, one person turned to the other - "Can you follow what they are talking about? " Several years earlier, their long-term neighbor informed them that a Russian couple had made him an offer for his house that he couldn't refuse. The Russian couple, Ana and AntolySokolnikoff, moved in shortly after and became friends with the Moore's. Ana started joining the same running group Greg and Jean belonged to on the weekend. They had also, unbeknownst to the Moore's, bugged their house because their employer wanted Greg and Alex's first invention that would send information back to the present day from the future.

"No, but I saw them working on a project in the garage when I came home," said Ana.

"Next chance we get, we will place bugs in their garage," replied Antoly.

Greg used the device they had mentioned to receive daily stock picks from the future. Once he began investing, his wealth grew rapidly. Soon, the information expanded to include stock symbols from international exchanges in countries like England, Russia, and Japan. In response, Greg established automated trading systems in each of those countries, allowing him to capitalize on global markets around the clock.

Once the wealth started accumulating, Jean quit her paralegal job to attend Law School at Georgetown, which was near where they lived. She was now the lead corporate council for all the businesses they owned, including real estate, high-tech manufacturing, networking companies, restaurants, and Greg's newest venture – rare-earth mining companies.

When asked about it, he had to say that he didn't know why he bought all the rare earth companies except that the daily information from the future had an extra note one day that said, "Buy all rare earth. "Alex explained what he had learned about rare earth but had to admit that he didn't know yet what they were going to do with it. At this point, there were plenty of customers buying it, mostly to make computer components and other high-tech equipment. The profits from those companies were funding grants for studies at various universities that wanted to study the properties of the various rare earth elements to see how they interacted with other things in the physical world. Greg was especially interested in the study at Colorado School of the Mines that was trying to find better ways of extracting and separating rare earth minerals from tailings from other mining operations like copper, tin, silver and gold.

***

The next day, after driving four hours to Greg's parent's house in West Virginia, Greg and Alex offloaded the contraption from the minivan.

"Looks like the flock of sheep has gotten larger." Greg gestured to a nearby pasture as his parents came out of the house and approached the car.

"Yes. The wool from the sheep is a good income, so it made sense to let the flock grow." Ginny replied.

"What do we have here," asked Frank, who was Greg's father. He and Ginny, Greg's mother, lived on a 40-acre plot of land that their ancestors had homesteaded in the 1600s.

A national park bordered it on one side, a Shawnee Native American Reservation on another, and the town of Moss on the other side.

"It's an anti-gravity device," replied Alex. Then he explained about his dream visit to THE LIBRARIAN.

Frank and Ginny already knew about his dreams and thought it was fantastic. They had heard of something similar from their church group, but Alex explained that although all the religious writings from all the religions were in there, it didn't feel like they had a strict religious focus.

"How does this work?" Grandpa Frank asked Alex.

"The beehive structures glued to the bottom of the board produce energy that will counteract gravity," Alex explained.

Frank had a good reputation as a handyman who could build anything. After a few minutes of back-and-forth discussion, he had a few ideas on how to improve the stability and control of the device. They showed Frank that metallic objects like a wrench would rise up and then flip off the board. They tried non-metallic objects to show that they remained on the board. Alex explained that the energy was being generated both up and down and that once sufficient weight was placed on the board, the downward energy would overcome gravity and lift the whole contraption upward. Greg volunteered to step on the board first, but Jean recommended using a large stone just to see what would happen. There were several large stones lining the driveway. They carried the device next to one of the larger stones. Greg and Frank maneuvered it onto the device. It immediately lifted off the ground, tilted, and then the stone rolled off.

"Need a way to secure it," Frank said. "Still, that's encouraging that it would work the first time. Good thing no one was standing too close, " He muttered, eyeing the tilted board nearby.

Frank disappeared into his workshop, then came back out a few minutes later with a sturdy net. "This is used to secure loads in the back of the truck when I need to haul something." He also had a long yardstick and pencil as well as a bag. "The thing tilted because we didn't have the stone in the center. Alex, I will show you a simple way to find the center of a square." Frank proceeded to place an X on the board with the pencil and yardstick, going from one corner to the opposite one and then repeating the process from the other corners.

"What if we have to move the stone around to get it in the exact center," Greg said.

Frank pulled some stakes and leather straps out of the bag. "Already thought of that," he said. He proceeded to put the stakes in the ground around the board, then attached the holes at the end of the straps to the stakes, positioning the straps over the board. "This should hold everything down until we get the stone placed correctly.

Once again, Frank and Greg wrestled the large stone onto the board. Alex was ready with the net and threw it over. There were hooks around the edge of the net they secured to the underside of the board.

"Now, the tricky part will be to release the holding straps at the same time," Frank said. They discussed several methods to achieve this, then settled on Frank and Greg on either side. On the count of three, they slid the leather straps off. The device took off so rapidly that they didn't have time to look up before it disappeared.

"Did anyone see where it went?" Greg asked the family, who had been standing around watching.

Marie answered excitedly. "It went straight up very fast, then just before it disappeared, I think it started going at an angle."

"Maybe the stone shifted under the net, causing it to veer off." Jean said."I'm glad there wasn't a person on it."

About that time, there was a commotion in the sheep field. They looked at each other, instantly realized what happened, and ran over to the field. One of the sheep was struggling, tangled in the net as the stone was partially draped over the other side. Frank and Greg worked to free the sheep.

"Doesn't look good," Greg observed after noticing that the sheep could move its head and front legs but not its back legs.

"I'm guessing that the stone broke its back," Frank said as everyone watching gasped and groaned.

Ginny walked back to the house, returned with a pistol, shooed everyone back, then placed the pistol near the side of the head of the sheep and pulled the trigger. She stood quietly for a moment, then said, "Well… Looks like we're having fresh mutton for dinner."

As they approached the house, Greg informed his parents that their house in D.C. was bugged, but they left the bugs in place but never discussed any inventions at home. "We should have a sweep of your house done, too, just in case. "Nevertheless, for the rest of the afternoon and evening, they talked about the device, how to control it, and what to do with the invention.

"Send it over to NASA," Jean recommended. "They have engineers specializing in how to control rockets and spaceships. Let them figure it out."

"That makes sense." Greg said, then he turned to Alex. "Any idea how high it went before it came back down?"

"Depends on how long it was up there," Alex replied. "What is everyone's guess on how long it was in flight?"

A discussion ensued, with everyone offering their opinions. After careful consideration, the final estimate was around 40 seconds. "Now, we need to determine whether the device was accelerating consistently or if it slowed down as it moved farther from Earth," one of them suggested.

"We'll rely on your opinion on that one son." Said Greg. "After all, it is your vision that allowed us to build the device."

Alex walked over to the window and stared out. The family knew this was his way of putting on his thinking cap to ponder a difficult question. "I think that the further it got from Earth, the weaker the effect was on the push against the Earth. Plus, if it started to tilt, then it wouldn't have much to push against. Since the energy goes off the top and bottom of the device, it should have floated over the earth and stayed at a constant altitude where the energy couldn't overcome the earth's gravity. So it must have come down sideways. Maybe the wind moved it over the pasture; maybe the stone shifted a little as it was rising, causing it to angle over the field. Anyway, I'm sorry about the sheep."

"Don't worry about it," Frank said. "At least we got a good dinner out of it!"

***

CHAPTER 2

"What are you thinking about?" Jean asked Greg as she woke up and noticed that he was already awake. He was lying on the bed with his hands clasped behind his head, staring at the ceiling.

"A couple of things. First, what is the hardest project in the world?"

"What do you mean?" She replied.

"You were telling me that our foundation is tackling water projects in Africa and the middle east, children's education around the world. Those are very worthy causes, but I'm wondering what's next. What are considered the hardest projects in the world?"

"Our foundation think tank always has World Peace and cheap energy at the top of the list, but so far, nobody has come up with good solutions for those," Jean replied.

"Hmmm, going to have to put some thought into that. It might be the Why question Dmitry posed to us. "Greg was referring to his Russian colleague, Dmitry Balinov, who had posited the question when they first met on why Greg had invented the device that could transmit information from the future at this point in history. People who discovered his trading method and were mimicking his trades every day were also becoming very wealthy. Dmitry Balinov was one of them. It resulted in mutually beneficial partnerships in Russia and all the former Soviet Bloc countries, especially businesses, to expand the networking and cell phone infrastructure. Greg already owned much of the internet backbone in other countries around the world and had plans to go into other areas that had little to no network infrastructure.

"Another thing I'm thinking about is that instead of getting involved with NASA, I want to use this invention to build spaceships. And if we can work out the aerodynamics for flying within earth's atmosphere, I want to start a new airline company that replaces all the gasoline-powered planes."

"I admire your ambition and drive, truly," Jean responded. "And that's one of the things I love about you. You've always been a visionary. To address the practical side of these ideas, let's sit down when we get home and draw up a business plan to lay out the expenses and logistics."

"A third thing I was thinking about is the paradox of the fax. I never would have thought to invent the device to send stock picks back from the future to our fax machine if we hadn't gotten that first fax." Greg said.

"Well, you might have. When you and Alex built that first experiment to transmit energy faster than the speed of light, then you decided that the only way that would happen is if it went through another dimension. So, you probably thought about uses for that invention and came up with the idea of sending information from the future. So, I've always thought that it wasn't a paradox but a logical and thoughtful use for the device." Jean explained.

"We've always made a great team." He replied, drawing her over so her head rested on his chest. He kissed the top of her head as they dozed for a few minutes, not yet wanting to get up to start their day.

***

He felt…

He didn't know what he felt. He could tell that he was sitting on a hard chair at a table, with his head resting on his arm that was tingling. He must have fallen asleep.

He groaned as he sat up and looked around. He was in THE LIBRARY. As he rolled his neck around, he glanced up and could see bookshelves full of books, seeming to endlessly rise into a fading darkness. He glanced around the room at the five doorways, assumingly going to other rooms. That made sense because each room had a hexagonal shape. He wondered how many rooms there were. He wondered where the entrance was located because he remembered always just arriving in the same room with a single table and chair.

He also remembered that THE LIBRARIAN was always there when he arrived, awaiting instructions for which books to fetch. Now, THE LIBRARIAN was nowhere to be seen.

He stood up and instantly realized that he was hungry and had to find a bathroom. Which door to choose? He peered through the door to his right. An exact replica of his room existed that way, with a single table and chair and five doorways. As he explored each doorway, the rooms all appeared the same.

He went back through each doorway, this time looking for an exit sign or any other sign. The only difference was that his original room had a book on the table. He couldn't remember what he was last reading, only that he had been reading books on so many subjects that his brain was swirling with ideas.

By now his feeling like his need to find a bathroom was getting more desperate. So, he picked a doorway to his right and entered the room. He realized that as long as he went in a straight line, he could always turn around and retrace his steps. Soon, he was running. Nothing changed. The rooms seemed endless.

He stopped, wondering why he was not breathing hard. Out of curiosity, he extracted a book from the nearest shelf and opened it to a random page. Gibberish. None of the words made sense. Now he remembered what he was just reading. It was an explanation of the library and how it could contain all the knowledge ever written or would be written in the future.

Now, an urgent physical need cut through his awe. He had to find a bathroom. He thought of THE LIBRARIAN, and suddenly, he was standing in the next doorway, holding a book open to a page. Alex grabbed it and searched through the gibberish for anything meaningful. One sentence simply said, 'Open your eyes'.

***

"Mom, Dad! Alex won't wake up." Marie said as she went into the kitchen.

Jean glanced up, looking worried. "What do you mean."

"He's twitching a little bit and moaning something," Marie explained. "I kicked his foot and yelled his name several times, but he didn't wake up."

Jean and Ginny rushed into the main room of the house where Marie and Alex slept. They had always slept on the floor by the fireplace during their visits to this old house since there were not enough bedrooms. The sleeping bags they used during their younger years had been replaced with very comfortable air mattresses. Jean knelt, rubbed Alex's arm, and gently called his name. Alex quieted down and became very still. Jean repeated his name while still rubbing his arm. She could see that his eyes were closed, but the eyes were rapidly moving back and forth under the closed eyelids.

"He's dreaming about something." She announced.

All of a sudden, Alex opened his eyes, took a second to focus, and saw his mother's worried face peering down at him. He looked around to notice everyone in the family standing around, looking concerned. Alex suddenly sat up, threw off his blanket, and bolted to the bathroom.

A few minutes later, Alex came out to the kitchen, drying his hands on a towel, and said excitedly, "Dad, I know how you can build your own LIBRARY."

***

CHAPTER 3

Greg blinked, still shaken from watching his son awaken from a trance. "Wait… How?"

"The best way to explain it is to imagine that all words in our language had four letters." Explained Alex."Then you create a document with all possible combinations of each word, starting with 'aaaa,' then 'aaab,' and 'aaac' until you get to 'zzzz.'Now, imagine you do this with all 26 letters of the English alphabet. This means that the longest word would be 26 characters. But add capital letters, the space character, and the punctuation marks and special symbols like the dollar sign or the British Pound sign and you have a complete library."

Greg thought for a moment."The programming would be fairly easy. To store all that data would take many terabytes, which is somewhat expensive these days. But disk prices have been coming down. The other challenge would be an index strategy and a clever search function."

"And you need a way to stitch together each section until you can read a complete book," Alex said.

"What do you mean?" Greg asked.

"Here's an example," Alex said. "If you search for a phrase such as 'the white sheep,' you would get many pages returned." he gestured out the window where they could see the flock of sheep in the far field. "You would get one page with that exact phrase, one page with it all in capital letters, one with partial capitals and partial lowercase letters. One page returned where that phrase is part of a full sentence such as 'The white sheep is eating green grass in the far meadow."

Marie joined the conversation. "Wouldn't most of this library be gibberish? Because you said earlier that all combinations of all letters would form a complete library. So a search for 'the white sheep' could return 'aaaa the white sheep xyz$%* is BN&*87 eating 987%&^)&%'."

Alex nodded. "Yes. Most of the library is gibberish. It does contain every combination of every possible word and symbol."

Frank wanted to share his thoughts. "That means it could also contain false information, such as 'toothpaste is made with volcanic ash."

"Exactly," Alex said.

"So, how do you know what is real." Grandma Ginny asked.

"That's where THE LIBRARIAN comes in. I think of a topic or ask a question, and then books start appearing on the table in front of me." Alex said.

"So, when you asked about anti-gravity devices, THE LIBRARIAN could have brought you thousands of pages of things that didn't work. How did he or they know the right books to bring?" Jean asked.

"That I don't know," Alex said.

"What does THE LIBRARIAN look like and sound like?" Ginny asked.

"Remember that this is my dream, so I'm convinced that my perception of THE LIBRARIAN is something my mind can handle. To me, it is a person in a shimmering purplish cloak with a big hood. The face is in shadow so I've never seen the face. The sleeves are long, so I've never seen any hands. THE LIBRARIAN doesn't speak aloud; I just think something and a book appears with the answer. It doesn't even communicate telepathically with me, but it somehow knows what I am asking or what I want to read."

This caused excited comments around the table as everyone imagined what it would be like to visit the library. This morphed into conversations where everyone shared what they would look up.

***

After they got back to Washington D.C., Jean's personal assistant, Priya, called with an update on the Y2K party preparations. Earlier in the year, the Moore's had decided to hold a contest with a $1 Million prize to one of their companies who had the best Y2K party. There were rules and stipulations involved, of course. For example, if the police were called for any incident at the party, then that company would forfeit their eligibility for the prize. The Moores generously provided each company with the same budget for funding the party. Marie had suggested that each party be filmed so all employees from all the companies they owned could watch the clips afterward. Greg and Jean agreed since they already owned a professional film company that made the hit cable TV series, "Castle Restorations."

This particular company stemmed from Moore's meeting the family of Marie's best friend, Aimee Satrat. The Satrat family owned a large vineyard in France that had an old castle in disrepair on the property. After many discussions, the families agreed to form a joint venture with the Moores to restore the castle and convert it into a luxury vacation property with modern facilities and conveniences. It was such a hit they decided to expand the company to restore castles and historical buildings in other countries. They hired Jillian Castor, a local news reporter in Washington D.C., to film all the restorations and air them on cable television. It was a huge hit around the world.

***

CHAPTER 4

"George has called a meeting at ten o'clock," said John to his group. They were part of a team that kept track of inventors and inventions for the U.S. Government. Their main source of information was the U.S. Patent Office, where hundreds of patents were filed every day. Most of it was boring work because there were many tech companies claiming to be the first to make an innocuous improvement to software, such as a new type of drop-down menu. This team was more interested in inventions that were considered impossible or were very futuristic. Eight years ago, they were informed by another government agency that a person named Greg Moore may be someone who should be watched. Greg and his son Alex had filed a patent application but had later retracted it because it didn't work. It was an interesting patent that claimed to be able to send information faster than the speed of light.

"Alright, settle down." George said to start the meeting. "Jane, let's hear from your group that monitors the patents."

"Nothing too advanced, but a few that bear watching, and as usual, there are several in the category of 'I wish I had thought of that.'" Said Jane. "And since everyone is always interested in patents of that category, here's one that caught our attention. It's for farmers and ranchers to use a low-cost computer board to open and close doors in water pipes. It uses solar energy for power and a little bit of software for the farmer or rancher to change the schedules with their computer at home."

"What did we add to the watch list?" George wanted to know.

"It's in the AI category. One of the big software companies filed a patent for software that claims to do better facial recognition."

"John, you're next," George said.

John's team had been assigned the task of tracking not only successful inventors but also others on the list deemed "persons of interest." Their homes, cars, and workplaces were all bugged, and the team monitored every recording. It was illegal, and everyone knew it, but no one cared. The team believed that for the U.S. to stay ahead in the technological race, the rules didn't matter.

John sifted through the activity reports of those being monitored. It seemed like a dull week, nothing particularly exciting or groundbreaking.

"However…" John said, his voice suddenly charged with excitement. "Remember that guy and his son we were monitoring a few years back? The ones who claimed they invented a faster-than-light transmission device?" Several heads nodded in recognition.

"Well, it looks like they've been working on something else, an anti-gravity device, to be precise. According to our recordings, they were conducting some kind of garage project over the weekend. They placed metallic objects on a board, and they were actually lifted off; at least, that's what it looked like. We sent a van to check it out, but when we got there, nobody was home. It seems like they've disappeared."

"That puts them back on the active watch list." George said."Find out where they went. And since they are not home, add one of those new low light, motion activated miniature cameras to their house and garage."

***

"Dmitry, there were people in Greg Moore's house and garage today installing miniature cameras. "Said Antoly, who was a neighbor of the Moore's. Dmitry Balinov was a business partner of the Moore's in Russia and one of the wealthiest and most influential people in that country.

"Maybe that means they are finally on the verge of inventing their device to send information from the future," Dmitry replied. "See if you can hack into the cameras; that way, we don't have to install our own."

"That should be easy." Came the reply.

***

CHAPTER 5

Marie and Aimee started attending MUN, the Model United Nations when Marie told her parents that her mandatory Government class was her new favorite course as a senior in high school. Marie had heard about MUN from her teacher, who had participated in those sessions when she was in high school. Marie talked Aimee Satrat, her best friend, into attending as well. After getting registered, they both chose the Crisis Council to participate in. The MUN, as Marie's teacher explained, was an organization where junior high, high school, and university students could participate in United Nations simulated programs, drafting resolutions, papers, and research on relevant world problems. The Crisis Council was a committee that received a made-up scenario of a potential world crisis. They had to form teams to work on a solution, write a paper, and deliver speeches.

While seated at the U-shaped tables in a large classroom at Georgetown University, Aimee leaned over to Marie and whispered, "That guy across the way keeps glancing at us."

"Well, we are two hot, crazy girls, right?"

"No, I mean like he knows us."

The proctor paused her speaking and gave them a stern look for whispering.

Marie furtively studied him without being obvious. He was a tall, handsome Native American youth with long, straight black hair. She listened to the proctor explain their challenge this year for the conference, which was, "What if polar ice caps melt enough to cause the sea levels to rise by one foot." In her subconscious mind, she was wondering if she knew him and, if so, where.

Suddenly, it dawned on her. It was one of the young men who lived on the reservation near her Grandpa Frank and Grandma

Ginny's place in West Virginia. She remembered meeting several of the tribe members when they came to her brother's birthday party when they were younger. It must have been six or seven years ago, but she could not remember his name. His name tag was turned just enough that she could not read it. An idea dawned on her. She looked directly at him and held her name tag out so that he could clearly read it. He looked down at his and realized that it was at an odd angle relative to her, so he squared his shoulders and held the tag so she could read his name. Victor. She nodded, then waved, with the intention that he knew she remembered him. He gave a slight wave back.

At the first break, Victor walked over and reintroduced himself. They exchanged the usual questions, quickly discovering they were all high school seniors. Aimee and Marie played soccer, while Victor and his cousin Jackson played basketball and ran cross-country. Victor mentioned that Jackson was currently in another room attending the MUN Security Council meetings. He explained that this was their sixth year at MUN, having started back in junior high. The girls admitted they hadn't heard of MUN until recently. After a brief, awkward silence, Victor broke the tension by asking, "So, where did you get your outfits?"

"These are Satrat and Moore originals," replied Aimee.

Victor paused as it sank in. "Those are your last names, which means that you made them."

"Yes. We have started designing and making clothes." Marie responded.

"Very nice." He replied.

"Would you like a jacket to go with your outfit?" asked Aimee. "We've never done any men's clothing, but we've talked about starting. You could be our first runway model."

Victor was wearing a starched white shirt and a department store tie with black trousers, which was the standard dress code for MUN. "Sure. How much would it cost?"

"Nothing right now. We're not charging this year while we are experimenting with different designs." Marie said.

One of the girls, who had been sitting at the tip of the U-shaped tables, approached them and said her name was Elizabeth. As they all shook hands and introduced themselves, she said, "I noticed your clothes as soon as you came in. Is it possible I could get an outfit, too. I would be willing to pay."

"Sure. We'll take your measurements tomorrow. I will bring a tape measure." Aimee responded.

At that point, the proctor called the meeting to order and continue with the next phase of the project.

About an hour later, Marie started to fidget as she realized that she had not taken a break earlier. She really had to pee. She looked at her watch to notice that they still had about thirty minutes until the lunch break was due. She glanced at Aimee and made a desperate-looking face. Aimee returned a similar look and Marie noticed Aimee was rapidly bouncing her right leg up and down. Marie assumed that Aimee was in a similar situation.

As soon as the proctor called a lunch break, the girls bolted for the restrooms, giggling all the way. Aimee almost went into the men's room as it was the nearest door. "This one," Marie shouted as she burst into the women's room.

Victor was just emerging from the men's room when Marie and Aimee came out. "I figured that you were desperate by the way you ran out of the room."

"Yeah, sitting there all morning sipping tea, then water, we really had to go," Marie replied.

As they were walking to the dining area, Aimee asked. "Victor, what do we do this afternoon."

"Research. The goal is to present an outline and summary of a plan this evening. The first two years we spent in the Georgetown library. We still need the library for some things, but mostly we use Google. Hopefully, it's better than last year."

By that time, Elizabeth caught up with them.MUN encouraged the students to form teams; they decided that the four of them would make a team. Elizabeth informed them this was her second year at MUN. "Don't worry about feeling lost." She said. "It's common to feel overwhelmed your first year."

Jackson was waiting outside the dining area with another young man, Kaden. Introductions were made. Jackson expressed surprise and excitement because he remembered the first time he and Victor had met Marie and Aimee. Lunch was boisterous as they all got to know each other.

"We'll identify tasks, and each takes one or two," Victor explained as they walked back to their conference room.

"I didn't see a list of tasks to choose from," Marie said.

"All we are given is the problem statement. It's up to us to create a solution. The first step is to think about what can happen and create a list of tasks that need to be done to arrive at a solution."

"Yeah. My dad always says when presented with a large problem, you must break it into smaller pieces until you get to the size of pieces your mind can deal with," Maris said.

"Exactly," Victor replied. "I learned that from watching my other teammates in earlier years. Here's my ideas on the tasks."

"First, Identify the country's most likely to be affected by rising tides. Second, create a plan to deal with displaced citizens. Third, establish a budget, with something called "Sources and Uses of

Funds. "It's a standard way of figuring out how much the solution will cost and where the money will come from.

CHAPTER 6

Jean stood in her top-floor office overlooking the Potomac when the desk phone buzzed. "Hello, Keith Williams, it's been a while since we talked," she said as she answered. She had been thinking about what to do since Bernice, the CEO of their real estate corporation, had announced her retirement. Keith had been the CFO of their real estate division for several years. Bernice had mentioned that he was a great hire by improving the money handling, upgrading the business management software and overall fiscal policies of the corporation.

"Not very good news from our San Diego office," Keith informed her. "Last month, the head of the accounting department for the West Coast division had told me that he was checking into a rehab clinic to deal with a cocaine problem. I sent Sally, one of our rising stars, out there to fill in. She just emailed me that there's something funny going on with the books."

"What have you discovered so far?" She wanted to know.

"That's all we know right now. I'm heading out there tomorrow to lead the investigation."

"Why not take your family along? They could use a break from this rain, too, especially with schools on break. I'll text you the number of our charter airline. "I will call them and put you on the approved list for future flights."

***

Keith called Jean a few days later to explain that there was an embezzling scheme in place. Invoices were being paid to a fictitious company. Keith was keeping their findings quiet until they could discover who was behind the scheme.

"Do you think it is the accounting manager with the drug problem?" Jean asked.

"He's certainly on the list of suspects. But we'll keep digging. I'll call when we have more information." Keith replied."And by the way, we are having a problem getting payment on a lease on one of the new buildings in north San Diego. It's a biotech startup. I talked with the owner, and he says he's trying to raise money to finance his venture."

"Send me his contact information, and I'll have my husband call since he's the more of the science guy."

***

The next morning at breakfast, Greg turned to his son. "Alex, have you ever heard of self-healing concrete?"

"No, but it sounds cool. Why?"

"I talked to a guy last night in San Diego who is starting a new biotech company to make it. He says it is something the ancient civilizations used to create buildings that would last. They mix some kind of bacteria in the water when making the mortar."

"Oh, I'm taking biology at school. Physics and math I understand but biology is not really my thing yet. Why don't you call Dr. Bergstrom at Johns Hopkins?"

Dr. Bergstrom was the head scientist at the brain research department who was leading the study on Synesthesia. Alex had been diagnosed with that condition when he was 5 years old, and the family had agreed to have Alex participate as a research subject. It was discovered that Alex's brain could quickly absorb complex topics. As a result, by the time he was in second grade, Alex was doing calculus and studying physics. In the eight years since he had started, Alex had gone from being a subject of research to participating in advanced projects as a part-time employee. Although he agreed to still take brain scans and other tests to further the research on Synesthesia, he participated in other projects dealing with hard physics problems. The agreement with Johns Hopkins was that he would continue to attend high school even though, in most subjects, he was way ahead of the other students.

"Good Idea. I'll call him later. I'm sure he has a colleague doing biological research." Greg replied.

"Or better yet, look it up in your LIBRARY," Alex suggested.

"Oh, that. I've written the software to create the content. That wasn't too hard. But the IT guys tell me that the server farm to hold all that data is not quite ready yet. Apparently, there is a shortage of disk drives, so we are waiting on a shipment to get the last few terabytes installed. And I haven't finished the search and stitching software yet. The algorithm to stitch the pages together is turning out to be more difficult than I thought."

Greg was referring to the LIBRARY, a digital archive designed to contain all knowledge ever written and even what might one day be written. This library contained all combinations of letters, numbers and symbols. A search would return exact hits, one page at a time. The challenge was to stitch the pages together since a complete book would have pages in different sections of the LIBRARY. The other challenge with the stitching algorithm was that there were more pages with the wrong information than with the correct information.

"While we are on the topic of complex systems, I've been meaning to ask what you think about building a quantum computer. It would help solve your problem because it would be much faster than an ordinary computer, like a million times faster." Alex said.

"Yeah, I've been reading about some of the big high-tech firms that have started building their own. They need near absolute-zero temperatures for the quantum chips to work. "Greg replied.

***

After breakfast, Greg drove to his office in the secure campus he had purchased a few years earlier. It had been a government project that had run out of budget, so Greg bought it. His first call was to Dr. Bergstrom who gave him the name and number of his colleague heading up the biological research department. Greg had an interesting reaction when he introduced himself.

"Are you related to Alex Moore?"

"He's my son; why do you ask?"

"Everyone knows the whiz-kid Alex even though he's never been on this side of the campus. What can I do for you?"

The remainder of the conversation was about self-healing concrete. The consensus was that it could be possible, but as far as this guy knew, nobody he had heard of was even doing research on it. Greg said he had Googled it, but no hits came back. When asked why he was interested, Greg explained that a new startup was forming to finish the research and make it a real product.

After another conversation with the biotech inventor Bruce Vendowski, Greg had a good feeling about the project and decided to invest. He called his wife.

"I'm flying to San Diego today to have dinner with that biotech guy you told me about. If it looks good, we might invest in that company."

"Take Keith Williams with you to help structure a deal. He's in San Diego investigating a possible embezzlement issue at our office."

During the flight, Greg looked up Bruce Vendowski. Impressive credentials, with an undergrad in Engineering at Stanford, a master's in biology from MIT and an MBA from Wharton.

***

After landing at the private section of the San Diego airport, Keith met him in a rental car, then they drove over to the building that Bruce had leased from Moore Realty (owned by Greg and Jean), but had not paid for. There was a flurry of activity as workers were doing a buildout of the former empty first floor. Bruce showed them where the clean-room chambers would be. Construction would start on that as soon as the right amount of funding came in.

Dinner with Bruce and Keith took place at a nice restaurant in the Gas Lamp district. Bruce was an interesting character with a total nerd vibe. Greg later described him to Jean as a thirty-something with a high forehead and a scraggly mustache. After a short discussion on the science behind the idea, Greg asked about patents. Bruce had the patent application filled out but needed the first round of funding to land before he could afford the patent filing charge and possible patent attorney fees. Greg nodded because he understood the process and the cost, having gone through it before. Keith wanted to know about the financing side of the deal, and Bruce was surprisingly well-informed about how to structure deals. He was initially asking for ten million dollars for a five percent stake in the company. Keith's initial reaction was that it was a high price to pay for such a small stake.

Greg jumped in with a question. "Why did you sign a lease and start building the space before you had the money?"

Bruce answered, "The funds are currently mine from mortgaging my house, which I inherited when my grandfather passed away recently. But that's almost gone. There was another venture capital company interested, so I signed the lease and got started when they looked like they were going to sign a deal. They backed out at the last minute, saying they were more interested in biotech firms that were doing human-based research on cancer, longevity, obesity and things like that."

Bruce also presented a plan for the use of funds. The most expensive items on the plan were the build out of the clean rooms and hiring the scientists that would help perfect the formula. Greg was also accustomed to that part of building a company, having been through it before and seeing what the salaries of scientists were these days. The only negative was that it could take a long time to prove that the concrete would last longer than normal concrete, up to ten years. But on the positive side, Bruce explained, if it worked, they would be selling the product to all infrastructure projects around the world.

Greg decided to go ahead with a deal but had learned through his charity foundation not to give all the money at once. So, he proposed a plan to Bruce to fund several rounds of financing, starting with one million dollars and free rent for one year, but added that stipulations would be written into the contract that more funding would only be available if certain goals were met. Bruce agreed. Keith agreed to stay in San Diego for another week to work with attorneys to structure a deal and arrange the financing.

***

"That Keith guy is amazing," Greg told Jean when he got back home. "We should find a bigger role for him in the company."

"I'm going to offer him the CEO position now that Bernice is retiring." She replied.

"Great idea. And we need to fly to San Diego at the end of the week to sign the papers for the investment in the biotech company." Greg said.

"Oh good, a nice break from this crappy November weather would be wonderful."

***

Greg and Jean had a nice few days in San Diego despite the bad weather following them. Greg had imagined Southern

California as sun-soaked and warm, but the forecast was all gray skies, drizzle, and wind. They definitely did not bring the right clothes. Jean had the perfect solution, "We're going shopping!"

The signing of the paperwork went smoothly. Despite the weather, the Moore's decided to don windbreakers and hats for a trip to the famed San Diego Zoo. It was, as Greg put it, "Better crappy weather than Washington D.C.".

We should bring the kids here," Greg said as they strolled to the elephant section. "They'd love it. This place is unlike any zoo we've ever visited."

"I believe our foundation is one of the donors of the conservation fund here," Jean said. She was more active with the foundation than Greg was. He had originally gotten involved in several water improvement projects in the Middle East and Africa but had not been paying much attention to other projects.

"By the way. American Express called and offered us their new black credit cards. It's supposed to be a way that vendors can recognize people with extremely high credit ratings, so if we want to buy something really expensive, they don't have to go through any credit checks." Jean said.

"Interesting," Greg responded. "Let's give them a try. And get some for our parents, too."

***

Back at home, over a dinner discussion, Marie and Alex were interested in the description of the zoo and their parent's trip to San Diego. Alex said he and Sam had made the freshman high school basketball team. The coach told them that they only made the team because they were in better shape from running cross country than the rest of the guys trying out. He mentioned that they would have to work hard on their skills if they wanted to see much playing time. Marie mentioned that she and Aimee had made several prototype dresses for different occasions, especially for prom. Marie was thinking about inviting Victor to the prom dance, even though he didn't go to her school. Jean told her that she would need to get special permission from the school in order to invite an outsider, meaning someone who didn't go to that school.

On Friday that week, Keith texted Jean and Greg and asked them to join a Skype conference call. "I have bad news and worse news." He informed them when the call started. "The bad news is, we've identified the culprits behind the embezzlement scheme and are ready to press charges." It appears that all three people in the accounting department were involved, which leaves us without anyone else here to do accounting except Sally, who said she only agreed to fill in for a few weeks and can't stay much longer. The detectives say they need to confiscate everyone's computer and our server and take any paperwork, which effectively shuts down our normal accounting process. Fortunately, it doesn't seem like any of our real estate agents were involved."

"How did Sally notice the problem?" Jean asked.

"First, I asked her to find out why their margin was a lot less than the other divisions. It took her a few weeks, but she finally tracked it down. Second, the other people in the department kept making it difficult to find anything. Third, two of the three people have not shown up for work in a few days."

"How much was embezzled?" Jean asked.

"About $2.2 million. It was done through fraudulent invoices to fictitious cleanup and construction crews whenever a property would turnover." Keith explained.

Greg chimed in, "Ouch. Is that the worst news, or is there more?"

Keith paused. "That's only the tip of the iceberg. The worst part is that Bruce has vanished. We may have been scammed."

Stunned silence was the answer from the other side, so Keith went on explaining. "I went to the building he had leased to check on the progress and to see if he needed anything from us. Everything is cleared out. I called the police when he didn't answer his phone. The detective assigned to the case went to the address he had put on the lease agreement. It turns out that it was a legitimate address and that Bruce had been staying there, but when the apartment manager let them in, the only item in sight was a cell phone on the floor. He called the local office of the FBI and asked them to get involved."

"So, he cleared out as soon as the million-dollar funds were transferred?" Greg asked.

"Appears so!"

***

CHAPTER 7

"Ok, go," Marie told Aimee. They were trying to ditch Aimee's security team because they wanted to go to a party that Aimee had heard about at school. Aimee, as the daughter of the French Ambassador, went to a private high school. Marie went to one of the local Washington D.C. public high schools.

Aimee got up from the table at the coffee shop and went to the bathroom. The bathroom window was large enough for an escape, but unfortunately, it didn't open. She pretended to stretch as she exited the bathroom and glanced toward the back door. One of her security guards was standing there. 'How did he know?' she thought. She waved and returned to the table. 'We'll have to come up with another plan,' she said. "The girls kicked around other options while finishing their tea and came up with an idea they were sure would work.

They exited the coffee shop, pretending to argue, and got in Marie's car, which was parked at the curb near the shop. She was driving the family's old minivan. Aimee got in the front passenger seat but left the door open. The girls were speaking in raised voices, loud enough for the two security guards to think they were having an argument. Aimee gave the security guards a minute to get to their car, then ducked down, slid out of the seat, crawled under the door and kicked it closed. She walked in a crouch to hide between cars in front of them. Marie drove off, looking in the mirror with satisfaction as the car containing the security guards followed her.

Marie drove at a steady pace to avoid losing the tailing car as she headed to the party. It was dusk, but there was still enough light to see that parking near the party house would be a challenge. She spotted a space as she drove around the corner, parked, got out and started walking toward the party.

The security guards immediately stopped, rolled down their window and demanded, in French, to know where Aimee was. Marie replied, in French, that Aimee was supposed to be with them. She explained that they had an argument and that Aimee had left to get a ride with them. The guards were confused and spoke to each other briefly. One jumped out to inspect Marie's car and, upon seeing it empty, jumped back in his car, then accelerated rapidly to go back to the coffee shop. Five minutes later, Aimee arrived in a cab.

As usual, they were dressed in their new Satrat and Moore designs they had made a few days earlier. They wore their creations everywhere, even to school or while doing chores. Whenever anyone asked them, they never responded, 'We made them,' instead, they said in an excited voice, "These are the new Satrat and Moore designs. "When asked where they got them, they handed out a card that said 'Satrat and Moore' in a fancy script, accompanied by a website. You can buy these online."

The party was crowded. The music was loud. Aimee introduced Marie to some friends and schoolmates as they made their way to the kitchen to get a drink. On the way, they passed a group getting beer in red plastic cups from a keg. They kept going, looking for wine or punch. A handsome young man was mixing drinks from different bottles. He handed Aimee a green cup and said, "Try this."

She took a sip. "Oh, this is good. What is it?"

"Mai Tai."

Aimee offered Marie a sip, who agreed that it was indeed good. He made her one of her own. The two girls wandered to the backyard, where everyone was dancing. Marie noticed they weren't really dancing just hopping with their hands in the air. They joined in.

The music changed to an upbeat techno song, and the crowd parted to form a circle. One of the boys set his drink down, entered the circle and started break dancing. They watched as a few other people traded off to take turns showing off their skills. Aimee chugged the remainder of her drink and announced that she was going to get another. Marie noticed her drink was not even halfway gone. She nodded as she turned to watch the dancing again. She didn't see Aimee stumble slightly before disappearing into the kitchen.

Marie watched, mesmerized, as the dancing got better and more athletic with moves she would have thought impossible. She wasn't sure how much time had passed, but it had been several songs, and Aimee was not back yet. Marie turned to look for Aimee and grab a refill. Her head felt woozy, and her legs a bit rubbery. The feeling got worse as she left the kitchen to see if Aimee was in any of the front rooms. Needing fresh air, she wandered out the open front door and was accosted by Aimee's security guards, who had returned.

Marie's brain would not function properly, but she managed to let the guards know that Aimee was there but had disappeared. One guard charged through the crowd to the upstairs floor. The other rudely pushed his way through the ground floor rooms, through the kitchen and to the backyard. He soon returned to make his way up the stairs, where Marie could hear a commotion. Both guards soon returned, one assisting Aimee, who was missing her blouse. The other followed, carrying her blouse. Once out the front door, they helped a crying Aimee put her blouse back on while several of the partygoers had their phones out, filming the event. Marie stood there in a trance, watching but not comprehending.

One guard approached to scold Marie but sighed heavily upon seeing her state. He took her by the arm, and the four of them walked out to the car. The guards had parked in the middle of the street with their doors open. There was an angry driver of another car who was trying to drive down the street. He was yelling that he would call the cops if they didn't move their car. He didn't have to call the cops. The lead guard called Aimee's father for instructions, then drove around the corner to Marie's car, then called the police, telling them the address of the party and mentioning illegal drugs.

Marie was strapped into the front passenger seat of her car. One guard drove her car, and they proceeded to the Moore's house, where Marie was escorted inside. Though still woozy, Marie had regained enough clarity to recount the night. She gave a short version of what happened, and then Jean took Marie to her room and put her to bed. Greg talked to the guards for a few minutes before calling Sebastien to tell him that Marie and Aimee would be fine and to thank him and his security crew for rescuing the girls.

***

Marie woke in the morning with a dry throat and a parched mouth. She grumbled as she made her way to the kitchen, hoping that nobody was there. No such luck. Both her parents had chosen to work at home that day, probably waiting to pounce and yell at her for sneaking out to that party.

To her surprise, they were calm and initiated a meaningful conversation with her, asking what she had learned. Marie apologized profusely in addition to giving a full recount of the party, the incredible break dancing, and then getting confused while desperately trying to find Aimee.

"The drugs are called 'ruffles'; they are given to girls to get them disoriented and helpless. Then, the guys take them to a room to have sex with them while their resistance is low. "Greg explained.

Marie chugged a glass of water and felt slightly better. She poured some orange juice as her mother cooked scrambled eggs and toast.

After consuming all that, she was still hungry. A ripe banana finished breakfast, and she finally felt full. She wandered back to her room, texted Aimee, then flopped on her bed and fell asleep again.

A ping from her phone roused her. "UGH," the message read, it was from Aimee.

Marie hit the dial button and heard water running and muttered speech coming from the other end. "Sounds like you are in the bath," Marie said.

"Very hot with lots of bubbles."

"That sounds great," Marie replied as she got up and headed to her bathroom, noticing that it was already 3 pm. She turned on the faucets, lit a candle, poured in some bubble gel and got undressed. She turned up the sound on her phone so she could hear Aimee over the noise created by the running water. Marie explained that she had already had a post-event conversation with her parents and that they had been gentle but firm in their admonishment.

Aimee recounted her side of the tale, saying that her mother, Monique, yelled at her for the first time in a very long while. Monique, normally a quiet, well-mannered person, had let Aimee know very sternly that she was in trouble. Sebastien, her father, had postponed meetings at the embassy to stay home until Aimee finally awoke just before noon to wander into the kitchen. He too, scolded her, adding to Monique's diatribe to explain this was an example of why she should not evade her security team. Aimee apologized profusely, made a piece of toast then said she was headed to the bath. They both admitted they still felt groggy and disoriented.

There was a period of silence before Marie heard music coming from the other side. Aimee had started a Loreena McKennitt station. "Good choice," Marie said as they kept the call open, laying back to soak in the soothing music.

An indeterminate amount of time later, Marie jolted awake as Alex burst into their shared bathroom. With his back to her, he threw open the toilet lid, zipped down his pants and forcefully started peeing. "ALEX!" yelled Marie. Startled, he jumped and turned, spraying pee all over the wall and floor.

"Arrhg!" he exclaimed, turning back to finish peeing in the toilet. "Look what you made me do!"

"You didn't knock or anything." She yelled at him.

"You didn't lock the door like you're supposed to!" he yelled back at her.

"Enjoy the show, perv?" she responded as she sunk under the remaining bubbles.

"You don't have any boobs, your skinny wench." He said as he grabbed a dry cloth from the cabinet to clean up his mess.

"Get Out!" she yelled, "You can clean that up later. "They heard giggling from the other end of the phone. Marie had forgotten that the call was still live.

"You don't have anything to laugh about either, you sexy toothpick," Alex said to the phone. He bolted back to his room, closing the door before Marie could splash him with more water.

"That was hilarious." Aimee told her, then after a few seconds of silence, "Did you see anything?"

"Yeah. Let's just say it's too bad he's my brother."

***

CHAPTER 8

"Five, Four, Three, Two, One!" the crowd shouted. "Happy New Year!"

The Moores decided to attend the Y2K party held at the headquarters of their real estate company in Washington, D.C. They had recently completed a 30-story modern high-rise just outside Washington, D.C., off Interstate 66, with a commanding view of the Potomac River. The top floor housed the executive offices and a large open space specifically designed for the Y2K celebration, which was planned to be converted into additional office suites afterward.

After all the videos were posted on the company website and all the employees voted, there was a tie between the Castle Restoration company party and the Greek Real Estate company party. The crew doing the castle restorations had grown quite large since it had started due to the numerous castles being restored simultaneously. It was a multi-national company with workers from many European and North African countries involved. They had decided to have the Y2K party in a partially restored castle in the south of Portugal.

The castle was a blend of Moorish style and traditional European style architecture. Greg had paid for travel for all sixty people from around the continent to get to the location. Some were staying at the castle; some were staying at nearby resorts. The camera crew did a fantastic job documenting the castle and the grounds, starting with the cliff overlooking the sea and the arrival of everyone at the costume party. The castle's majestic towers and fortified walls exuded an air of ancient splendor. Its ornate walls and splendid courtyards were adorned with elaborate patterns and calligraphy. The hues varied from pale blue to a deep ocher, which complemented the greenery of the gardens. The camera crew boss decided to mark her calendar to return to get new shots of the blooming flowers in spring. The elaborate water fountains and water channels were in the final stages of restoration and would be done by spring.

Inside, the rooms were ornate with a blend of opulence and simplicity, showing a history of art and architecture. Stained glass windows, intricately painted ceilings, detailed floor tiles and carved wooden beams echoed the rich heritage of the Moorish culture. It had been built at a time when the Moors came across from northern Africa to rule Spain and Portugal. The restoration crew consisted of Spanish workers as well as architects and specialized craftsmen from Morocco who had knowledge of ancient methods of building. This castle is a testament to the rich diversity of Spain's cultural tapestry.

The party started early with a sunset dinner overlooking the Atlantic, then a lively gambling room with music and drinks and a grand prize to the person who won the most chips for the evening. One hour before midnight, the party shifted to the castle ballroom, where an orchestra was playing a variety of modern and old-style classical music. A choreographer was hired to teach a traditional sixteenth-century dance, which turned into a source of laughter as many guests clumsily stumbled through the steps.

Dance contests for the best waltz, the best jitterbug and the best break dance took place. At midnight, the champagne flowed freely as everyone counted down to welcome the new year. The party went strong for another two hours before everyone started drifting off to bed.

The Greek party was similar, being held in a large villa the Moore's didn't even know they owned but vowed to visit after seeing the video for the Y2K party. Everyone was dressed in traditional Greek outfits. Dinner was a long affair, only a portion of which was recorded by the camera crew, who apparently stopped filming after being cajoled into joining. A traditional Greek 'Glendi' shows the spirit of 'Philoxenia,' which is the love of strangers accompanied by the desire to make guests feel welcome. Hosts of these parties go to great lengths to make everyone feel welcome, whether close friends, family or newcomers.

After dinner was a variety of games and competitions, two of which looked rather dangerous – a spear throwing and an axe throwing competition. The other games were rather mild in comparison but looked fun nonetheless. The ping pong ball toss into a row of fishbowls looked easier than it was; only two out of about a hundred balls landed successfully, while the rest bounced around wildly before falling off the table. Flower garland tossing onto pegs set into a board mounted on the wall was equally challenging. There were a variety of other games filmed by the crew as they meandered through the crowd.

This was the only family affair of all the parties, with children being allowed to attend. By the time the dancing started about an hour before midnight, the camera crew got great shots of the smaller children asleep in various locations around the room. At first, the dance seemed subdued but soon picked up as traditional Greek music and dances started. There were cute segments of children learning traditional dance steps. By midnight, the crowd was quite boisterous, and the countdown to welcome the new century was very loud. One of the reasons this party got so many votes and eventually the winning vote by Greg and Jean was the finishing segment, where the entire party moved the dancing out to the chilly morning air on the veranda to watch an absolutely stunning sunrise. The party showed no sign of slowing down. The food kept coming, the music continued, and children were waking up and joining again. Elders had gathered at a long table, clapping in rhythm to the beat, tapping their feet and swaying in sync with the music. The energy of the event transferred to the viewers of the videos, who said they felt the sense of community generated by this party.

***

CHAPTER 9

Alex and his best friend Sam were eating lunch in the school cafeteria. "Dude, we ought to invent the Invisibility Cloak from the Harry Potter books!" Sam said. "How would that even be possible?" he continued after a moment. After no response from Alex, he glanced over and saw him lost in thought. "Earth to Alex," Sam said and waved a hand in front of his face. "What are you thinking about?"

"Do you think we'll make the varsity baseball team?" Alex asked. He and Sam had been playing baseball since little league, starting when they were 6. Plus, they had been taking Karate lessons for several years, and both ran on the Cross-Country team at the start of this school year and the prior year when they were freshmen.

"Maybe. With this size of school, there are a lot of people trying out for baseball. But we did make the JV team as freshmen." Sam replied. They had learned last year that this school had a varsity, junior varsity and freshman baseball teams.

"Hmmm, you'd have to bend the light away from it or make it absorb the light somehow," Alex said.

"What the bleep are you talking about?" Sam asked.

"Your suggestion to make an invisibility cloak," Alex replied.

"Impossible," Sam said. "But you'd have to admit it would be super cool! Or invent a 'Beam-Me-Up' device like they have on Star Trek."

"Not as impossible as you might think," Alex explained. "I'll just have to think about those for a while."

Sam had known about Alex's special condition called Synesthesia and his participation in studies at John's Hopkins Research Institute. As a result, Alex was already at university graduate level in math and physics, even though he was in his sophomore year in high school. What Sam didn't know was that Alex had shown his dad the basis for their first invention of sending information from the future back to the present day. Alex had envisioned the hardware side of things, and then Greg had written software to control the content and logic for that information to come to their fax machine at home.

***

Jean and Greg flew to London at the recommendation of another billionaire they had met after mentioning that they needed a private security firm. They were staying at their Mayfair flat they had purchased a few years earlier. It came with a live-in husband and wife team that had worked for the prior owners. Sawyer Kenworthy, the owner of the security firm, sent a car for them. Jean and Greg enjoyed viewing the different historical buildings as the car wound through the streets of London.

After explaining that they needed added security because several situations had occurred, such as Greg's kidnapping a few years earlier, and they had been targets of several cons. as the reasons they needed increased security, Sawyer gave them the background of the security company and his transition from British Military SAS team to providing security for corporations and high net worth individuals.

Jean and Greg were impressed with the offers and signed up for services right then, even though they were outrageously expensive. Sawyer assigned them a project manager who would oversee the teams in various countries that would engage wherever they were. The British project manager, Rory Hunter, would meet them the following morning for a security sweep of their flat and the common portions of that building. Greg had a question for Sawyer, "We've been using various charter flight companies but have talked about getting our own plane. What do you recommend."

"There are pros and cons for each, but for security purposes, it is better to stick with one or two companies you trust because they constantly spend money on security and upgrades," Sawyer explained. "We also have three of our own planes if you choose to use them."

Jean told him which companies they regularly used, and Sawyer approved several of them that he was in contact with.

A sweep of the building the next morning and their flat uncovered several older-style bugs that Rory explained had probably been there for more than thirty years. He also explained that there was no way to tell without a lot of other equipment who was receiving any of the signals. The sweep team also found some bugs in the lobby and one in the old lift. All were promptly removed. A regular schedule of sweeps was agreed upon. Rory was given contact information for the live-in housekeeper and her husband, who had also been involved in the morning activities and future planning.

Rory also gave them lessons on common security awareness and procedures. Plus, the Moore's learned they would get assigned a driver in any country they went to if they gave 48-hour notice or were flying on one of Sawyer's planes. Rory had also arranged for their U.S. security manager, Pike Mason, to meet them at home and their office buildings for another sweep.

On the plane ride back, Jean mentioned, "Rory could have kept talking all day. I just love his Scottish accent."

Several days later, Pike Mason called to schedule a security review of their house and offices. Greg had his main office in a secure campus he purchased years before when the U.S. government had started the construction but decided to abandon the project due to lack of budget. The campus was complete with a 24-hour manned guard shack at the front gate. One of the buildings was occupied by

Lawrence Woollcott and his team, which did military contracts to build and test special devices. Another building housed Greg's office and the office of the head of Campus Security, retired Colonel Raymond, who had regularly been encouraging Greg to increase security for his family and businesses. There was no need for Pike Mason to sweep for bugs on this campus as the Colonel did it regularly. But Pike did find several bugs and cameras in their house, one in the car and one in the garage. Greg and Jean agreed to leave the bugs in the house and car there, and they informed the children about the bugs and warned them not to talk about any inventions at the house or in the car.

Colonel Raymond had been Greg's first hire on the secure campus. When he purchased the property from the U.S. Government, he was handed the keys by a recently retired Colonel who had overseen the building of the property. The campus was about seventy-five percent done and needed more construction. In the conversation about his intentions for the property, Greg realized he needed help to finish the build-out and to hire a security staff so he offered Colonel Raymond a job on the spot. Greg often reflected that it was one of his best hires as the Colonel quickly became a mentor and friend even though he was about twenty years older than Greg.

***

"Other than the embezzling you discovered, how are you liking your work life?" Greg asked Jean one night as they were getting ready for bed.

"I just love it!" Jean exclaimed. "If you had asked me ten years ago where I saw my life going, I would never have envisioned being the CEO of CEOs."

"Is that your title?" Greg asked.

"I don't really have a title, but that sounds like a great one," she replied.

Jean had the idea several years earlier to create a holding company to oversee all the other corporations. Greg watched her grow and blossom as she built all the corporate structures, hired people and managed boards of directors. Greg attended some of the meetings since he was technically on all the boards, but he preferred to focus on the logistics and tactical aspects of the companies.

"I see you like an orchestra conductor, heading all these companies. "Greg told her. "Always knowing what strategy to apply to all these moving parts."

She snuggled next to him. "I'm grateful that you are taking care of all the issues that crop up when implementing my ideas. "Then she snuggled closer.

"What about the bugs?" he whispered in her ear.

"Let them listen!" she whispered back as she kissed him.

***

Greg came home from his office and saw Alex and Marie standing by the mailbox looking like they were having a deep conversation. After he parked in the driveway, he walked toward them. "Go away, Dad." Marie said, "We are planning a surprise for you."

"Is it better than the taser-proof jacket you made me before? "Greg asked.

Both children shrugged and said, "You'll see."

Greg walked into a silent house. Then he remembered Jean said she would be late due to a business acquisition meeting. One of their companies was acquiring another company that was struggling. It was her first acquisition, and she said she was learning a lot from the specialty firm she hired to oversee the process.

Over dinner, Alex asked, "Dad can your manufacturing company make a spool of thread made out of special materials?"

"I don't think so; it mainly makes electronic components and circuit boards," he replied. "Why do you ask?"

"It's for the surprise we want to make you," Marie replied.

"I'll put out some inquiries and see what I can find," Greg said.

Jean came home around 10 pm, tired but elated. Greg smiled as she had a few bites of the dinner he had saved for her, chattering all the while about her day. As they went upstairs toward their bedroom, Jean suddenly stopped talking and looked at Greg. "Here I am, prattling on about me. You look like you want to say something."

"Can you handle managing more companies?" he said, pointing at the bug in the ceiling fan.

"We can probably make it work," she said with a nod. "What kind of companies?"

"I don't know yet." he said as he wrote 'Come to my office tomorrow' on a pad they had been keeping by the bed. Then he continued speaking, "I have a vague idea for several new ventures, but it's going to be very expensive."

"How expensive?"

"VERY," came the reply.

***

"Wonder what that's all about?" Ana said to her partner Anatoly as they were listening to the recording the next day. They were one of the two groups who had bugged the Moore's house to find the invention. They had told their boss back in Russia that they were sure that the hardware had already been built, but they had not been able to find it, nor had they heard the family talk about it again.

Jean was waved right through security when she arrived at the guard gate at the campus that housed Greg's office. Greg had ordered lunch on the patio from the chef who was employed on the campus.

"So, tell me about this new idea." Jean inquired.

"Actually, it's two ideas," Greg replied.

"First, Alex has been talking about creating a quantum computer. I want to build one."

"Wow, how I see why you said VERY EXPENSIVE last night!" Jean responded. "But tell me, do you have any knowledge of how to do this?"

"Sort of, there have been plenty of articles online about the basics. Quantum computing has been at the forefront of big computer companies for several years. I need to hire the best and brightest hardware and software engineers to start a research company to build a quantum computer. And I have an empty building on this campus with subterranean basement levels that would house fairly large teams if needed."

They ate in comfortable silence for a few minutes, each absorbed in their own thoughts. Jean looked at Greg and said, "You said there were two ideas; what is the second one?"

"The counterterrorism thinks tank group I started a few years ago has come up with some ideas on how we can better react to threats against our family. They gave me a synopsis but are putting together a full presentation for both of us. I think it's going to need some new inventions, so I need to either buy a specialty manufacturing company or create one."

"We certainly have the money. But I'm worried whether you have the time to take on a new project of this magnitude." Jean said.

"I'm learning from you to hire the best people to run the companies and trust them to do most of the work while occasionally getting involved to set strategic goals."

"Then I would recommend that you hire yourself a personal assistant. Mine has been a lifesaver." Jean counselled.

"What qualities should I look for?" Greg wanted to know.

"Someone who did not turn their brain off after high school. Organized, efficient, assertive, good with people, can listen well, can delegate and someone who is a gadget nut."

"What does that mean?"

"Someone who loves to test all the new products that come in the market, like new cell phone versions, even new coffee makers." She said.

"Will you help me interview?" he asked.

"Sure. In fact, I'll have my assistant, Priya, put out the notice and set up the interviews."

***

After lunch, Jean left to go to her office, located on the top floor of one of their business buildings, where she oversaw all the other businesses they owned, even the ones overseas. As she settled into her newly renovated office, she felt a profound sense of accomplishment and personal growth. Every element of the design was chosen with care and intention, creating a space where she could flourish. It is a peaceful space overlooking the Potomac River, which she occasionally gazed over when she was in a contemplative mood. This office is a manifestation of her accomplishments and personal growth. It has modern amenities for pampering herself when she needs it. A separate room for yoga, with massage tables for her and possibly a friend, and another room strictly used as an executive lunchroom, complete with an award-winning chef whom she paid very handsomely to pamper her and her team. But her favorite was the bathroom and shower with a very large closet that was filled with her favorite shoes, handbags and outfits, including many Satrat and Moore designs that the girls made. She enjoyed being their experimental test dummy whenever they attempted new designs.

This office, as she told the architect, needed to be not just a place to work but a sanctuary that embodied her dreams and aspirations. It must be a place, she insisted, where she can draw strength from the inspiring environment she helped create.

Jean attributed the success of Moore's many businesses to her practice of having high tea twice per week, on Tuesdays and Thursdays, with her executive staff members. She couldn't remember who started the tradition of coming to the meeting well-dressed, but everyone soon adopted the style. Someone told her she started it by appearing dressed in a new outfit from her daughter. Jean made the stipulation that discussions were not limited to business, although it morphed into business first, then a wide variety of social topics, including family, hobbies and upcoming weekend activities.

***

Greg stopped by the Colonel's office and mentioned that he was looking for a top-notch assistant and wanted to get his take on the type of person that would be well-suited for the job. "That's easy." said the Colonel. "Either get an Army S4 or someone who has been a military adjunct."

"Explain," Greg said.

"An S4 is a logistics and supply officer. If you can find a good one, they can be worth their weight in gold. But be careful, it's also a department where slackers end up."

"Do you know anyone like that available?" Greg asked.

"Let me make a few calls." The Colonel responded.

"Send the names over to Priya; she's coordinating the interviews," Greg said. "Also, do you know who I would talk to in the government if I wanted to buy an abandoned missile silo?"

"I will also make calls on that topic." The Colonel responded with raised eyebrows.

"And FYI, I'm starting a new company to build a leading-edge supercomputer. I'm thinking that Building C will be a good place to get that started." Greg informed him.

"I'll get a few of the security crew, and we'll do a walkthrough." Replied the Colonel.

Greg wandered down to his office and made some calls to find a company that created special materials. After getting passed around to several people in one of the companies, he realized he needed to know more about what Alex had in mind because he couldn't answer most of the questions from the design engineer. Alex was home from baseball practice, so Greg called him on his cell phone and added him to the call. Greg explained to Alex the purpose of the call, but Alex was hesitant to say much because it was for the surprise gift planned for Greg. Before Greg hung up, he made sure the design engineer had his phone number and a promise to call him with a price estimate. About an hour later, the design engineer called Greg. "Without revealing too many details, what your son is asking us to build is practically impossible without new specialized equipment that we don't have. I'll have to ask the finance guys if we have the capital to buy something like this."

Several weeks later, Greg and Jean were in the offices of the specialty manufacturing company just outside of Colombus, Ohio, discussing an offer to buy the company so they could infuse the capital to buy the equipment they needed. The decision to make an offer to acquire the company came after a discussion with Alex, who informed them that with the ideas of other products he had in mind, they would need a special materials manufacturing company that could do custom orders.

Jean had done her homework, looking at the financial figures of this company. She and Greg came up with an offer they thought was fair. The current owner wanted a much higher price, but after a few back-and-forth offers, they settled on a price. Greg helped close the deal by saying that they wanted to keep all the current management, engineers and employees in place.

Over dinner at an upscale restaurant in a revitalized section of Columbus, the current owner, Marvin, asked, "What is your son going to do with this material?"

"We don't know," Greg replied. "He has been an inventor since he was a young age, so make him whatever he wants to build. I don't need to know the details, just the price tag. Besides, one of the reasons I picked your company to acquire was that you build the absolute-zero temperature devices I'm going to need to build a new high-speed computer system."

"What does your son do for a living?" asked Marvin.

"He's still in school," replied Jean. He is involved in a research program associated with Johns Hopkins. A lot of their ideas come from brainstorming sessions. Our son says it's his role to figure out how to build these ideas. He won't tell us what this current project is because he says it's a surprise gift."

Alex was in kindergarten when he started his relationship with the Johns Hopkins research program. First, he was the subject of study on Synesthesia after it was discovered he had that condition. He had struggled to read and had said that words in a book quickly turned to colors. Later, he started contributing to various advanced discussions, and then he was invited to participate in some of the experiments and in the brainstorming sessions.

***

A month later, Alex and Greg flew to Colombus, Ohio, to inspect the first components created by the new machine Greg had purchased. Greg and Marvin sat in a business review meeting while Alex and the material engineers worked out kinks in the creation of his invention.

A text from Alex came over Greg's phone. *'Dad, I'm going to add another invention to the list because the first component we are making is going to be too heavy for what I need. Plus, the second part will help create some lift without an energy source.'*

Greg knew instantly that Alex was talking about the anti-gravity device they had invented before.

"When you said your son was in school, I thought he was at a university level. But it looks like he's in high school." Marvin remarked.

"Just finished his sophomore year of high school," Greg answered.

"Well, he took charge of my PHD guys like he knows his business," Marvin said.

"He's taking PHD level math and physics classes through the university while he's in high school," Greg explained. "He wanted to stay in high school for sports and to be with his friends."

"What sports is he in?" Marvin asked.

"Mainly baseball. He and his friend decided to run Cross Country to stay in shape. His baseball coach encouraged him to try out for the basketball team to learn other skills that would help him with baseball.

"Impressive," Marvin remarked. He and Greg exchanged stories from when they were that age and discovered they had similar interests.

Another text from Alex. *'We're going to need some of the rare earth material.'*

***

Alex and Sam were given a choice of being on the varsity team but not getting much playing time or staying on the junior varsity as starters. In a meeting with their parents, both boys decided that they would rather get more playing time. The parents agreed. The first game was a scrimmage between the varsity and junior varsity teams. The JV team almost won since Alex and Sam got a few hits and drove in several runs. The higher-quality varsity pitchers saved the game for them. After the game, Sam threw his glove with force into his locker. "I'm a better shortstop than that clown." He said, referring to the guy on the varsity team. Alex agreed.

***

"Greg, we have a problem," his wife said over the phone. "The new BBQ restaurant that opened last month in Baltimore is getting hit by a protection racket. The other shop owners in the strip mall say it's been going on for years."

"Have the police been notified?" Greg replied.

"Yes, but the other shop owners say the police never do anything," Jean explained.

"Anything on the security cameras?" Greg asked.

"Yes, do you want me to have the manager make a copy and send it to you?" Jean wanted to know.

"No. I can access it from here. Give me some time to come up with a plan. Oh. About what time did this happen? It will be easier to find the right section." Greg said.

"Yesterday at about 2:30 pm, according to the manager," Jean said.

Greg called over to Colonel Raymond's office, which was just down the hall. "Colonel, we have a problem."

Greg was accessing the security footage from that restaurant while explaining the situation to the Colonel. They both watched as two large men came into the restaurant, asked to speak to the manager then looked around. One spotted the security camera that covered the front area and gave it a nonchalant salute. "Anything from the parking lot camera?" asked the colonel.

Greg queued up the videos from that camera, then fast forwarded to the approximate time. A few minutes later, both men came out of the restaurant, got into a late modeled SUV with the license plate clearly visible, then drove off.

"Obviously, they don't care about being seen," Greg said. "We can give this video to the police."

"Do you realize that it will be cheaper to just pay the guys than to pursue this?" Said Colonel Raymond.

"Really?" Greg asked. "It just seems wrong to let it go."

"You'll be keeping the status quo and keeping the peace because if you succeed in bringing down one organization, another will take its place. It will be a never-ending battle." explained the colonel.

"What happens if we don't pay?" Greg asked.

"They trash the restaurant, or scare away customers, or maybe the Health Department starts creating fictitious violations. Could be any number of things."

Greg called Jean but had to leave a message. "Jean, Greg here. Have the manager pay the toll or whatever it's called for protection. Proceed with filing a police report anyway. We'll figure something out."

After the colonel left, Greg sat at his desk and wondered how hard it would be to track down a license plate. He owned all the networking companies in this area, so it could give him an edge in hacking into the Department of Motor Vehicles (DMV). Plus, he had a secret gadget that would make his intrusions undetectable. His manufacturing company made the underground connectors according to his design. The gadgets had a false flag mode that allowed him to send a signal with a special header that made it seem like it was coming from another segment of the network. It's what allowed his investment fax to seem like it came from a random number every day.

Greg logged into the DMV public web page and browsed around for a few minutes but never found a way to search for someone else's license plate. But looking at the URL for those web pages, he was able to get an IP address. He knew if he wanted to cross the line and break the law, he could use that address as a starting point to get into the database that contained names and addresses related to license plate numbers. Then, he could track down the vehicle owner. But then what? Maybe followed those two men to see who they worked for so he could find the head boss. Greg started daydreaming about doing wild things to the boss and anyone in his organization, like hacking into their bank to freeze their accounts or turning off the electricity at their home and businesses. But with a heavy sigh, he realized that he probably wouldn't do anything. He also realized that he should take this challenge to his counter-terrorism unit to see if they had any clever ideas.

***

The next day, Greg had three people to interview for his assistant. The first one was a young girl just out of high school who wore such a short, tight skirt that all the security guys who worked with Colonel Raymond made an excuse to wander into the building to get a cup of coffee. After talking with her for 30 minutes, he wished her well and had one of the security team escort her back to her car.

"Jean, did you pre-screen these interviewees? "Greg asked.

"No, not personally. You'll have to ask Priya,". she replied. "Why, what's wrong?"

"Not the right fit for this position and didn't seem to be excited about working outside of normal daytime hours. Plus, she asked more about vacation time and other benefits. "Greg replied. "Hey, got to run; the next person is due any minute. Oh, do you want to meet somewhere for lunch somewhere between our offices?"

"Not today, I got some conference calls with the west coast offices. How about Friday?" Jean replied.

"That works. It seems like Friday is becoming our normal lunch date. I've been trying to keep Friday noon free just for that purpose." He said.

"Me too. Love you. See you tonight." Jean replied.

Greg's next interview was a former army captain named Mike who had been a squad leader before he had been injured. He convinced the army that he could still serve despite having a metal leg. He said he hadn't been thrilled about moving to the logistics division but was glad he did. Mike explained that he ended up doing his job and his boss's job because his boss was always doing some busy work and 'delegating' his normal duties to Mike. Greg liked him; he had a good sense of humor, was still very fit and seemed willing to go anywhere at any time for any project.

The third interviewee was a retired pilot who said he was bored with retirement and was looking for something to do. Craig was likable, gregarious, and well-dressed. Greg had always thought that pilots were detail-oriented, and Craig appeared to fit that mold. He reminded Greg of Lawrence, his former boss and current business partner. Greg made a sudden decision not to offer Craig the assistant job. Instead, he had a different idea.

"Have you ever had a security clearance?" Greg asked.

"No. But nothing in my past would prevent that from happening." Craig replied.

"Do you know anything about building products or manufacturing?" Greg asked.

"What kind of products?" Craig wanted to know.

"I'm building a new type of supercomputer, and I need someone to oversee the whole project. I need someone who can manage any type of project and is good at building teams. You don't have to know anything about the science behind the product but need to know enough about it to understand the reports from the engineers and scientists."

"I'm interested, but the only things I've built are things around the house, like a bookshelf and a spice rack for the kitchen." Craig thought for a second, then said, "I built my computer system about five years ago, but that's really just putting the right parts into the right slots from a kit."

"How are you at managing people?" Greg wanted to know.

"Never did it professionally, but I believe I'd be good at it. In addition, I know I am good at teaching because before I retired officially from the airline, I taught classes for a few months while modernizing the content and course material."

Greg liked this guy, so on the spot, he offered him the position to start up the new quantum computer division. They agreed on a salary, and Greg told him that someone from Human Resources would reach out to get the paperwork started. In parting, Craig said, "I'm excited about this, much more than being an assistant, but I probably will only last a few years before I really want to retire. I see my job as building a smooth-running company and making sure I train my replacement.

Greg laughed as they walked out to Craig's car, which was a Mercedes Maybach. Greg whistled and said, "Nice ride!"

Craig said, "It was my wife's present to me for my retirement. At least now I have somewhere to drive it."

CHAPTER 10

July 2000: Net worth $1.9Trillion

"Anybody up for a driving vacation to Wyoming?" Greg asked the family.

"Why, what is out there?" Marie asked.

"Your dad bought an abandoned missile silo," Jean explained.

"Cool!" Alex said.

"We bought a new RV for the trip. And your Grandpa Frank and Grandma Ginny are coming too, in their RV." Greg said.

"What about your mom and dad? "Marie asked Jean.

"They are in Scotland working on the next castle restoration project. That's the project where the archeologists are involved because they found a tunnel under the castle leading to a burial mound. Jean said. "Apparently, they like being stars of the cable TV show Castle Restorations."

"Maybe we can go see them after this trip before school starts again. "Alex asked. "I'd like to see what the archeologists are doing."

Jean glanced over at Greg, who nodded. "I don't see why not." She said.

The morning they left, the weather was overcast and muggy. Dark clouds threatened rain. After doing a walkthrough of the RV, explaining how things worked and talking about safety rules while driving, the family headed off. Jean immediately cranked up the air conditioning. Greg commented that it seemed everyone in the city had the same idea because the freeway was packed. They inched along for about 45 minutes before traffic loosened l up. Jean called Ginny with an updated ETA. It wasn't long before they were at cruising speed, rolling past farms with some plants already knee-high. The farms were interspersed with stretches of forests. Soon, the landscape was more forest than farms.

Just after noon, they arrived at the grandparents' house, had lunch, then headed west. Alex and Marie wanted to ride in Frank and Ginny's RV, leaving Greg and Jean to themselves. Jean had been on her cell phone most of the morning during the first part of the trip, but this part of the country had intermittent cell phone coverage, so she told Greg she was going to close her eyes for a while.

Frank had the route all mapped out. They were heading toward Wright, Wyoming, the closest town to the missile silo. They zig-zagged on back roads until they got to Interstate 70. The plan was to stay on I70 until St. Louis, then head northwest to Lincon, Nebraska, then northwest through Scottsbluff on Highway 26 until they arrived at I25, and follow that to Douglas, Wyoming, before turning north on 59 to Wright. The trip was to take three days. They planned to drive until mid-afternoon each day and then stay overnight at an RV park. Marie and Alex were excited to learn that the route out of St. Louis was part of the wagon train trail the settlers took when the western part of the United States was populated.

The first night, Jean commented, "This is the right way to go camping."

Ginny laughed and replied, "It's called Glamping or glamor camping."

Once the stabilizers were lowered, the sides of the RV expanded into bedrooms and additional space. Marie and Alex flipped a coin to see who got to stay in the extra bed in their grandparents' RV. Marie won. They started a fire in the pit between the RVs and started cooking burgers. Their neighbors on the other side stopped by to introduce themselves and remind the Moore's of the ice cream social starting at 7 pm at the main cabin.

When they left, Frank leaned over toward Greg and spoke in a low voice, "Let me guess, the silo has to do something with the anti-gravity device."

"Yep.Going to build a spaceship. I've hired a few folks away from NASA and Boeing had them sign all sorts of NDA's. I call them my AstroX team. They are currently working in my office building in Arlington, with Colonel Raymond overseeing the project, getting them anything they need for now. He knows they have a blank check. So far, expenses have been minimal, except for the high-end CAD-CAM computers and large graphics printers. Oh, and their salaries. These guys are expensive!"

"What about the logistics of actually going into space?" Frank asked. "You know, space suits and stuff."

"That comes later," Greg replied. "This team has promised to put together a list of people needed to staff a full-fledged space program. And I had an architect draw up plans for an assembly plant next to the silo. The missile silo came with 800 acres of land surrounding it. I plan on hiring locally to create the building."

"What about secrecy?" Jean wanted to know. The entire family had been listening to the conversation. Greg had a bug detection device and had gone over both RV's before they left so he knew everyone could speak freely and had told everyone that.

"My thought was to explain that I am building airplanes to start a new airline, which is true in a sense. By the time anyone realizes that it's really spaceships, we'll have several already built." Greg said.

"What about safety and control?" Jean asked. She was referring to their initial test in a field next to Frank and Ginny's house where their original design went straight up for about 40 seconds, then came down in the neighboring field and killed one of the sheep.

The burgers were ready, so the family loaded their plates with food. Greg answered, "The space experts I hired said they have most of that figured out. Colonel Raymond said they destroyed a few ceiling tiles in their initial tests with the models they built but have since gotten things under control. They also recommend we coat the spaceship with the same material as the stealth bomber so it is hard to detect."

Alex and Marie glanced at each other. Marie shrugged and said, "Now is as good of a time as any."

Their mom asked, "Time for what?"

"We have a surprise that might help with the secrecy." Alex said, then continued, "Let me go get it."

"Um, wait," Marie responded. "Too many people around. We should finish eating, then go inside the RV to show everyone."

"Now I'm intrigued. What could you possibly have that will help with secrecy on a spaceship project?" Greg wanted to know.

Both children smiled and said, "You'll see."

It wasn't long before they finished dinner and were cleaning up when Alex left to go inside the RV, where he had his duffle bag. A few minutes later, the rest of the family followed, crowding into the narrow space. "Where's Alex?" Frank said as they all looked around. "I thought he came in here."

"Right here." Said Alex in a normal voice, then his head appeared near the bathroom door, but nobody.

Ginny, being the closest to Alex, squealed and jumped back. She jostled Frank, who fortunately was sturdy enough that he didn't fall over. "What the heck!" Frank said while the others were watching in stunned silence. Marie was grinning and hopping from foot to foot, obviously excited at what they were seeing.

The rest of Alex's body slowly appeared, then disappeared again. The family gasped! Marie giggled. "Alex figured out how to build an invisibility cloak. "Soon, everyone was passing it around, commenting on how light it was.

"This is a story I want to hear," Frank said, with agreement all around. The family put away the cloak and then sat around the fire pit while Alex explained his work with the manufacturing company in Columbus and all the trial-and-error tests they had undertaken until, finally, something worked.

Marie told her part of the story. "Originally, we envisioned a cloak made of special thread. Alex was going to figure out how to make the thread, and I was going to sew the cloak. There were some promising trials with different rare earth materials until Alex decided that one of the rare earth materials worked better than the rest and it should be made like those Mylar blankets that are sold in camping stores to keep people warm in emergencies."

"And I worked with Marvin in Columbus and his engineers until we got it just right. By the way, he needs you to call him as soon as you get this. He wanted to tell you himself, but I talked him into giving me the prototype to surprise you with." Alex said

Greg laughed. "It sure is a surprise. I can think of a thousand uses for this. And I certainly will let the spaceship team know about it."

"What about a patent?" Jean said. "You know, protect your rights."

"Well, we probably should, but then the whole world will know about it," Greg said. "Too bad there's not a secret patent department that wouldn't publish this to the rest of the world. Dad, are we going to be anywhere near Columbus on this trip?"

Frank responded, "Yes, we go right through there tomorrow morning; we are only about 1 hour away."

Greg grabbed his phone from where he had it stashed by the driver's seat to call Marvin, the prior owner of and current CEO of the manufacturing company Alex had mentioned. "Marvin, it's Greg Moore. I know this is last minute, but we're going to stop by tomorrow on our way through Columbus."

Marvin chuckled, "Got your present, did you? I was wondering when Alex was going to give it to you."

"Yes. And quite the surprise it was, too. I'm flabbergasted." Greg said as the rest of the family headed up to the ice cream social. Greg gestured that he would finish the call and join them in a few minutes. "If you're available about 10 or 10:30 tomorrow, we'll be pulling up with two big RVs, so tell your security guys not to be alarmed. We'll talk about the manufacturing process and plans I have to make more."

"OK, see you then."

It was already hot and humid by the time the family packed up and got on the road. The clouds in the sky were perfect for guessing what the other people in the RV had seen. "I see a turtle" one would say, then the others would point to the cloud formation. Or, "I see a bear head with extra-large ears. "Greg and Jean also taught the children to play the license plate game. This is the game where they would look at the license plates of all the cars and trucks passing them, then write down the state it was from. The object was to get all 50 states. "No way we're going to get Hawaii or Alaska," Marie stated. Greg told her that it was quite possible, but she said she didn't believe him and that she would have to see it to believe it.

Greg and Alex pulled into the parking lot of the manufacturing company. Marvin met them at the front door. "I thought you said you were bringing two RVs," he said.

"It appears that we shared all our S'more supplies with the rest of the campground at an ice cream social last night, so the rest of the crew stopped to get more." Greg countered.

During the ensuing meeting, Greg explained he would need enough of the cloaking material to cover the building they were in by this time next year. Marvin surmised, "You want to make a building disappear?"

"No, but that's not a bad idea either. It's just an easy way of estimating how much I'll need for a special project. "Greg explained.

"Well, that depends on how much antimony and thortveitite crystal you can get us," Marvin said. "Those are the main ingredients."

"How did you figure this out?" Greg wanted to know.

Alex answered, "Well, I needed a crystal structure to play tricks with the light and reading about different minerals, this one looked promising when I saw its atomic structure. I also needed something like Mylar blankets to use as a base. But Mylar didn't work too well, so I went through the periodic table, reading about each one and its properties. When I got to Antimony, I knew that would work. Marvin's chemistry department figured out how to heat a mixture of the two to get the materials to bond together."

"Eventually, through trial and error, we got the process down. But the cloak comes with a warning because the antimony dust is poisonous to humans. It's ok once it's processed into the cloak, but in raw form, we must wear the protective suits to make it". Marvin said.

Greg pondered, "On the one hand, I want to apply for a patent for the invention, but on the other hand, it may be better not to let the rest of the world know about it yet."

"Well, you can apply for a top-secret patent." Marvin explained." It goes into a different database than the general patents."

"There is such a thing?" Greg asked in wonderment.

"It was started during World War I, primarily for military inventions," Marvin said. "We have one. We had filed a regular chemical patent for making another special product for another customer. Someone from the Secret Squirrel department of the government visited us and said they were going to put it into the top-secret patent files. That way, if anyone else invents something similar, we're protected."

Alex giggled at the words 'Secret Squirrel'. "Is that a real department?" he asked.

"No, but I don't know what else to call it because they never explained what their department really was," Marvin answered.

"OK, Alex, write up a patent application like I taught you a few years ago. I'll review it and hold onto it for now, but we'll have it available. "Greg said.

Marvin offered to provide Alex with the access he needed to the right people in both the chemistry and manufacturing groups so he could get the wording right for the application.

As Greg was driving the RV out of the parking lot, Alex called his mom to find a meeting place. After he hung up, he said, "Dad, what are you going to use it for?"

"I'm going to cloak the spaceships," Greg said with a playful glance at his son.

"SWEET!" was the only reply.

***

CHAPTER 11

It rained heavily on the trip from Colombus to St. Louis. Greg and Frank had the windshield wipers going full speed most of the way. Ginny had the foresight to get some walkie-talkies while they were shopping in Columbus so they could talk to each other while on the road without using cell phones. They had just communicated that they would skip the St. Louis Arch visit since it was raining so hard, but when they got closer to the city, Frank, who was in the lead RV, called back and said he could see the trailing edge of the storm. They decided to drive to the arch and do an assessment then. By the time they got to the site, it was just drizzling, so they decided to go anyway. The parking lot near the Arch was not very full. The line to get in was not very long either. Greg paid for the tickets and the family got in the elevator to the top. Once they got to the top there were Ooh's and Aahs as they could see the breathtaking panoramic views of the landscape over the Mississippi River on one side and the skyline of the city on the other.

They decided to have a late dinner in St. Louis before going to the campground Ginny had called to reserve spaces the day before. The family walked down the sidewalk through the long garden that bordered the Arch, then wandered several blocks through the city until they found a restaurant. Greg muttered while they were walking, "Someone should create a website that would make it easy to find nearby restaurants and assist with the navigation to the place. Call it 'FoodFinder' or something." On the way back, they were accosted by a homeless man with a long, scraggly beard and wild hair. He mumbled something about the spare change in a nonthreatening way. Greg instinctively reached into his pocket before realizing that he had not carried cash for several years. Fortunately, Jean and Ginny had thought ahead and had gotten cash for the trip. They each gave the guy $100. He looked at them in disbelief, then silently turned into the nearest alley and disappeared into the darkness.

Marie and Alex were curious about being homeless and kept asking questions that the adults didn't know all the answers to. In the discussions that followed, they surmised that although it was enough to get food and shelter for the night, he would probably spend it on booze and drugs. This led to more questions, which led to a discussion on addictions to alcohol and various drugs. It also led to a discussion on homelessness, where some people were forced into it by life circumstances and some by choice.

"Why would anyone choose to be homeless?" Marie asked.

Greg answered first. "To be unencumbered by owning anything. There is a series of books I enjoy about a guy who wanders around the country on foot or by bus with only the clothes he is wearing and a folding toothbrush in his pocket, sleeping in motels and eating in diners. He has money from his military pension, so he is not poor like the guy we just saw."

At the insistence of the children, Jean listed a lot of the projects around the world that their charity foundation was involved in. Greg filled in details of the projects where he could, as he had visited several in person. Marie and Alex responded that they had no idea this was going on and were glad to get the opportunity to hear about the foundation.

The rest of the trip was uneventful except for a few aggressive and impolite drivers wanting to pass them once they got off the freeway and onto the back roads in Nebraska and Wyoming. Greg called ahead to the Sheriff in Wright, Wyoming, just before they arrived. The Sheriff had an extra set of keys because they occasionally had to go on the land to chase off squatters. Hunting was technically not allowed but that was too hard to patrol and prevent.

The property was undulating grassland with one medium-sized building near the chained entry gate. The sheriff opened the padlock on the gate and handed Greg the key ring, stating that the other keys were for the building and the silo door. The building was empty except for evidence of rodent droppings everywhere. The silo door was stubborn and creaked when opened. There was no electricity to power the lights and the elevator, so the group agreed that they would leave the door open overnight to get some fresh air circulating, then return the next day with flashlights to explore the silo.

The RVs were parked right next to the silo door. Early the next morning, after another campfire breakfast, Ginny and Jean volunteered to stay above ground while everyone else descended ladders and ramps, exploring side rooms and alcoves at each level until they made it to the bottom. It was past noon when they finally exited, filling the ladies with tales of what they had discovered. The end result, as Greg put it, was a giant hole with lots of cement. Now he wasn't sure what he was going to do with the silo. His original idea was that the silo was a perfect place to build spaceships undetected, but now he realized that the 800 acres surrounding the silo were a better place for a manufacturing plant. It would also need a small town to house the workers, engineers, maintenance people, pilots and other support personnel. This was going to be more expensive than he originally thought.

***

Greg was reviewing his plans via a telephone call, thinking to himself that it would be great to have a TCPIP based conferencing application that would allow many people to join a call remotely through their computers. Oh well, he thought, another project to table for later.

The manufacturing plant buildings were done. One building received all the raw materials and created parts. The other, larger building was to assemble the final pieces and put on the cloaking material. The town buildings were the last thing to be finished. A civil engineering firm had been hired to create the foundations, but once they saw the plans and the need for housing for the workers, they drew up plans for a complete sewer system, water purification system and other things necessary to support a small town. Two entire acres were devoted to solar panels. The hilltop a half mile away was going to house the row of giant windmills. The original entry road that had been built sturdy enough to support large trucks that brought in large missile parts was now covered in cracks and weeds. This needed to be torn down and rebuilt from scratch.

He and Jean started a conversation about what an ideal town would be like. Marie and Alex joined in. The family enjoyed weeks of dinnertime discussions on this topic and even extended invitations to their friends to join. By the end of the first month, there was a long list of ideas on what should be included. Greg was reminded of a quote he had heard in his youth that a camel was a thoroughbred racehorse designed by a committee. He was hoping his town would turn out ok, but there was no way all the ideas would be adopted.

Greg did like the 'no cars in town' policy because he didn't envision too many houses being built. But it turned out that enough houses were built that an electric shuttle bus ran from one end of town to the manufacturing plant. There was a large parking lot for employees driving from Wright, and town residents used the lot for their cars and RVs. The town was large enough to register as a town, which means it got its own postal code, which means it needed a post office. A tri-space building was suggested for the purpose of a post office, a coffee shop and a library, which was nothing more than a few rows of bookshelves around the coffee shop where residents left books and traded for other books. Greg and Jean supplied the first few stacks that had been accumulating in their house.

There was no bar or restaurant, so an enterprising fellow from Wright approached Greg to borrow money to build a steak house, dance hall and saloon in between the town of Wright and the manufacturing plant. It turned out to be a great investment.

***

September 11, 2001

Greg had gotten to his office early. He had woken at the usual five am to go for a run but decided to start work early, so he made a to-go cup of tea in his travel flask, grabbed an apple for breakfast and headed into his office. He worked in silence for a while, then began hearing the office wake up as other people started arriving. Colonel Raymond stuck his head in Greg's office and waved, then headed toward the kitchen. He knew the Colonel's routine was to turn on the TV and watch the morning news for about twenty to thirty minutes while enjoying a cup of coffee. The next thing he knew, the Colonel was yelling at everyone to come to the kitchen. They all stood in stunned silence as they watched the videos of the airplanes striking the Twin Towers in New York City, then later as reports and pictures of the Pentagon after another airplane struck that building.

Suddenly, Greg realized something and hurried back to his office. With his daily fax coming from the future, he should have known about this. Why wouldn't he send himself a note on a prior fax about this event? At first, the faxes had been coming on paper, but he had figured out a way of sending them to a file on his computer so he could automate the stock trading process. So, he opened the folder containing past fax files and read one. At the top, it said, 'Terrorist attack on 9/11/2001, NYC and D.C.', followed by a few more details. He opened several more and saw that the same note had arrived on earlier days as well. If he had been paying attention, he would have known about this and been able to alert the proper authorities.

With a heavy sigh, he realized that he needed a way to detect extra notes on the page and send them in a text message to his phone. He was a good programmer, so searching for extra text and extracting it from the page was not much of a challenge, but sending a text to his phone took a bit of research and required another API or application programming interface that he had to download. It was several weeks before it was perfected. But in the end, he was happy with the result and was confident that if anything else like this happened, he would not miss it.

***

CHAPTER 12

January 2002: Net worth $3.5 Trillion

"Hey, Sis, can I get you to make a tuxedo for me and a dress for my prom date?" Alex said.

"You should have called a few months ago. We're really busy with custom orders from famous people because all the spring awards shows are coming up." Marie responded. "And we still go to classes during the day. Plus, I've applied to get an internship at the Louve with an art restoration expert."

Marie and Aimee became overnight sensations after designing and making a series of dresses for teens. The success was meteoric due to a clever internet campaign run by their friend Elizabeth they had met at MUN. They had made her a dress that she started showing off on her web page she had programmed herself with the help of her older brother. The main theme was to show off 'Satrat and Moore's originals, and Elizabeth's brother had worked out the tedious programming required to purchase clothes with a credit card. Not only were there pictures of all the clothes Aimee and Marie had made, but they also started posting short videos of them drawing the designs, selecting the material and sewing the clothes. Aimee was the main designer. Marie made most of the clothes. They both did the material selection and cutting.

"Do you have your measurements already?" Marie asked Alex.

"No."

"Get Mom to do it; she knows how."

They had already made men's suit jackets for their fathers and for a few of their friends at the MUN conferences. This time, they tried some daring new styles. Alex loved it. He even posed for

Elizabeth to take a few pictures and a short video to post on the website.

***

The first spaceship was in the initial stages of assembly. The structural cavernous hexagons were built into the fuselage and wings. Several designs had been proposed, from a bell-shaped structure to one that resembled the stealth bomber. Greg opted for the one with wings that looked like the stealth bomber because he wanted an aerodynamic version needed to fly within Earth's atmosphere. He decided he was going to start his own airline company and replace all the gas-powered planes with this new generation of travel. The bell-shaped craft could come later when he needed to just get to space and back without flying to different points around the globe. He also challenged his aerospace engineers to come up with giant flying containers that could replace all the trucking and possibly most of the ships. Greg already had plans to open new manufacturing plants in different areas but was holding off until the timing was right.

***

Alex was the hit of the prom. Not only had he grown three inches in his senior year of high school to a height of six feet, one inch, but he had filled out nicely due to his training in different sports. Aimee had commented that it was certainly a pleasure to measure and fit him for the jacket and trousers. Sammy commented that he wished he had put in a request for one of their jackets. Instead he had to borrow one of his father's old jackets that was too tight since Sammy had also grown several inches that year.

Both Alex and Sammy made the varsity team again in their senior year. Alex stayed at his customary third base. Sammy moved to shortstop, which he preferred. He had been playing second base the prior year because the short-stop position was taken by a returning senior who was quite good.

There were college and professional scouts in the stands for most of the games. The coaches explained the rules and procedures of when and how they could be contacted, when they could sign letters of intent for colleges, what the different types of scholarships meant and much more.

After the first game of the season, they had been approached by several universities with invitations to visit before signing letters of intent to attend that university. Alex and Sammy had already decided that the University of Texas in Austin would be their top choice because that school had been in the college world series more often in the last ten years than any other school. By the third to last game of the season, they did not have any interest from the University of Texas, so their coach called the other coach to find out that they would not get much playing time and would have to play outfield. Again, it was a decision to take a second-choice school to get more playing time or go with their first choice and not get much playing time.

Sammy ultimately persuaded Alex that the University of Texas was the right choice. "This team is going to the College World Series again next year. Just look at their pitching. Besides, we'll get into the lineup on the strength of our bats." It didn't take much coercion to persuade Alex because he had heard that the coaching staff was very strong as well. It was a big announcement in the Washington D.C. area when they signed letters of intent. They even made the ESPN magazine's episode of the top high school picks.

Alex was drafted by the Colorado Rockies, whose representative explained that several years of college was preferred. He could either turn professional when he turned 21 or after three years at the university level. Then, he could expect several years of semi-professional baseball. If he was still performing well, he would be invited to play at the professional level.

Sammy reported a similar experience after getting drafted by the Oakland Athletics. He said he didn't care who drafted him because it was likely to change before they ever got to the pros. Alex and Sammy were already planning to drive a car down to Austin and not fly. Greg had offered them a ride on one of his planes, but the boys decided they wanted to see more of the country by travelling on the roads.

Alex was taking a beautiful girl named Nicole to the prom. Sammy was taking his girlfriend, also named Nicole. They had decided to call her 'Pete,' a shortened version of her last name, Peterson. Nicole was a shy, petite girl at the top of her class. Alex had asked her on a date the prior year when she had asked him for help with her math homework for the third time. Most of the time he would glance at the problem, tell her the answer, then leave it to her to figure out how to arrive at the same conclusion. Other times, he would explain how to get to the answer and let her arrive at the answer. They would often do homework at her house, where her mother was always around. Alex would sneak a kiss when the mother was in the other room absorbed in her afternoon soap operas.

Pete was athletic, a leading swimmer on the high school team and threw shotput, discus and javelin on the track team. She had joked with Sammy the year before that she had bigger pecs than he did. She was the leader of the group, always talking, always asking questions, and always leading the planning for the group. She was, as their friend, a Ukrainian exchange student, said, 'An assertive American woman.'

Pete had joined their group one day a year ago, coming up to Sammy, putting an arm around his shoulders and saying casually, "How's it going?" Sammy was smitten after that. Pete delighted in challenging Alex to solve hard math problems in his head. After a few weeks of that, she said it got boring and switched to talking about other science things.

On one of their frequent double dates she started with, "What are stars made out of?" And Alex would explain about the different types of stars and what they were made of.

"Do you think there are Aliens?" Alex explains that the probability is there due to the billions of galaxies, stars and planets, that statistically, there had to be other populated worlds.

"Are there other dimensions?" Here Alex had to be careful because he had made a device years ago that would send information from the future. The theory was that it was going through different dimensions to arrive in the past. So, all he answered was 'yes.'

"Well, how do we get there?" Pete asked.

"Nobody has figured out quantum superposition yet." He explained, thinking to himself that this could be one of his next projects. He hadn't visited THE LIBRARY in a while. Maybe this would be a good subject to go to sleep with, which would usually trigger a dream of him in THE LIBRARY asking about a specific topic.

"What the F does that mean?" Sammy blurted. Sammy knew about Alex's condition and his advanced studies and that he understood most advanced physics and math topics. The girls didn't know about it.

"It means how to be in two places at once. Or instead of superposition there is another theory that means we have to transfer out our molecules to another dimension, then stitch them back together again in the exact same way on the other side. Like in Crichton's book *Timeline."* Nicole was looking at him in amazement and something else, maybe… fear? Pete just shook her head and asked, "How do you know all this stuff?"

"I read a lot, mostly science books, some science fiction. Lately, the scientists have been posting articles on the internet, so it's easier to stay current." Alex responded. "Also, since I get off at noon, I go either go over to work with an astrophysics group in Arlington or get on a conference call with the physicists at Johns Hopkins. It's too far to drive up there, then get back for baseball practice."

"So, when your face is in your phone, that's what you are doing?" Pete asked in amazement, then continued, "The rest of us are scrolling through social websites."

***

Alex paid for the pre-prom dinner since he had been getting a salary for years plus had been receiving royalties from his patents. He started his own corporation with the help of his mother when the royalty payments started coming in. As the senior year of high school started, he was fairly wealthy in his own right, but he never flaunted it. He did buy a new Camero when he got his driver's license but traded it in for a Range Rover four-wheel drive when he got his first ticket in the first week of driving. He had considered the popular Hummer but decided against it when he tried to park it in a tight spot during the test drive.

The foursome decided to go to a popular Indian restaurant. Nicole had never been to one. Sammy had voted for BBQ, his favorite, but had been outvoted. He didn't really mind. Like a typical teenage guy, he would eat any type of good food offered. It was one of Pete's favorites, as it turned out. Alex drove to the prom in his roomy Range Rover and dropped them off at the curb before circling the school parking lot to find a free space in a remote corner.

The prom was loud with a wide variety of music, with songs of different genres represented. Rap, reggae, blues and hip-hop were dominant, with a few slow jazz songs. Near the end, an old classic rock song came from the Moody Blues. Even though there was a no-kissing rule, it was still crowded enough that the school monitors and proctors were probably not going to catch them; Alex kissed Nicole. She responded enthusiastically. After they broke their kiss, Alex noticed Pete dragging Sammy out the door of the gymnasium. He just smiled. Soon after, Nicole and Alex slowly wandered out to his car. He opened her door for her and received a warm smile in return.

"Where to?" he asked.

Nicole hesitated, looked like she was going to say one thing, then said, "Feel like ice cream?"

Alex started the car and then suggested that Nicole text Pete to meet them for ice cream at their favorite shop about a mile from the school. Alex picked the last table for four after he and Nicole waited in line to get their treat. It seemed like half the school was there after the dance. An instant after they sat down, another couple sat down at the open chairs. Alex informed them that they were saving them for their friends. The response he got was a rude stare and a shrug. "No other seats available." Alex decided not to make a big deal. They sat in silence, eating their treats. When they were done, they stood up and left. The weather had been nice earlier, but as they exited, they noticed that the wind had picked up and was getting quite chilly. Alex gave Nicole his coat as they walked toward his car. About that time Pete and Sammy came trotting down the road.

"Where have you been?" Alex asked.

"Behind the football stadium!" Pete answered.

"Doing what?" Alex wanted to know.

They both responded with a shrug and a smile. Alex and Nicole exchanged a glance and a laugh. As they piled into Alex's car, they all agreed to go to Alex's house because he had the Xbox and a very large TV screen in his living room. Nicole picked the dance competition game, which she won handily. Alex and Sammy both tried at the expert level to the laughs of the girls. Alex's mom, Jean, came downstairs, got a drink of water and watched for a few minutes, smiling at Alex when she caught his eye. Nicole and Pete had texted their respective parents with pictures of the dance competition with a short explanation that they were ok and would be home later. About an hour later, they all collapsed on the couch.

Alex pulled Nicole in for a kiss. She leaned in for a heated response. When Alex's hands started roaming, she stopped him, whispering, "I'm not ready yet." He stretched out on the couch, pulling her close so she could relax with her head on his chest. It wasn't long before he could feel her breathing settle into a steady rhythm. Alex watched Sammy get up, go to the bathroom, and come back to grab Nicole's phone out of her clutch to take a picture, which he sent to her parents with an explanation: 'Too much dancing.' He did the same with Pete's phone since she had fallen asleep on the other end of the couch. He then switched to one of the first-person shooter games that he played until dawn. Alex finally fell asleep watching him run through scene after scene, racking up points.

***

July 2002: Net worth $4 Trillion

"Five, Four, Three, TWO, ONE... LIFTOFF!" said Tom Mcloughlin, the pilot of the spacecraft, as he pressed the button on the invisible spacecraft. The team had a list of inventions and patents waiting to be filed about the creation of the craft. Once the basics of the hexagonal-shaped anti-gravity devices had been improved and sufficient controls were created to stabilize the craft, it didn't take long to build the spaceship itself. Numerous unmanned flights had gone to space while the engineers fiddled with perfecting the controls. The inaugural manned flight consisted of Tom

McLoughlin and Jax Lunders, the copilot. Greg had wanted to go but Jean insisted that he wait until at least the second or third flight, depending on the safety results of the first few missions.

Greg, who was normally not a pacer, was pacing back and forth behind the ground control consoles. He didn't know why he was nervous, perhaps because he couldn't see anything. He was worried that the military would spot the spacecraft and come to investigate. He was worried about a million things that could go wrong. Greg was an avid reader of science fiction and other books in the international intrigue genre, and something always went wrong.

Tom was in constant communication, keeping a running dialog going about the progress. This was planned because there were no visuals so the people on the ground had come up with the idea of letting Tom keep talking throughout the flight. Plan A was to go up to orbiting altitude, just above where the geosynchronous satellites were, test the maneuverability of the craft, do one orbit of the earth, and then come back down. They didn't have to worry much about the heat upon re-entry into the atmosphere because the controls placed on the anti-gravity device allowed a smooth and slower speed while descending. Plan B was created if everything was going well. Tom had permission to go into space beyond the altitude of the space station to test the ion propulsion system that would be needed once they were outside the gravity well of the Earth.

The shape of the craft was like the Stealth Bomber, except that it had a much larger fuselage to carry more passengers. Greg preferred this design because he wanted a visible version of this craft to start his own airline. Manufacturing had already begun on a prototype of the plane that he planned on revealing to the public when the timing was right.

Greg was already thinking further into the future and had created a think tank group containing what he was calling his AstroX brain trust, where X stood for physicists, chemists, cosmologists, AstroThis and AstroThat. Basically, any talent needed to go off planet and explore space. He had given them free rein to discuss and create plans for anything they could dream of, including Asteroid Mining, Planet Colonization, Interstellar Travel, and the hard one, Interstellar Communication.

Alex had jumped at the chance to join the think tank with the stipulation that his high school schedule took priority. Greg remembered when he told Alex about that stipulation and remembered that Alex thought about it for one second before agreeing because, as he put it, he was only going to high school to continue playing baseball.

"I'm glad you are passionate about playing baseball." Greg stated, "But it's important to pay attention in all your other classes. There is a saying, 'Be here now,' meaning, give your full attention to whatever you are doing at that moment."

"That's good advice, and I try to use practical examples to keep me motivated to pay attention in each class."

"Can you give examples?" Greg asked.

"I pay attention in English class as we are learning sentence structure because I remember all the corrections you made on my first few patent applications. I pay attention in Spanish class because the baseball team has a few really good players from South America. I pay attention in Geography class; well, for one, I like it and second, going with you on your different trips has made me appreciate the different countries and cultures more."

"Those are great examples, and I'm glad you are getting good grades in all your classes."

Greg turned back into Tom's monologue. "We've cleared the list of tests we wanted to do at this level. Everything went smoothly. Heading for more altitude, initiating Plan B."

"Tom, Greg here. Anything you are worried about at this point?"

"Just about who will win the office pool about when the anti-gravity devices will lose effect, and we have to kick in the ion drives."

Tom was referring to the differences of opinion that various groups had about what altitude the ion drives would need to be started. The geophysicists had one guess, which was a range of altitudes. The mathematicians had a more precise altitude for their choice. An office pool was started. Everyone put in $100. The pot was almost $10,000, with most people siding with the mathematicians. There and been a heated debate on how to measure the point in time the effectiveness stopped. An agreement was reached that it would be at the point when acceleration would start decreasing. Alex heard about the pool and created a third category, which was the point when all dampers were removed from the anti-gravity device. His theory was that the ship would do its final acceleration at that exact point and then rely on inertia to keep traveling before the ion drives would be needed. Greg thought it sounded practical, so he and a few others put their money in that category.

"All dampers off," Tom said as he slid the control level to the end. "Wow. We just jumped further than we thought; we are now way outside our planned orbit."

"Everything OK?" Greg asked over his headset.

"Acceleration is slowing, speed is higher than we thought it would be due to the big jump to get outside the gravity well. Initiating ion drives to turn and head home. Got to burn off some of this speed before entering the atmosphere, or we'll cook."

It wasn't long before Tom and Jax opened the hatch and lowered the ramp. The entire staff was out there, excitedly greeting them with high fives and hugs. In the ensuing debrief, Greg mentioned that there should be a special MVP award for the team that contributed the most to the success of the mission. They went around and around, not arriving at a consensus until Tom stopped it all with his opinion. "It's got to be the quality control team. This is space, and anything can go wrong at any time. They should get the award for their diligent testing of every component, every part, every aspect of the mission." After that, it was a unanimous decision. Greg then promised a bonus to everyone involved and an additional bonus to the quality control team.

The next day, Tom and Jax were airborne, inside the gravity well of the earth, conducting a long list of tests. They were nervous when they hovered at 5,000 feet over the nearest Air Force base, but they were not detected, so they went around the world at various points of interest, doing tests before returning home. With the success of this mission, Greg dialed a number to talk to a person he had been both excited and nervous to talk to – The head of the Air Force advanced technology group. He had wanted to talk directly to the General who headed the Joint Chiefs of Staff, but apparently, because of the chain of command, he had to start somewhere to convince that person that a meeting at higher levels was warranted.

Tom McLoughlin had been an advanced test pilot with the Air Force before Greg hired him and knew just the person to talk to. Instead, it took a series of calls to land the right person who could then go directly to the head of the Air Force, who could then get Greg in contact with the President's military staff. Without revealing too much to the people they originally talked to, Tom explained that there was a 'new type of propulsion system' an inventor created and wanted to know if the Air Force was interested. A one-star General named Jonas 'Ace' Venator, a former pilot, was now heading the Advanced Technology and Research Division.

Tom's former Colonel had made the introduction, suggesting that before the call, Greg had put together a short biography of himself and a brief description of his invention. General Venator had read the information and was intrigued. Greg had only described the invention as an 'undetectable propulsion system,' which he thought was enough to get anyone interested.

After a brief round of introductions, the General wanted to dive into the specifics of the invention and how it worked. Greg and Tom convinced him that a demonstration would be a quicker and more effective use of time.

"Just tell me where you are, and we can be there in a few minutes if you promise not to shoot me if I suddenly appear in front of you," Greg said.

"Explain." Said the General.

"Well, let's say you were at Andrews Air Force Base. I would say go to Hanger X and make sure there is a clear space in front of it to park a 747-sized aircraft. I could meet you in 30 minutes at that spot, and you'd never know until we were standing right in front of you."

Complete silence. Then, "I'm deciding whether you are crazy or if this is real."

"How about meeting us in a non-military setting like your home if you have a large enough yard to park a 747, or tonight at a nearby golf course when it's empty." Greg offered.

"There is a nearby golf course, but I wouldn't want to damage it by landing a large craft on the fairway."

"This is a vertical landing and takeoff. No damage. Not even a divot." Greg said.

"Non detectable by radar?" asked the General.

"Yup. This has been tested by hovering at various altitudes over many military bases around the world without detection. It has some improvements on the stealth bomber coating as well as the new propulsion system.”

More silence. Then, “This would be the point I would normally hang up, but I’m working on some pretty advanced stuff right now, so I’m going to go out on a limb and believe you. Meet me tonight at 11 pm at these coordinates.”

That ended the call. They looked up the coordinates. It turned out to be a non-working farm pasture in a remote part of Ohio. Tom’s guess was that the General either worked at Wright-Patterson AFB or he could call someone to get a fast ride to these coordinates.

Greg called his assistant, Mike and asked him to track down any information about the owners of the property. Mike was an absolute wizard at getting information on anything Greg asked for.

“Tom, let’s take a ride.”

“Where to boss?”

“Space. I want to go to space.”

“Call Jean and tell her. She made me promise that you would call her if you ever asked.”

Greg nodded and then called Jean. It was a lengthy conversation about safety, with Greg handing Tom the phone several times to answer Jean’s questions. She reluctantly agreed on the condition that he promised that he would call her the second he was back on earth.

Before they left the building to board the craft, Greg stopped. “Tom, I assume there’s no cell reception up there.”

“Nope.”

Greg wound around the desks to the main flight controller’s desk. “Here’s my cell phone. It’s unlocked. I’m expecting a phone call. Answer it if it rings and patch it through, please.”

“I’m off-shift in two hours, so I’ll pass it through to the next shift.”

"Thanks."

During the fifteen-minute flight, Greg was sitting in one of the comfortable seats in the passenger section, talking to Tom on a headset.

"Tom, how is the pilot training program going?"

"Actually, Jax is filling in the details when we are not flying. He's taken an interest in participating. We're getting to a point where it will need a review of the first draft of all the material from a professional trainer.

"Excellent. Is there a special version of the training material for military pilots?"

"There will be. And a different version for space pilots. And a different version for military space pilots."

Greg paused as he remembered the full list of proposed tests that had been in his email the month before. Tom had recommended a large variety of tests that assumed that other nations would eventually get this technology and air battles may occur. Greg shuddered at the thought, but he couldn't be naive enough to think that these planes would only be used for peaceful purposes.

After they cleared the Earth's gravity well, Greg was invited to the cockpit to view Earth. No conversation was necessary as the three of them gazed in wonderment at the sight. They had all seen pictures from prior space missions, but the pictures could not match the actual experience. No wonder the astronauts called this the blue planet. It was more than just the color; it was the brilliance of the hues, the whites of the clouds, and the deep blues of the oceans. Greg decided that it was something everyone must experience for themselves, and he found himself wondering how he could give this gift to every human who wanted it.

"Spin us around; let's take a look at the stars." Greg requested.

As they sat there looking through the window, absorbed in their own thoughts, Jax interrupted. "What's that?"

"Where?" both Greg and Tom said.

"One o'clock."

They both leaned forward as if getting closer to the glass another foot would help. Then, they noticed a dot of light growing closer. It must have been travelling at great speed because it changed from a small dot to a glowing, golden orb.

"Ahhh…" Greg said, not knowing what else to say.

"WTF…" Tom said.

Jax didn't say anything else as he was busy ensuring the video system was recording.

"We don't have any weapons on this craft," Tom said, mentioning Greg's decision to leave those off so they could get a functioning prototype completed sooner.

After about one minute, they all had to blink several times to make sure they were seeing clearly. A large human in a golden bubble was hovering in front of the window.

"Greetings." It said with a wave. The sound was coming over the internal speakers.

"Greetings." They all said simultaneously.

Then Greg spoke first, "Who are you?".

"Identities are not important right now. The important question is why I am here. With the inventions to produce this spacecraft, plus other inventions that Mr. Moore has and will create, it puts Humanity in a position to advance to the next level."

Realization quickly dawned on Greg's mind, like a welcome beacon shining on a dark night. Like a warm feeling that crept through one's body after realizing the answer to a long-ago question. It was something Greg and Jean occasionally talked about after Dmitry Balinov, one of their Russian business partners had asked in that first meeting, "WHY?". Why was the fax-based technology invented by Greg and Alex, and why at this point in history?

The being in the bubble confirmed that exact thought. "Mr. Moore has been pondering the question of WHY for years, ever since the first invention proposed by his son Alex."

Both Tom and Jax turned and looked at Greg. "I'll explain later," Greg informed them.

"We have been watching your progression with great interest as human technical capabilities have accelerated over time. Your technical advancement has outpaced your social, cultural and political progress. I am here as a messenger. Your planet must prepare itself to be invited to participate in an Intergalactic Federation."

Greg's first thought was, "WTF!!!!" followed by something he said out loud, "You said 'prepare.' What does that mean?"

"Some of your science fiction writers got it right when they said aliens usually laugh at earthlings because they don't have a planet-wide governmental system."

"Do you mean that in order to be invited to this Federation, the Earth must have a single governing body?" Greg asked.

"Yes. Once that is done, we can talk about joining the Federation, choosing Earth's representatives, and participating in galactic business."

Greg's mind went in multiple directions at once. He instantly had so many questions. The dilemma was which one to ask first. "Why us?" he finally decided to ask next.

"Just you, Mr. Moore. You have been chosen to drive the next phase of advancement toward a global governing body. We have been waiting for someone altruistic enough to put these inventions to use for good causes only. The other two need to continue completing the tasks you hired them for. If they have an interest in getting involved in planetary governance in the future, there is confidence you will find a way for them to participate."

"Do you mean something like the United Nations or the G8 or the European Union?" Greg asked.

"In the base concepts, all of these groups serve as starting models to accomplish what is needed."

Greg switched direction with his questions, "Should the world government be based on a certain political theory, like Democracy, Socialism or any of the myriad of choices."

"Does not matter. Everyone on earth must agree on how this governing body should be based."

"Does that mean that other planets in the Federation have different political systems?" Greg wanted to know.

"Yes."

Greg's mind continued to race in different directions. "I'm going to assume that I am not the first contact to be given this task."

"That is correct."

"So, Atilla the Hun, Alexander the Great, the Romans, Hitler, Napoleon, the British Empire. All these were contacts who decided that global conquest was the best answer for creating a united government."

"Mostly correct. Hitler was the only one on that list who did not have a personal invitation. He read an ancient manuscript obtained and deciphered by his archeological team and decided on his solution. After what Earth calls World War Two, certain leaders were visited, which led to a more peaceful outcome by creating the United Nations."

"How do we get any nations to agree to be governed by the United Nations?" Greg asked.

"You'll have to work toward a solution. If I tell you, it comes under the category of having the messenger cause too much influence. The 'how' is up to the people of earth."

Greg suddenly remembered something he had read a while back about China's Ten Thousand Year Plan to dominate the world. Perhaps Russia's expansion after World War I and II was a different type of answer.

"And why now?" Greg asked.

"Something stated earlier. Your social, political and cultural advancements are outpaced by your technical advancements. It is somewhat common in the world. Now is the time to devote your efforts and resources to bringing alignment to the goal of preparing Earth to join the Federation."

Greg switched trains of thought. "Lately, we've had major incidences based on religious differences." He was referring to the Twin Towers attack in New York City

"Those are known as intra-planetary skirmishes. Those don't need to be solved to be invited to the Federation. It's something you may want to solve to achieve world peace."

"One last question," Greg said. "If I bring back other people, will you come to have another conversation?"

"If you bring the right people." With that, the golden glow rapidly retreated, faster than it had arrived.

Tom, Jax and Greg watched in stunned silence until the final dot of light blinked out.

It was a full three minutes of silence before Tom shook his head hard as if to clear a strike that left him stunned. "Let's go home."

After another moment of silence, while watching Tom and Jax turn the craft around and start heading to Earth, Greg said, "There are some things an NDA just doesn't cover. I trust you'll keep silent about this?"

"Who would believe us."

At that moment, the communication system to Earth came back on. "… HEAR US". Someone was shouting.

"Major Tom to Ground Control, Loud and clear," Tom answered.

"Glad to have you back." Answered a relieved voice. "We lost you for about 10 minutes."

Greg was stunned to realize that the conversation with the being in the bubble was only a few minutes. With his mind going in a million different directions, he suddenly remembered the late-night meeting with the General.

"Relax," Tom said. "We have time to get dinner at the chow hall before we meet with him. Food's way better there than the protein bars and MREs we carry here for emergencies." Tom was referring to the fact that Greg had hired professional chefs and paid them and their families extra bonuses to be stuck in his secret facility in Wyoming.

Everyone had already eaten by the time they landed, so Greg, Tom and Jax grabbed a table near the window. The chef informed them that the food had already been cleared, but he could warm up the leftovers if they desired.

"You wouldn't happen to have any nice steaks on hand?" Greg asked.

"How about elk steaks? I bagged one the other day and was about to cook some for myself and the kitchen crew."

"Perfect."

"I don't envy you. That's a monumental task." Tom said, bringing the conversation back to the visitor in space. Jax nodded.

"As you can imagine, my brain is in overdrive trying to decide what to do next," Greg responded.

At that moment, one of the staff from the control room came running in with Greg's cell phone. "It's your wife."

"Oh, crap. I was supposed to call her as soon as we got back."

That was exactly what Jean said as soon as Greg pressed the unmute button. "Sorry, Jean, we're in the middle of an important debrief. I'll fill you in tomorrow privately."

Jean knew exactly what that meant, so she didn't press for more information. Being married this long had its advantages, and they often knew what the other meant without lengthy explanations. She said she was just glad he was back safely.

"We're also flying to meet an Air Force General at 11 pm at some abandoned farm in Ohio. I'm going to offer him a version of the plane."

"I thought you weren't going to open that can-of-worms."

"I should have talked to you again, but it won't be long before word gets out anyway. And I want to go ahead with the idea of creating an airline company like we talked about before. And I believe you'll want to come with me on the next space trip."

"Wow. That's a lot of big topics to hit me with at once."

"Yeah. We don't get to do anything small anymore, do we? Oh, dinner is here. We just landed a few minutes ago, and the chef is preparing a special meal of elk steaks and something green."

"Broccolini." Said the server as he set the plate in front of Greg.

***

CHAPTER 13

The General was waiting at the edge of the field as Tom maneuvered the craft to have the door open about 50 feet from where he was standing.

"Lights on or off?" Greg asked Tom.

Jax answered. "Lights on. It makes it look like you are stepping out of a portal with the lights behind you."

Greg grinned and mischievously pressed the button to open the hatch and lower the ramp. "Hello, General, Greg Moore; care for a tour?" Greg approached and shook hands with a stunned General who was dressed in jeans and a light jacket.

Greg gave him a moment to get over his disbelief before taking him inside, introducing him to Tom and Jax, and then giving a tour of the rest of the craft.

"Have a seat; we'll talk about the technology."

"One second." Said the General as he walked to the door and waved to someone. He spoke into his watch, "Stand down. Everything's fine here."

"Security detail. Can't go anywhere without them these days." Explained the General.

"I have a security crew, too, but now that I have this toy, I don't need them all the time," Greg replied.

"Ok, let's hear it."

Greg started, "The propulsion system is proprietary, as is a part of the cloaking. The basis for cloaking is the same as the stealth bomber."

"Wait. How did you get the specs for the stealth bomber? That's top secret."

"I asked the Russians…"

"The Russians have the plans?" interrupted the General.

"No, they said they were trying to steal it from us," Greg replied.

"Then…"

Greg wanted to tell him that he had Alex look it up in THE LIBRARY, but Greg felt that the door should not be opened right now. Instead, he said, "I hired a bunch of the best aerospace and aeronautical engineers away from NASA, Boeing and other companies to create this craft. I gave them a mandate to cloak it. This is what they came up with. Don't ask me to explain the details; I barely made it through Physics 2 at college."

"How many can I get my hands on, and when?"

"This is the prototype. My manufacturing plant is creating civilian versions, uncloaked, of course. The big announcement is next month as I announce a new airline company. That will give us time to design a weaponized version with your team."

"How much?"

"Something in the billions, I'm sure. Prototypes always cost more. The bean counters told me this one cost about 15 billion. But with manufacturing efficiencies, we can probably shave off a billion or two. Then it depends on how crazy we get with weapons."

This time, the General laughed, "I had an insane number in my head."

"Want to take a ride?" Greg asked.

"Where to?"

"Name it. We've tested it near several secure locations and were undetected." Greg said, not wanting to get himself in trouble by saying they had actually invaded the airspace of several foreign countries and hovered over their military bases.

"How about Wright-Patterson Air Force Base." The General offered.

"That's no fun. Pick a base in Russia."

Again, stunned silence. The General looked Greg in the eye and realized he was not kidding. "You're serious."

"Yup. Been there. Done that. Have you back before sunrise."

"As much as I'm tempted, let's do something with the most advanced radar and sky surveillance system in the world today – Cape Canaveral."

Greg put on his headset. "Tom, what's the ETA for around trip to Florida and back."

"About an hour unless you want to land and put your toes in the water."

***

After dropping the General off at the farm at the conclusion of a successful trip, Greg asks Tom to drop him off at home. It was 4 am when Greg lowered the landing gear at the soccer fields near his house. With the lights off inside the craft, his exit was virtually undetectable. It would look as if he just appeared out of nowhere and started walking. He wanted to walk home, even though it was about a mile and would only take 20 minutes if he went directly home. He needed the time to think. He needed time to switch his brain from military contracts and starting a new airline to a much bigger project. Preparing the world to join an Intergalactic Federation was a monumental task. He zipped up his jacket to ward off the chill and walked for about an hour, then headed toward his house. A text to Jean that he was arriving in a few minutes and got an immediate reply that she would unlock the front door. He texted back that she should put on some walking shoes and a light sweater. Jean was waiting outside.

"I think we should be ok to talk outside," Greg said as he took her by the hand and started walking down the street, referring to the fact that they knew their house was bugged and monitored by who knows how many groups.

"This means it must be big," Jean said quietly.

"Bigger than anything else we've ever tackled, bigger than anything either of us could have imagined. And it answers the looming question we've had for a while, WHY."

"Meaning, the Dmitry question of Why us and Why now?" asked Jean.

"Exactly. And now we have an answer."

Greg was silent for a bit, "Just wondering how to start."

Jean was anxious and wanted to blurt something like, "Just get on with it; the suspense is killing me." But she sagely said nothing, just squeezed Greg's hand in encouragement.

Greg started with the wonderful view of the earth and the rotation to see the stars, then the golden light appearing. That set the stage for the rest of the tale. At some point, Jean had stopped, moved in front of Greg and was staring directly into his eyes. Greg was so engrossed in the tale that he wasn't aware that they had stopped. When he got to the part where they were invited to join an Intergalactic Federation, Jean's legs seemed to lose all strength, so she sat on the curb in front of someone's house and tugged Greg's hand to have him sit beside her.

"And we have the video in the spacecraft. I watched it on the way back to make sure it's good quality. And that's why I need you to come with me on the next trip. He, or it, or whatever it was said, he would appear for another conversation when I brought the right people."

Jean lay her head on Greg's shoulder for a while as they both sat in silence. As she stood up and pulled Greg to his feet, she said, "And now we know why."

They walked in silence for a while; Jean said, "We need to do something I've been thinking about for a while, but now it's for a different reason. I've been grooming several people to take on increasing responsibilities because I'm working too many hours. You are, too. Our whole life is consumed by our work. I was thinking it would be nice to take some downtime, but now…" she left the thought hanging with the understanding that Greg would know exactly what she meant.

"You're right. But maybe we can do both. Take some downtime as we start working on setting up the foundation for moving forward with this new project. However, there are some things I have kept as personal projects. I can think about who to turn them over to or who I need to hire to hand them off to."

"Same here," Jean replied. "I've been working on it for a while, but maybe I approached it wrong. I was giving multiple people bigger roles in running the holding company, but I may have created a monster because there is an internal power play going on."

"Is any of them a clear leader?"

"No, they each have their strengths, but if I had to choose today, I couldn't."

"Well, you don't have to choose today, of course. But if someone doesn't become the obvious choice when you are ready, then consider bringing in someone from the outside to take over."

"I've thought about that too. I'm thinking that Keith Williams, the CEO of Moore Real Estate is actually the best choice."

"Oh, that's perfect! He's fantastic." Greg replied.

"Yeah, but Bernice assured me that LaKesha is ready to take over and is already doing most of the work anyway."

"Interesting. What else."

"Priya and Mike are getting married."

"You mean…"

"Yes, our personal assistants have been dating for a while now. Mike proposed last month. You've been out in Wyoming, so you haven't seen Mike in person for a while. He wanted to tell you personally."

"Geez. I've been so self-absorbed in my own projects that I didn't even notice."

***

CHAPTER 14

"Tom, can you track down Sam? I can't reach his cell. Left a message but haven't heard back from him." Greg said.

"Sure. He's probably in the plant solving manufacturing problems. Anything in particular?" Tom asked.

"I'm going to need a smaller, personal version of the plane."

"Cloaked or uncloaked?"

"One of each. And how is the pilot training program progressing?" Greg asked.

"The first course is scheduled for next month. We're recruiting from former military and commercial pilots. Invitations have already been sent out. You need to finish deciding on salaries and pay scales. We are also recruiting for maintenance engineers and other support staff." Tom said.

"Isn't your wife the head recruiter?"

"Yeah. First, she always tells me that your idea to hire the spouses has really helped create this small town you've built here in Wyoming around the plant into a really nice community. Second, she says if you don't start making decisions on things she needs, then she's going to make them herself."

Greg promised to call her soon. He also realized she would make a great mayor of the private town.

***

Greg drove to his office on the secure campus to catch up with the Colonel and the other projects. Mike followed him into his office as soon as Greg walked into the building. Greg asked for one minute, then jotted notes on a piece of paper for things he had to do.

Alex: *Baseball tournament*

Marie: *What the heck is she up to this summer?*

Visit Nicholas Koumistas in Greece, as we promised 2 years ago.

Delegate everything.

Hire more people?

"Go." He said to Mike as he finished the last note.

Mike went through his list of everything Greg needed to do, some of which he knew about and some of which were new items. Then he announced his upcoming wedding. Greg warmly congratulated him and told Mike he was sending him to London to get a custom-tailored suit. Priya had already arranged for Aimee and Marie to make her dress.

Greg met with the AstroX group he had hired to finish the design of the spacecraft. They ran through a list of improvements for both the spacecraft and aircraft versions. Greg could sense their excitement and asked the team leader about it. He responded that the group was very excited to have discovered an addition to the hexagon shaped devices that were the basis of the antigravity device. They had gotten a Titan beetle, which had been the basis of one of the large beetles that should not have been able to fly due to the ratio of its body mass to the wing size. They magnified the underside of its outer shell two thousand times under a microscope and discovered a tiny hair in the center of each hexagon. Adding a similar metallic thread in their spacecraft version added power and efficiency. A demonstration on a larger scale device showed a vortex being created around this central thread. At the end of the meeting the team leader informed Greg that all team members expressed interest in going to space, something Greg promised the group that they would get to do soon.

The next meeting was with the quantum computer group. Craig informed him that the single quantum chip computer was done. There were demonstrations of what it could do. The next phase would be to create a version with multiple chips that would exponentially increase the power and speed of the hardware. Greg choked at the budget for this next phase but learned that multiple quantum chips in a single computer would replace an acre of a server farm of silicon-based computers. A discussion ensued about the need for compilers and languages that were needed to build applications. Greg asked them to send him a recommendation report on what was needed. Greg's own pet project to house THE LIBRARY and stitch together whole books would have to be set aside for now.

Mike and Greg flew to Wyoming. In a meeting listing all the things the town needed, Greg appointed Tom's wife as mayor, gave her a handsome salary, and set her budget at $70 million to expand Mooretown, as it was officially being called. Needing to delegate a lot of other tasks still on his plate, Greg promoted Sam, the manufacturing plant lead engineer as the new CEO of the Aerospace company. They had a lengthy meeting where Greg shared his ideas for the future progression of the space efforts as well as the commercial airplane division. Sam was excited at first, then got worried when Greg shared more of his visions for the future.

Greg laughed as he saw Sam's face change from enthusiasm to concern. "Don't worry, you get to hire your own staff, and I'm going to loan you Mike for a short time until you can get your own personal assistant. And hire Tom McGlaughlin as your Chief Operating Officer, although you might have to promise him that he can still keep flying for a while." Sam nodded in relief, and then his expression changed once again to astonishment when Greg mentioned a starting salary.

"My wife's going to kill me; she's already saying she doesn't see enough of me now," Sam said.

"So, hire your wife. It's been a great tradition so far at this facility. I've met her; find her a job where she can wear a hard hat and boss people around."

"I know just the job. I'll start her on the receiving dock where the big trucks come in. That way, she can get a hard hat AND a clipboard." Sam said.

***

"Hello, Dmitry. Can you meet in person next week?" Greg asked while on a phone call with his main Russian business partner.

"How about your new house in France, Chateau d'Armainvillers?"

"You know about that? The purchase is just completed, and we have not stayed there, but that would be a good location."

"I thought about putting in a bid once I saw it was on the market, but what am I going to do with yet another mansion?" Dmitry replied.

"Bring your family." Greg offered. "I assume they like being spoiled. Sebastien Satrat and family will be there as well."

"Why are we meeting? What is the subject?" Dmitry wanted to know.

"The largest project ever undertaken in modern times. It will take a person of great influence to move it forward."

"Very intriguing. See you there."

***

CHAPTER 15

"Nice house," Dmitry said in his understated humor as the families concluded a tour of the chateau and grounds. It was a great summer day with billowy white clouds dotting the sky. A slight breeze rustled the trees, making the tour of the extensive gardens a delightful experience. This chateau was on par, and some said it was bigger and better than Versailles.

"What is nice is that the prior owner discretely added the most modern amenities and security systems. It even has its own cell phone tower disguised as a tree." Jean explained.

"The Tour de France is riding nearby tomorrow; I would like to go." Stated Svetlana, Dmitry's wife, in heavily accented English.

Dmitry explained, "She was an amateur cyclist, progressing toward the professional ranks before we got married. Now she occasionally rides, but her duties as Minister of Education keep her busy enough that she doesn't get to ride often."

The adults headed toward the patio, where the chef had prepared a tea service. Marie, Aimee Satrat and the three Balinov children said they were going to explore the house more. The six adults sat at a large, sturdy oak table with a white, lacy tablecloth. There was tea, coffee, juice and water available. Sliced fruit, finger sandwiches and small bowls of a variety of nuts were spread along the center of the table.

"We're interested to hear about this grandiose project," Dmitry stated, nodding toward his wife to include her.

"Yes, you were very mysterious on the phone. We are also intrigued." Sebastien Satrat added, also nodding toward his wife, Monique.

"First announcement is that I have a new invention for an antigravity device. It's been used to create a spaceship and will be used for a new generation of airplanes. About the grand project, instead of me explaining, I want you to watch a short 6-minute video taken during my first space flight." Greg said.

At that point, Mike, Greg's assistant, brought four iPods with earbuds. Then sat at one of the remaining chairs at the table. Dmitry had a problem getting his video started, so his wife leaned over and pressed the right button. Mike had edited the video to include short clips containing views of the earth and the Milky Way with some nice classical music in the background. Then, as the golden globe started to appear, the sound switched to the cockpit audio with Jax stating, "What's that?". The Moores sat quietly, watching the faces of the others as they watched the remainder of the video. Dmitry's face was stoic, not showing anything. Svetlana was the most expressive as she sat straighter in her chair with one hand holding the iPod and the other daintily covering her mouth. Sebastien leaned forward and placed his other hand over the top of the device to reduce the glare since he was sitting on the side of the table with the sun at his back. Monique had a surprised look on her face, with wide eyes and arched eyebrows.

Silence surrounded the table as the adults simultaneously pulled the earbuds from their ears. After a brief pause, Dmitry said, "And now we know why."

Greg spoke after a moment of silence. "I propose that we limit the viewing of this video to this small group for now. We may have to show it to select individuals in the future to get their buy-in."

Dmitry looked around the table, then said, "Why me? Why did you think of inviting me to be one of the first people to see this message."

"I asked Jean who, of all the people we know around the world, would be the most influential in getting an effort of One World Government to succeed. She said, 'Call Dmitry.'"

Marie and Aimee wandered outside to the table and grabbed a finger sandwich. Noticing the silence at the table, Marie thought it was fine to interrupt. "Um, Dad, did you notice all the cars in the huge garage?"

"Yes, they came with the house. The sheik who owned the house before us said he had no interest in shipping them back home, so he wondered if I wanted them."

"Well, that makes sense. I wondered why you paid full price for the house when anyone else would have negotiated for a lower price." Dmitry said with amusement.

"Can Aimee and I take one for a ride?" asked Marie.

"Did you get your international driver's license yet?" asked Jean.

"No. I've been busy with studies and MUN research. Same with Aimee."

"I'll take you out later in one of the sports cars of your choice." Replied Greg.

"What is the topic of discussion today?" Marie asked.

"We are discussing whether one world government is possible," Greg replied.

"Oh!" replied Aimee excitedly, "We had that challenge last year at MUN."

"That is the challenge where Victor won the best solution and best speaker awards," Marie said.

"Can you give us a synopsis of the solution?" her mother asked.

"Sure. First, finish getting all nations into the United Nations. Second, create a constitution and get it ratified by all nations. Third, change the charter of the UN to be a governing body, and get signoff from every nation. This third one will be the biggest challenge because that means that the heads of state will have a higher authority to answer to." Marie explained.

That kicked off a lively back-and-forth discussion, with Marie and Aimee answering the questions and leading the discussions. After about 30 minutes, Marie offered to call Victor Shawnee, who was not only a friend of the family but a distant relative on Greg's side of the family. He was a member of the Native American Shawnee tribe, and he had decided to use that as his last name when he registered for Sorbonne University.

"Victor, can you get a cab and come to the Chateau d'Armainvillers, and bring a copy of last year's MUN solution with you. A cab driver will know how to get you here. Oh, and bring an overnight bag." Marie said on her cell phone as she invited Victor.

"Ooh, fancy. What's up?" asked Victor.

"A new study group has formed at the chateau, and they are interested in our solution."

"Ok, I'll be there in about an hour or so."

With that, the group decided to retire to their rooms for a brief rest before dinner. Victor arrived two and a half hours later with a tale of heavy traffic out of Paris and several closed roads due to the Tour de France riding nearby. Greg had been summoned to pay the cab fare. The cab driver was apologetic over the size of the fare due to the detours, but Greg waved off his apologies and gave him a healthy tip. Marie appeared, telling Victor that she would get him settled in the bedroom and that they had been waiting for him before dinner started. She took him by the hand and led him to her bedroom. Greg noticed this with interest and a raised eyebrow. Everyone was informed that dinner was being served.

Victor was introduced to the group with Aimee excitedly telling the group about the story of Greg's ancestor marrying into the Shawnee tribe. She had heard this story from Victor's great-great-great grandfather, Running Bear, who they estimated was now over 100 years old. Victor explained that his name was really Young

Wolf but he had taken the English name of Victor and used the tribe name as his surname.

Talk then turned to MUN, and since Victor had more experience than Marie and Aimee, he explained the structure, the challenges they were presented with every year, and the process of researching, writing and preparing a solution and a speech. The adults listened with rapt attention as Victor had a way of speaking that captivated his audience, just like his grandfather.

When the talk turned to the subject of one world government, Marie gave Victor a synopsis of what had already been discussed earlier, and then he filled in the details of the rest of the solution they had presented at MUN. The adults commented on how detailed the solution had been and congratulated Victor for winning the prizes for best solution and best speech.

"I'm curious about your recommendation for a federalist style of government for the U.N.," Dmitry asked.

"Most people either don't understand the term federalist or have a misconception," Victor explained. "At its basic definition it is simply a hierarchy of government structures that are at times independent and other times dependent or subservient to the higher levels of government. For example, in the U.S. we have elected city officials, then county, then state, then federal. Other countries have similar structures, but some have different structures. All we would be adding is another level on top of the federal or country level, no matter what style of government has been adopted by each country, where style means Socialist, Democratic, Dictator, and so on."

There were nods around the table as everyone absorbed what he was saying. "Now imagine a future U.S. election ballot with an added section for people to vote for their U.N. representatives." More nods, then a question from Greg.

"My brain is jumping ahead on logistics on how to get this to work. One of the challenges is going to be to get everyone on the planet the ability to see candidate speeches and read about their policies."

"Yes. And although the internet has made great progress over the past four or five years, the majority of the world still does not have adequate internet access." Replied Victor.

Greg looked over to his assistant, Mike, and nodded. Mike was already making a note about a future task for Greg to take on. Greg then glanced at Dmitry, and they both nodded, silently acknowledging a task to expand and improve network coverage in the countries where they had partnered to have joint ownership of the internet backbones.

Jean turned to Victor and asked, "What are other challenges to this effort?"

"Getting everyone to agree that the United Nations should be the One World Government will be a monumental task. This task will take on different forms of influence in different countries because most countries while agreeing that One World Government is great in concept, in reality, they would never relinquish control over their individual countries." Victor said.

"My thought exactly." Said Dmitry. "Russia will be very difficult to persuade."

"What if there was a way to form a worldwide group who could excerpt the right influence on their respective countries. What is everyone's opinion on the success of this idea?" Greg asked.

Everyone tried to speak at once, then stopped. Greg proposed they go one at a time, starting with Jean on his right. They each went around the table, giving a short one or two-sentence answer. The final consensus was that everyone thought the project was possible but that it would take many years and a lot of money to make it happen.

Greg concluded the evening with a statement, "I am thinking about using Chateau d'Armainvillers as the central headquarters for this project. There is enough room to invite influential people from different nations to study this initiative and work toward a solution."

As the group broke up, Aimee and Marie said they were taking Victor for a tour. Svetlana shepherded her children toward their bedrooms. Sebastien and Monique stepped outside on the patio to get some fresh air. Jean and Mike were talking. Greg pulled Dmitry aside and told him that he was now trading in every country that had a stock exchange and that he had business partners and government contacts in those countries, similar to the arrangements he had in Russia. Dmitry said he knew about most of Greg's foreign trading but didn't know that he was in all those countries.

Greg said, "If I get you a list of names of my contacts in each country, would you be willing to help identify who would be the most influential? Then we will invite them here to the next conference."

"Sure. I would be happy to help. But first, I want to know if you have invented a device that sends information from the future."

"Yes, do you want it?" Greg asked.

"Of course, but why would you just give it to me?" Dmitry wanted to know.

"I'm getting the use out of it that I need. Second, it's considered old technology. I've got a research and development company that is making some amazing things surrounding that concept." After a brief pause, Greg continued. "I assume you have a copy of the patent my son Alex and I filed years ago. Simply turn the magnets ninety degrees, change them to be electromagnets instead of magnetized iron bars and build a device surrounding them capable of creating intense heat." Greg explained.

"So that is why you retracted the patent. It would not work as designed, but you figured out a new design that would work!" Dmitry said with a sly grin.

"Yes, but we decided not to send the new design to the patent office once we got the signal to return at twice the speed of light. We felt that the world was not ready for such an invention."

With that, Greg and Dmitry separated. Dmitry headed to the bedroom suite to find his family. Greg headed over to Jean and asked if she was ready to retire for the evening.

On the way back to their bedroom, they encountered Marie who informed them that Alex texted with news that his team was invited to Jamaica for the next baseball tournament. Earlier that year they had won the U.S. national high school baseball tournament and won the Japan High School Baseball Invitational Tournament. Their coach had decided to accept the invitation for the summer Caribbean tournament because he learned that many of the top players from Central and South America would be attending. Greg and Jean immediately checked their phones and noticed they had gotten the same text.

Jean replied, "How exciting! Send the dates, and we'll be there."

For the next two days the team compiled a list of tasks that needed to be done. Dmitry would identify the most influential people in each country that they would then invite to a future conference. Svetlana would work within the Russian government to promote favorable views of the One World Government idea. Sebastien would do the same with the French Government, in addition, he would make contacts within the United Nations to see if there were already similar discussions in place. Jean would take on a similar task within the United States, but hers was a monumental challenge because the Moores had little to no governmental contacts. Monique volunteered to plan the next conference and all the logistics surrounding that. Greg had a very large challenge to spread internet access and cell phone access across the globe because they all agreed that was the best way to get the messages out to the world's citizens. Marie, Aimee and Victor agreed to help wherever they could, but everyone insisted that they continue their university studies as a priority.

***

The next day, the group walked down the long scenic tree-lined cobblestone driveway to the public road and found a place to stand to watch the Tour de France. Most of the Chateau's staff were already there. People were lining both sides of the road as far as the Moores could see. It was still one hour before the Tour de France riders were due to arrive, but they didn't mind the wait. It was a warm, slightly breezy day. They quietly chatted with the other spectators and learned that most people were avid fans, having traveled around France to find places to watch the riders come by for the day. One guy explained the different jersey colors to Greg and Jean, who were newcomers to the sport.

Everyone knew the lead riders were coming soon when the official helicopter hovered overhead, then circled the Chateau grounds before slowly inching up the road. Then, a group of motorcycles came next. The crowd excitedly pointed to a group of six riders coming up the road. Greg was amazed at the speed; he estimated they were going over thirty-five miles per hour. One guy started a timer on his phone and then explained to Greg that it was to tell how far behind the peloton or main group was. He had already told Greg that the race was going to turn east, away from Paris, at the bend in the road ahead and ride another forty miles to the finish line. It was due to be a sprint finish if the peloton could catch the lead group. It was the final day that the group contesting the green sprinter's jersey could get enough points.

Almost three minutes went by when the person with binoculars announced he could see the main group coming up the road. They went by so fast, and there were so many colors that it was hard to determine who was in the lead. Greg said he did catch a flash of yellow, a guy wearing all yellow, from his helmet to his shoes. The expert next to Greg explained that with only three minutes to make up over the last forty miles, the lead group was surely going to be caught. He also said that the team leading the peloton was all from the sprinter who was wearing the green jersey and that if they could catch the leaders and then lead him to victory today, then he would most likely keep the green jersey by the end of the tour.

The chef had brought a large folding table with a variety of afternoon treats for anyone in the crowd. He was surrounded by people talking about the wide variety of treats as well as the quantity. There was a lot of discussion on this year's Tour de France and the fact that the yellow jersey had changed hands more than usual. Jean commented that it seemed like complete chaos. Greg concurred. Still, they agreed that it was exciting to see so many people enthusiastically following the sport.

***

Greg and Jean stayed a few more days at the chateau and then called the charter airline company they used in Europe to visit Nicholas Koumistas, the president of their Greek real estate company. This was their first visit since they hired Nick several years earlier. The Moores were surprised by what Nick had accomplished, not only in Greece but in nearby countries throughout the Balkans as well.

The economy in Greece and surrounding countries was very depressed. Unemployment was at all-time highs. The Greek government had imposed what they were calling Austerity Measures. Public employees and retirees had their salaries and pensions cut in half. Social programs had been disbanded. People were abandoning homes they could no longer afford. Nick took advantage of the situation by buying houses, villas and condos that were in foreclosure, modernizing them and renting them for much less money than the original mortgage payments. As a result, many people who were on the brink of being homeless were grateful to be able to stay in their residences.

Jean and Greg were staying with Nick at his large villa, which Nick explained that he moved into after the British couple had abandoned it the prior year. It had been their second home, but they couldn't afford to keep the payments going. There was a large staff at the villa. Housekeepers, groundskeepers and a chauffeur, which Nicholas explained, were retired public servants who needed to do something to supplement their pensions. When a new property became available, the crew that went in and fixed up the property was a mix of retired school teachers and young people who had been unemployed. The same model was used in other countries that Nicholas had expanded into. The model only worked because of the economic situation and the insistence that Moore only wanted the company to make a very small profit, which Nick explained was currently at 2%.

For the next few days, Greg and Jean visited several of the properties. There were a dozen apartment buildings in Athens that now had full occupancy due to the low rent being charged. The university had sold the dormitories when they couldn't afford the mortgages. It was one of the first big set of properties Nick had purchased and renovated. They drove southwest and toured an absolutely gorgeous seaside resort that was stunningly whitewashed on the outside. The interior was also nicely appointed, although somewhat dated. The property was on the market. Jean, whose nose was better than Greg's, could tell something was wrong when they walked in. Nick agreed with her perception that the plumbing and sewer connection needed a complete overhaul, which caused Greg to reminisce about the first apartment building they had purchased in Washington, D.C.

On the list of potential properties were several other seaside resorts on the Peloponnesian Peninsula that were popular with British citizens. It was further away from Athens, so they scanned through pictures online instead of taking a lengthy car or train trip. Jean approved the increased budget for both the purchase and the renovations, stating that they would have to come back next vacation to stay at one of them.

Nick was keeping his salary very reasonable and told the Moores that his bonus was being able to move his family into one of the nicest villas in Greece. Jean, being the CEO of all the companies, approved of this business model and told Nick to keep expanding and to call her if he needed more capital. Nick responded with a list of planned acquisitions and the budget to fix and modernize them. He had also called the Castle Restoration crew and informed them that there were properties around Greece that they may be interested in restoring. Jillian Castor had been on a visit and would be sending her husband, who was the lead project manager, to do more detailed investigations.

***

CHAPTER 16

July 2003: Net worth $6 Trillion

It was a busy week for Greg and his assistant Mike. First, they flew to Wyoming to unveil the new airline and airplane based on the anti-gravity device. The commercial version was uncloaked and dampened so that it would not achieve the heights to go outside Earth's gravity well. They took the first plane on several stops to a few different states and countries. The first was to Washington, D.C., to pick up Jean and her assistant Priya. The next was to Scotland to see the archeological dig next to the castle restoration project that had uncovered a tunnel leading to an ancient burial mound. Jillian Castor was there to lead them around the site and film everything for the next episode of the popular cable television series Castle Restoration. Jean's parents, who were heading the castle restoration company and had expressed interest in going to Jamaica, boarded the plane with the rest of the group.

A quick stop in Paris to pick up Marie and Victor, who were dating. They both expressed a desire to go to Jamaica to watch Alex's baseball tournament. The next stop was back to Washington, D.C., to pick up the baseball team, coaches and any of the family members in the area who were going to the tournament. Finally, Jamaica, where Mike informed Greg that the Prime Minister had requested a meeting.

At all the airports, a crowd of reporters and on-lookers were gathered to see the new aircraft. Greg had a speech prepared that he repeated at each location. However, in Jamaica, there was only one small television crew to greet them. Greg did the obligatory speech, and then, off camera he asked the reporter where the crowd was.

The reporter informed him with a laugh that they were all at the public terminal and that he had been paying attention to the landings in other countries and had noticed that they had all taken place in private airports. Greg joined in the laughter as the family entered the caravan of buses arranged by Mike and Priya.

The accommodation was luxurious. Mike and Priya had arranged an entire beachside resort for the family and baseball team. It was a new resort that was originally slated to open in one month but had been persuaded by an offer of extra profits to open early. Mike informed the owners that the family and team would stay out of the way of the remaining construction.

After a hectic breakfast where Greg and Jean watched in humor as the coaches attempted to get the group of teenage boys fed and on the busses to go to the stadium for their first practice before the tournament, Greg welcomed his daughter Marie and her boyfriend Victor to their breakfast table.

"Sleeping in today?" Jean asked.

"With the time zone shift, we ended up walking on the beach at midnight," Victor explained.

"Enjoy the day off. You can either plan your own thing today, connect with Mike and Priya, or just hang out at the beach." Greg offered. "Alex's first game isn't until the day after tomorrow."

Jean informed them, "We've been invited to lunch at the Prime Minister's villa at 1 pm."

"Interesting," Marie replied. "What does he want to talk to you about?"

"He probably wants one of my airplanes."

***

"This way, please."

Greg and Jean followed the butler through the villa out to the back lawn, where a man and a woman were seated at a table set for four people.

"Pleasure to meet you, Mr. Prime Minister," Greg said as they shook hands.

"Call me P.J.," the Prime Minister requested.

"I'd like to introduce my wife, Jean," Greg said. "She is the CEO of all the companies we own."

"And an attorney, if my research is correct." Said the Prime Minister. "Let me introduce the U.S. Ambassador to Jamaica, Sue McCourt Cobb."

"Pleasure to meet you as well." Both Greg and Jean said as they shook hands with the Ambassador, then took their seats as lunch was served.

"I understand your son is in the baseball tournament we are hosting." Said the Prime Minister.

"Yes. He plays third base and is one of the two power hitters on the team." Jean said.

"I would like to invite you to use my stadium box for the games. I have cleared my schedule for the final games of the tournament, but you are welcome to use it for the entire time."

"I understand that you converted the main soccer stadium to a baseball field for this tournament."

"Yes, the main baseball stadium suffered some damage last year in the hurricane and the repairs are not yet complete. Plus, the locker rooms are nicer in the football stadium."

"How about if we sit in the team section of the stands with the other parents for the first part of the tournament, then join you in the box if our team makes it to the finals," Greg said.

"That is a perfect solution."

"Do you know a Mr. Monsoon?" Greg asked the P.M.

"Yes, why do you ask."

"He places a large bet against my son's team and accuses several of the stars of cheating so that they will not be able to play," Greg responded. "Do you have any influence with him?"

"I can threaten to shut down much of his illegal business, but that may take longer than this tournament will last."

The Ambassador, who had not said much up to this point, offered her opinion. "I must caution you that he is a dangerous man to cross."

"If you can get him a message that his silent business partner would like to speak to him, I would appreciate it," Greg said.

"You are a part owner of the cable and cell phone business on the islands. I will assume that Monsoon is also invested in those businesses." Said the Ambassador.

"Yes," Greg replied as they finished an excellent lunch of spiced grouper, jasmine rice and cold mangos. Then, they were offered a choice of coffee or tea. Jean chose tea. Greg was normally not a coffee drinker but had heard about the world-class beans produced on the island.

"Excellent coffee," Greg said after taking a sip.

"Yes. We take great pride in the beans grown here on the islands. It is one of our primary exports. And, of course, I pay a bit more to have the experts pick out the best batches for me." Said the PM, who then gave a brief history of the island.

When the PM changed the subject to Greg's new airplane and asked how he could get one of his own, Greg countered with an explanation of their One World Government initiative. He basically hinted that if Jamaca would back a vote to make the United Nations the governing body, a new airplane earmarked for Jamaca could find its way to the top of the list as the demand for airplanes was currently very high.

"You will want to meet with Pat Durant. She knows more about the inner workings of the United Nations than anyone else I know. Pat is Jamaica's permanent representative to the U.N. since 1995." Said the Prime Minister.

Immediately after lunch, the Ambassador returned to her office, called her boss at the U.S. State Department and relayed the conversation about OWG. Her boss listened thoughtfully, then responded that this was not the first time he had heard about the subject. He told her he would await her full report, then hung up.

***

Alex waived to his family as he trotted out to take his turn at batting practice. The weather forecast predicted rain, so the officials shortened the warmups and announced that the game would start about 15 to 20 minutes early. The family was prepared and had worn rain gear and brought umbrellas.

The American team had easily won the first two games; this one was the quarter-finals against a decent team from Argentina. Greg had learned that many professional baseball players came from South and Central America, including Argentina, where it was a major sport.

Greg noticed a large man with dreadlocks approaching. He locked eyes with the man to indicate that he knew the man wanted to speak to him. "Monsoon would like to a word." He said in a deep voice with a Jamaican accent. Greg and Jean had discussed several options and had developed a plan to respond to this situation. It all started when Greg had gotten a notice on his cell phone to check his faxes and discovered one from the future that said, "Monsoon intends to file a grievance of cheating against several players on the American team, causing them to be ineligible until an investigation is concluded."

Greg followed the large man to a luxury skybox, where he was introduced to "Monsoon". Greg had done his homework and knew that his actual name was Fredrick Belvidere. "Hello Mr. Belvidere."

"Ah, I see that you have done your homework." Said Monsoon.

"Well, we are business partners in the island network and cell phone businesses."

"Yes, but you never come to any of the meetings. Instead you have your local attorney attend in your stead."

"I know. It is a small venture for me, and I am already working too much, but I do keep an eye on the progress and the quality reports." Greg said.

"Help yourself to any of the food, the rest of my family will be here shortly. May I offer you beer or wine?"

"Tea is my drink of choice, but I will save that for next time as I hope this will be a short meeting," Greg said. "I assume you got word that I wanted to meet."

"Yes, and I am intrigued about what you would be interested in talking to me about," Monsoon said.

"I would like you to withdraw the claim of cheating against the American team," Greg said.

"How could you possibly know about that?" Monsoon said incredulously. "Can you read minds?"

"No, that has not been invented yet," Greg replied. "It came to my attention as soon as the draft was written by the Jamaica Baseball Commission. You can tell them to withdraw it."

"You have no leverage against me!" Monsoon blustered.

"I know you are considering placing a large bet against the American team if they win this game and go to the semi-finals. The claim of cheating against the star players will force them to sit out, then likely lose the game, making your bet successful."

"How could you possibly know that? It is impossible unless you can read my mind."

"It is a guess on my part, derived when the draft of the cheating claim was brought to my attention," Greg said.

"Then what incentive do I have to withdraw the claim," Monsoon said.

"I leave you alone to conduct business as normal."

"Are you threatening me?" Monsoon asked.

"Look, Monsoon, we don't want to start a feud. It wouldn't benefit either of us."

"I don't see what you can do to me and my organization."

"Have your security guys look out on your back lawn," Greg said.

Monsoon made a call, talked for about a minute, then said, "They see nothing."

Greg sent a text that said, '*Tom, go ahead with the plan.*' Then to Monsoon, "Now have your men check again."

Tom had landed the cloaked spaceship in Monsoon's rather large backyard and had one of the crew jump out and do something; then they took off again.

Monsoon called again listened to a brief explanation on the other end, then hung up. With a perplexed look on his face, he said, "How the hell did you get past my security to plant a circle of American flags on my lawn?"

"To paraphrase a famous science fiction writer, 'Any sufficiently advanced technology is indistinguishable from magic.' And if I can do something like that, imagine what else I can do."

"Like what?"

"Let's start with some of the non-violent things that would make your life miserable. I'm thinking of perhaps intercepting all your phone calls and texts or randomly interrupting them. Or, capture all your emails and publish them in public. Or, even better, turn off the electricity in any building you enter." Greg explained. "I'll be gone in a few days, and you can go back to business as usual. Our paths may never cross again."

"Ok. I will not proceed with the cheating claim." Monsoon said. "But tell me, how did you find out about the claim? Do you have someone inside the commissioner's office?"

"Before I visit anywhere, I do some investigations, looking for things that would affect my family. Remember, I am part owner of the network and cell phone companies here on the islands, and I can easily get information from anyone connected to these networks." Greg said.

"You mean like hacking?" Monsoon asked.

"Precisely!" Greg said emphatically. It was not the truth, but it was a concept that Monsoon could understand. With that, Greg left the sky box and made his way back to his seat. He gave Jean a thumbs-up sign as he approached.

It started drizzling in the top of the 5th inning, then it turned to rain in the top of the 6th inning. A quick conference between the coaches and umpires resulted in the decision that the rain was not heavy enough to call the game. With the American team leading by one run, the first batter in that inning was the power hitter for the Argentinian team. Alex dove to catch a scorching line drive that would have been a foul ball. He caught it for the first out but landed heavily on his ribs directly on third base. Greg could hear the oomph as the wind was knocked out of Alex. He lay there for a few seconds, then raised his glove with the ball inside to show the umpire that he had caught the ball. Then he rolled on his back, gasping for breath as the coaches and trainer rushed from the dugout to his side. Greg and Jean rushed down from the fifth row to observe. After about two minutes, the coaches helped Alex up. As they were escorting him off the field, the coach told his parents that they were taking him to the medical center inside the stadium to get an X-ray.

Later that day, Alex and his coach made their way back to the resort in time for dinner. The diagnosis was bruised ribs, nothing broken. They would have to make a game-day decision on whether he would be able to play in the next game tomorrow.

***

"Dmitry, I have an update on the One World Government project after my meeting with the Jamaican Prime Minister and the American Ambassador to Jamaica," Greg said. "You are on speakerphone with Jean, Marie and Victor. We are still in Jamaica, waiting for our son's baseball tournament to proceed."

"Yes, I saw on the internet they have won all their games," Dmitry said.

"True. But Alex was injured yesterday, bruised ribs, nothing broken." Greg explained. "But fortunately, the games may be rained out today. It will give him an extra day to heal. The coaches have him doing light stretching today in the hope that he will be better by tomorrow."

"Good. Keep me posted on his progress. Now, what is your news."

"Since Jamaica is in the British Commonwealth, we not only have to convince the Prime Minister and their U.N. Representative to vote for One Government, we also have to convince the Royal British Representative as well."

"Hmmm, I see," Dmitry replied. "It may be easier to go directly to the source so that all countries in the British Commonwealth can be influenced from the top down."

"So, how do we get an audience with the Queen?" Jean asked.

***

Alex was able to start the next game but said he was going to have trouble swinging the bat. In his first at-bat, he tapped a surprise bunt down the third base line and safely made it to first. Sammy hit a triple off the centerfield wall to score Alex. The remainder of the game was a pitcher's duel. The game ended 1-0 in favor of the American team. That put them into the final game the following day against a very strong team from Mexico.

The next morning, Alex's bruise looked even worse than before, but he said it felt better, even though he said he didn't sleep well. At the field, Alex did the regular warmups but skipped batting practice, saying that his ribs were too sore to do the twisting motion to bat. Greg could see him talking with the coaching staff about what they were going to do. Apparently, they were going to keep him in the game because Alex stepped to the plate to open the game. That was the first time he batted first all season. Normally, he batted third and his best friend Sammy batted fourth. The plan from the coaches was for Alex to bunt toward third, but he noticed that the third baseman was playing in toward the grass. They were expecting the bunt. Alex stepped back, looked toward the dugout and got the sign from the coach to hit away. Knowing that Alex was injured, the pitcher threw a fastball straight down the middle. Alex swung as best he could but did not have his regular power. It was a late swing, too, but it ended up being a blooper over the head of the first baseman. Alex made it safely to first base.

The pitcher glanced at Alex several times and noticed that he was not taking a normal lead off the bag. He concluded that Alex was not going to attempt to steal, so he ignored him. The next batter hit a line drive to the shortstop for the first out. The following batter hit a slow roller toward third base, and it looked like it was going to be a double play to end the inning. Alex was thrown out at second, but the runner made it safely to first. Sammy was up next and hit a home run to put his team up 2-0.

Throughout the remainder of the game, the teams kept trading leads with the score 8-8 at the end of regulation play. The other team did not score at the top of the inning in overtime. For Alex's team, the first two batters hit outfield fly balls, making it two outs. Alex was up next. He had hit two singles all game but decided that he was going to ignore any pain and stiffness and swing as hard as he could. He let two strikes go by, then two balls. The pitcher sensed that Alex was still injured, so he pitched a slider low and inside. Alex was ready for it. With a golf-like swing, Alex got a solid connection on the ball and lifted it high in the air toward deep center field. He couldn't tell how far it was going to go, so he ran with all his might. As he rounded first, he could see the outfielder leaping to catch the ball at the top of the wall. He couldn't tell if he caught it, so he kept running hard. He kept watching the outfielder and noticed that he just stood there and did not throw the ball back into play. That was when he realized he had hit a home run! The team was going crazy, jumping and yelling as he rounded third and into home. He jumped up and down on home plate as his team surrounded him, yelling and pounding him on the back, which hurt like hell, but he didn't care; he had won the game.

***

CHAPTER 17

"This is either a spectacular Hollywood production with a cheesy dialog, or it's real." Said Prince Phillip after he watched the six-minute video of Greg's encounter with the glowing golden orb. The Queen sat silent, watching the faces of the Moores.

"It's easier to convince someone that it was made by a talented special effects team, but I assure you it is real," Greg replied, then continued by explaining his cloaked spacecraft, a version of his publicly announced new airplane. The Prince immediately started asking questions.

"How fast were you travelling?"

"Not exactly sure. The pilots said we had stopped accelerating but were still moving at a high rate of speed. I could get that answer, though." Greg replied.

"The actual speed is not important; the question was more about whether you were stationary or moving. And if you were going at a high rate, then the being in the orb was keeping pace with you." The Prince explained. "And you don't appear to be headed toward the moon; what was your actual bearing?"

"We would have had to turn twenty degrees left to go to the moon. The pilots tell me we were headed toward Saturn. I haven't shown this to my astrophysicist team because I wanted to keep the audience as small as possible – you are the 9th and 10th people to see this video. Tom, our pilot, said as best he could calculate, the orb originated from one of Saturn's moons, but without further analysis, he couldn't tell me which one." Greg explained.

"One World Government." Said Queen Elizabeth. "If you can convince us to back your initiative, then supposedly all the Commonwealth nations would fall in line due to our influence. Smart."

"We prefer the federalist model, where all countries remain as sovereign nations, instead of abolishing all governments in favor of a ruling world government," Jean said. "Similar to the model of your commonwealth system, or maybe a combination of that and the E.U model."

"It will still be difficult to get every country to vote in favor of any initiative to change the mandate of the United Nations to become the ruling entity. How are you going to influence each country?" asked the Queen.

"A series of workshops are being planned over the next year whose audience will be the most influential people in each nation," Jean explained. "We are still discussing who will be invited to each workshop. For example, does the first one include only heads of state, or do we start with influential people in each nation with the intent of convincing them to take the message back to their respective countries."

"I've read your Treatise on One World Government." Said the Queen. "It seems to be based on a MUN paper from last year."

"Yes, the original paper was authored by a small team, with the spokesperson named Victor Shawnee. I added the legal sections after researching the different legal systems around the world." Jean replied.

"Yes, every year, I read some of the higher-quality papers published by the MUN projects. I believe the challenges the students get are real-world and very intriguing. The Royal Family supports the MUN initiatives throughout the Commonwealth as it is one of the most beneficial efforts for young people."

"Our foundation is also a large supporter of MUN around the world ever since our daughter started during her senior year of high school," Jean said. "We supply facilities for meetings, computers, logistics for travel, lodging and food for the students."

The Queen looked at her husband. "You've been silent yet seem to be lost in thought."

"I'm thinking more about the Galactic Federation. You can figure out this One World Government effort without me. I'm more interested in what form the Federation takes, what advantages it will bring, where it meets, who will be the representative from Earth and other questions." Said Phillip.

"Ah, a man after my own heart!" Greg explained. "It's something I have spent a great deal of time thinking about since the encounter. Why do I get the feeling that you are not surprised by this event?"

"We have documents going back centuries of the same request to have one government ruling the world. That was the start of the British Empire. Eventually, it got too big to manage and collapsed under its own weight. More recently, Winston Churchill's private papers talk of a visit requesting the same thing after World War II. Britain worked hard to help establish the United Nations." The Queen explained. "Currently, I am in favor of your plans to morph the U.N. to become a governing entity, so I will back your effort."

"And at the end of the video, this entity stated it would return if you brought the right people," Philip stated. "Who would be in that group?"

"We've been thinking that it should contain people who are not convinced to vote for the initiative by other means," Jean replied.

"Are you interested?" Greg asked.

"Yes, absolutely."

That concluded the meeting, with the Queen stating that she would provide assistance and that perhaps they would meet again in the future.

***

CHAPTER 18

"Keith, you've been the CFO of our real estate corporation for six years and are doing a fantastic job," Jean said as the meeting with her Chief Financial Officer started. "Are you interested in the top spot when Bernice retires?"

"Absolutely," he replied. "And I've been grooming our head accountant to take my place as soon as he finishes his Master's in Finance next spring."

"Bernice also brought up LaKesha's name for future considerations as CEO but thought you would be a good choice right now."

"Yes. Bernice and I have been mentoring LaKesha for some time now. She is currently Chief Operating Officer and doing a fine job. She says she wants to get her MBA and has enrolled in a program called an Executive MBA, where she attends courses alternate Fridays and Saturdays for eighteen months. That way, the company gives up one day per week of her time, and the following week, she gives up one of her weekend days. I've looked at the curriculum and the professors, and I think it's a marvelous program."

"Is LaKesha related to you?" Keith asked.

"No. She is married to a man that my husband used to work with. He is Bernice's grandson. We met Lakesha just before she graduated from college. I was impressed, so I hired her right after graduation." Jean said, then continued, "You said you wanted to meet with me about something else?" Jean asked.

"Correct. There is a rumor that the U.S. House of Representatives will have a vacant seat for Virginia in two years. I'm thinking about running. I qualify because I live just across the border of D.C. near Arlington."

"Oh, right. Your house is in Riverwood, if I remember correctly, from when you hosted a holiday party several years ago. That's fairly close to the office, right?"

"Yes, about 10 minutes in normal traffic."

"How are you preparing for this transition?" Jean asked.

"Studying constitutional law, watching C-SPAN – the mostly boring Congress Channel and WIKIPEDIA has been quite helpful since its inception a year or so ago. It contains explanations of the different branches of government, how they relate to each other and, more important for me, the processes of government." Keith said. "Meaning, how bills and resolutions get passed."

"If I wanted to get something passed, how would I go about it?" Jean asked.

"First, find someone to write the bill. Or write one yourself and get someone in Congress to sponsor it. Then it goes for discussion, then a vote in the House. If it succeeds, it goes to the Senate for more discussion and another vote. Then it goes to the President for either signing or veto."

"In order to ensure it gets enough votes in both the House and Senate, how do I persuade enough people to vote for it?" Jean wanted to know.

"Give them something they want, like help fund their next campaign or establish a big business in their state or district to help with employment. It could mean finding a way to help them get one of their bills passed."

"That sounds like a lot of work because there are hundreds of people to influence," Jean said.

"That's where the Lobby groups come in. They contact each Congressperson or Senator to find out what they want. They even have people who will write the bill for you."

"Keith Williams, I believe you will make a fine Congressman. I'm willing to be a major donor to your campaign if you will help pass whatever it is I need to get passed."

"Tell me more about what you are interested in getting passed." Keith wanted to know.

"A bill or resolution to get the United States to agree to change the United Nations Charter to become a One World Government," Jean said.

"Wow. I didn't expect that. I was thinking you were going to ask for something favorable for your businesses. How did you get interested in One World Government?" Keith asked.

Jean did not want to bring up the Galactic Federation, instead, she used the story that the original group had agreed on and was a true story on its own. "As you know, the Moore Foundation is taking on big projects all over the world, water projects, disease eradication, education, homelessness, etc. We've concluded that projects like these would be easier to do if we had One World Government. I've written a Treatise on One World Government that I will send to you."

"You need to post that on the internet," Keith said.

"It already is. Let me send you the link." Jean said as she got out her phone and texted Keith the URL.

"Let me know when you need money for your campaign. In the meantime, if you want the CEO position in the interim, work with Bernice to start transitioning. Then we'll make a formal announcement and plan her retirement party."

"By the way, there is already a group of people, mostly academics, who are talking about One World Government," Keith said.

"How do I get in touch with them?"

"GOOGLE IT"

***

Several days later, Jean farmed out her normal daily duties to her assistant and various Vice Presidents, then spent the rest of the day crafting an email to the group she was calling OWG Original Group, which consisted of Greg, herself, Dmitry and his wife Svetlana, Sebastien and his wife Monique, Marie, Aimee and Victor. These were the people who knew about the invitation to the Galactic Federation being the reason for the push toward One World Government. The plan was to use the normal list of advantages of OWG to convince others to back the movement. Only those who strongly resisted the effort would be told about the Galactic Federation and possibly offered a ride to space to meet the golden orb being.

To: OWG Original Group
Subject: Status of effort to get U.S. backing

A Lobby group that focuses on Special Interest Groups like us has agreed to help write any bills and resolutions we need and then help get the votes needed to pass them. They are very expensive, but I assume that's one reason why we became super wealthy – to afford to back the OWG movement.

They explained that one of the best ways to get the votes of Congresspeople and Senators is to become a major contributor to their campaigns. That is another pile of funds we need to have ready. Each Congressperson and/or Senator will also want something favorable in their District and State, such as a new business or help with a special project, which means more funding.

There is another group, mostly academics, who has been working on the OWG issue and would love to have other people join their efforts. They've got good material on their web page and even a first draft of a World Constitution. (it needs some work, but it's a fine start). I talked to one of the academics, who seems to be the de facto leader of the group. He's excited to learn that we are serious about making this happen. I assured him that we have funding and backing from people around the world who can move this forward. He recommended that we all get a Skype account so we can start conference calls and chats. BTW, their site has an interesting page on the history of OWG movements – it appears that historically, there have been many attempts over the past 100 years to create a central world government.

This is going to seem like an impossible project, but let's stick with it!

Jean

***

There was almost an immediate reply from Dmitry in Russia. Jean calculated that it must be almost 2 am.

It has become very dangerous to discuss this topic in Russia. We'll have to find another way.

Greg must have been online in Wyoming because his reply was immediate as well. *Offer him a ride to space?*

***

Monique had planned the first conference at the Chateau for late September. She said the large ballroom would seat 75 people comfortably. The hallway just outside the ballroom would contain stations for coffee, tea and juices. Bathrooms would be a challenge, especially since most of the attendants were men. The invitations went out to the wealthy people who had been following Greg's trades in the various countries, which included several heads of state and other political figures from different countries. The goal was to convince them to use their wealth to influence legislation and votes to create a world Government. The main speakers and leaders of the breakout workshops were the academics and politicians who had been working on this issue for several years. Most of these speakers came a week early to help perfect the presentations and the papers.

***

Greg's new-style planes were busy shuttling people to France. The planes still caused quite a stir wherever they flew. The French government had been alerted to the conference and was interested in sending a few representatives. Somehow, the Queen of England discovered the dates before they were announced. She sent a note with a list of Commonwealth representatives to invite. Eighty invitations were sent out with the hopes of getting seventy to attend. Fifty responded, which turned out to be a good number because many of them brought interpreters.

Greg kicked off the conference with a five-minute talk, welcoming everyone and explaining the purpose of the meeting. He also talked about the protocol of the meeting such as raising a card with your name and country name when you wished to speak. He then mentioned to the audience that there would be no need to 'leak' anything to online media since all recordings and other content would be put online. Monique had also arranged a film crew to record the entire event.

Greg turned it over to Wolfgang Schmidt, a former East German resident and current professor of political science. Wolfgang was also a United Nations Representative from Germany. He had been writing and publishing about One World Government for years. The website that Jean had found the most helpful material, including a proposed OWG Constitution, had been written by a group headed by Wolfgang. Today, Wolfgang's PowerPoint presentation walked the audience through the highlights of the pros and cons of having an OWG.

Pros:

1. Economic: one currency, easier trade, normalizing taxation, fixing capital movement

2. Security: No need to fund individual armies. Peacekeeping troops would be supplied by the United Nations. Ideally, no more wars.

3. Open Borders: People would be free to migrate where the jobs were in a controlled fashion.

4. Justice: Similar laws and rules in each country. International Court of Justice

5. Education: Standard structure and standard material, equal opportunity to learn

6. Communication: standard access to open communication media (eventually)

Cons:

1. Autonomy: Countries not willing to live under a higher ruling authority and not willing to agree to economic, judicial and educational standards.

2. Uncertainty: Fear of eventually removing country designations and having one big brother government. Concern that, eventually, a loss of language and culture would be a long-term result.

Immediately after point number one in the Pros section on Economics, many cards were raised. Wolfgang mentioned again that questions would be taken after the Pros and Cons were listed. He explained that each of the points would be discussed in detail throughout the remainder of the day. Later, Jean expressed delight that the question and debate period was very respectful as everyone seemed to be knowledgeable about Roberts's Rules of Order.

The agenda for the following morning was the topic of how to morph the current United Nations into an organization that could become the governing body for the world. The main takeaway from that session was to first fix the corruption and imbalance of influence in the current United Nations structure. The second takeaway was an agreement that a bicameral representation structure was needed, similar to the United States Congress and Houses of Representatives and England's Upper and Lower House, which many countries emulated. The third takeaway was an insistence on a method of checks and balances so that no one branch of the government had absolute control. There were many other ideas and concerns listed that would eventually need to be addressed.

The afternoon contained breakout sessions for each of the topics in the pros and cons. The most popular was the Economic and Security sessions. At a break, Greg was talking to one of the African delegates who was skeptical about the OWG idea.

"Would this centralized government help us with our rebel problem? There is a group of rebels attacking the capital."

"What do they want?" Greg asked.

"Either to rule the country or to create their own country."

"Interesting. The United States gets requests every year from groups who want to establish their own nation within the United States. Most of these are Native Americans. There are strict guidelines for becoming your own nation within the United States. You may want to research these requirements if the rebels are willing to negotiate." Greg said.

"If you could help with that, I would appreciate it. Here is my card."

"Sure. I would be happy, too. Actually, if you think about it, this is the Palestinian question and would make a great discussion topic at this conference – 'Who should qualify for separate nation status.' If I recall, there was a great deal of discussion and negotiation after the breakup of the Soviet Union, so we should have a broad basis of examples to choose from. Now, we have all those new or returning nations in the Balkans, like Montenegro and Macedonia. The One World Government is likely to run into this on a continual basis."

The African representative had been outspoken in the security breakout session, saying he was doubtful that removing military force from each country was a good idea. Otherwise, he stated, it would be too easy for a presidential building to be overrun by rebels to create a new government. A consensus was reached by the group that, at the very least, a Presidential guard would be needed in each country.

Greg, using his natural left brain, listed the other choices for dealing with rebels, from wiping them out to negotiating a settlement to full capitulation and letting them take over the government. It was a good debate as the African representative had opposing points for each one Greg brought up.

Standing nearby was an elderly woman with a cane, whose name tag only said 'Isa.' She leaned into Greg and said, in an accent that Greg could not quite place, "Logic does not apply to human conflict." Greg nodded, taking in her point. He introduced himself and then said, "I noticed that your name tag does not have a country designation." Her reply was, "I live on a ship."

In a dinner discussion with the Swiss representative, Jean learned that he was already in favor of a One World Government. Jean took the opportunity to turn the conversation to playing tourist in Switzerland.

"That depends on whether you want luxury or rustic." He spoke.

"Tell me about both."

"If you want to be pampered, just about anywhere has upscale residences, especially around Geneva." He replied. "For Rustic, Lauderbrunnen is a dead-end canyon with spectacular scenery, caves, waterfalls and hiking. If you are going to go there, stay in Wengen. It's a small town where cars are not allowed."

The third day was much the same, with deeper dives in each subject. The final result was a great list of what needed to be done, as well as ideas on how to achieve the goals. Several people stayed up late each night, putting all the content on the web page with Marie being the driving force of the late-night sessions. Each day, they awoke to many constructive comments as well as posts by internet trolls calling them idiots and other names. Greg had hired an internet manager, who he instructed to remove those non-constructive comments.

The final result from the conference was a fairly good outcome. Greg and Jean felt that they had a good agreement on the idea from the attendees that a single world government would work if it was done properly. However, most had stated that it would take a lot more convincing for their respective countries to vote on joining such a federation.

***

CHAPTER 19

October 2003

"I need to go back to the office in D.C.," Greg said to his wife, Jean. "The scientists requested a meeting, and they said, 'not over the phone.' Then the airline plant in Wyoming has had an outstanding request for a meeting, but they won't tell me what it is."

"I guess I'm lucky. All my pressing business can be done over the phone and Skype." She replied.

"But I need a few days of downtime to just do nothing," Greg said.

"Sounds good to me. And after a conversation with the Swiss representative at the conference, I know just the place. " Jean said, then she sent Priya a text to book a nice room in Wengen, Switzerland, for five days. "Pryia will make reservations. And I told her and Mike to take 5 days off too."

"Where are we going?" Greg asked.

"It's a surprise!"

Priya texted back 2 hours later with the itinerary, stating that Greg and Jean had first-class train tickets the day after tomorrow.

Greg texted the head of security at the Chateau, Dirk, and arranged a ride to the train station for the morning of the trip.

On the way to the train station, Jean asked, in French, "Is Dirk a common French name?"

Dirk responded, "I will answer in English to practice. Dirk is very uncommon in France. My father was a huge Clive Cussler fan, and we had all his books in the house. Several were even signed by the author. He named me after the main character, Dirk Pitt." Greg was also a fan and had read several of the books, so they chatted about their favorites during the ten-minute drive to the station.

Several hours into the trip, Jean remarked, "We should do this more often." At first, they had been busy texting the various leaders of their respective companies and projects, then agreed to put away their phones and watch the scenery.

"What should we do more often? Put away our phones or take a first-class train ride through Europe?"

"Both."

The first leg was to Basel, Switzerland, then a twenty-minute wait to transfer to a train to Interlaken, then a one-hour wait for the transfer to Lauderbrunnen. A brisk walk to the other station to catch the cog train in Lauderbrunnen got them there with five minutes to spare before it left. There was a pamphlet on the seat describing the train and its history. Greg read some of the highlights to Jean.

"World's longest cog train. Narrow gauge. Opened in 1893. Apparently, the cogs don't engage until it gets steep."

The station manager in Wengen gave them directions to the Grand Hotel Belvedere, stating, in very good English, that it was on the far side of town and that they would have to walk because no cars were allowed in Wengen.

It was cold and sunny as they stepped out of the train station. Fortunately, they both had roller suitcases. Greg was pulling Jean's larger, heavier-wheeled case, and she had his medium-sized one. After about five minutes of walking into a cold headwind, Greg stopped in a shop and bought gloves and a ski hat for both of them. Jean picked out a beautiful long scarf. It was deep green with a vivid mauve stripe down the center. The tag on the scarf said, in German, French and English, 'Hand Knit by Yvonne.' The shopkeeper informed them that these scarves were highly sought after, as well as the accompanying Afghan blankets. Jean unfolded one and gasped at the exquisite shell-shaped pattern. She decided they would make great Christmas presents and picked one that was a royal purple with intermittent off-white stripes for Marie and one that was gold and silver for Alex. The last remaining two she purchased, intending to give one to her parents, who were still in Scotland on a castle restoration project, and Greg's parents, who were house-sitting Greg and Jean's house in Washington D.C. These blankets were rather bulky. After Jean remarked that there was no way they would fit in her suitcase, the shopkeeper had the perfect solution – she would ship them to any address in the world.

On the walk to the hotel, they weren't breathing too hard despite the altitude being about three-quarters of a mile high and the fact that neither had been running much lately. Greg had laughed after inquiring in the shop about how much further it was to the hotel. It was only another five minutes! After being told by the station master that it was on the other side of town, he had imagined it to be a much longer walk.

As they checked into the hotel, they learned that since it was between ski season and the summer hiking and biking season, the hotel was mostly empty. They also learned that they had the grand suite. And they learned that the hotel kitchen was closed until ski season started in one month. There was only one restaurant open in town for the five days they had booked; it was a five-minute walk in the center of town. It would be serving breakfast, lunch and dinner.

Their room had stunning views of the Jungfrau region, with majestic mountains whose tops were already covered in snow. They unpacked and collapsed on the bed for 20 minutes, laughing about how tiring it was to travel almost a full day. Greg almost fell asleep but decided that a trip to the bathroom took priority; he groaned and headed into the spacious bathroom with shiny gold faucets. He used the facilities, splashed water on his face and felt rejuvenated.

Jean was snoozing, with one leg dangling off the bed like she was getting ready to go somewhere. Greg decided to let her snooze as he stood staring out the window at the glory of the mountains. After a minute, he drew his focus to the back of the hotel. They were on the top floor. He spotted a hiking path snaking up the mountainside. Since it was almost dark, he decided that it was not a good time to go out. They had both packed their running kits. He would be sure to show the path to Jean tomorrow.

Jean slept for about 45 minutes before getting up and heading into the bathroom. By then, Greg had his computer out, answering emails. "Anything urgent?" Jean called from the bathroom.

"Not really. I'm glad I hired good project managers and CEOs. Most of them are requesting meetings, but I told them to send status reports because I'm on an impromptu vacation for the next five days and not even doing conference calls."

They dressed warmly, wandered through town holding hands, and passed the only restaurant open, zigzagging through the few side streets in town. It looked like most of the buildings had shops on the lower floors with residences above. There was one small grocery store, several hotels, a few tourist shops, and a sports shop where the owner was changing his front display from summer gear to skiing equipment. There were a few other restaurants that had a closed sign and one bakery/chocolate shop. They wandered back to the restaurant, relishing the warmth that enveloped them as they entered the foyer and coat check area. Stuffing hats and gloves in the coat pockets, Greg and Jean traded their coats to the attractive teen girl behind the half door for a ticket.

"Looks like I owe you some money," Greg said, referring to a discussion they had during their walk, whether the restaurant would be fancy, with waiters wearing tuxedos, or down-to-earth with waiters wearing rustic clothing. Greg had guessed it would be fancy,

Jean the opposite. It turned out to be somewhere in the middle, closer to Jean's guess, as the waiters were in warm corduroy trousers, comfortable-looking hiking boots and heavy long-sleeve shirts. The Matre-d had a traditional green felt hat with a feather.

Greg said the venison from the traditional section of the menu caught his eye. Jean went with ox-tail soup and a salad. They noticed a Satrat wine on the menu from their friend's vineyard in France and got a bottle of the Burgundy. Since they had promised to keep business discussions to a minimum on this trip, they turned to other subjects. Greg told her about the running path he discovered. Jean said she wanted to go to that little grocery store they had passed earlier just to see what was different. Greg thought that was a good idea.

Dinner was served. They traded bites, exclaiming how good all the food was. Jean remarked that the news from Alex was good. He and Sam had finished cross-country finals at the University of Texas in Austin, where they had both been walk-ons to the team. In his email, Alex said both had done better than expected on a tough course as both had finally gotten under the vaunted 16-minute mark for the 5k run. The other note he shared was that Sam had finally beaten him by 2 seconds after years of coming in close behind. Neither had gotten a medal, but the team did place third in the conference. As usual, Alex said his grades were all A's so far, just mid-way through the semester. Greg and Jean had just caught up with Marie because she attended the conference at the Chateau. They discussed her dating Victor and agreed that they were both happy and that it seemed like a natural, easy-going relationship. Jean said at first, she was surprised by them sharing a room at the Chateau but reflected on her own journey through life at that age and realized that she was completely comfortable with the arrangement.

They leisurely strolled back to the hotel, holding hands. Getting back to the hotel, they peeled off layers of clothes, crawled under the sheets and duvet, and then intertwined for a perfect ending to the evening. Greg woke Jean up in the middle of the night for another, more vigorous round that left them both breathless. Jean fell asleep with her head on Greg's chest. As the first rays of sunshine brightened their large bedroom window, they woke up in the spooning position with Greg's hand cupping her breast. They both woke up simultaneously and quickly disengaged to head for the bathroom. Jean won since she was closer. He went in when he heard her brushing her teeth.

In an unspoken agreement, they dressed in their running kit. Greg wondered aloud how many layers they would need. He said the window felt cold, but he could not see any breeze blowing the trees around. Greg chose a cotton sweatshirt with a hood. Jean chose a long-sleeved running shirt paired with a light nylon jacket and a wool ski cap. They both had high-tech running gloves in case it was cold enough to wear them.

They exited through the restaurant to the back patio to do extended stretching for ten minutes then headed over to the path. The skies were lead-gray, with heavy, low-hanging clouds, which the front desk person said was a typical late-autumn state. But no rain or snow was predicted. Fortunately, it was not as windy as the day before.

They started side-by-side at an easy jogging pace, then the trail quickly narrowed to a single wide path. Greg took the lead. He noticed that he could either take a steep path up the hill or turn right, paralleling the town and zigzag up the hill. He took the easy route. After one minute, they both stopped simultaneously. Greg said loudly, "OXYGEN!" Jean laughed and said, "Definitely not used to the altitude." They were high enough to overlook the whole town and down the valley to Lauderbrunnen. "Let's take the train down to see the caves later," Jean said.

They hiked for about an hour through the scenic forests and meadows before turning back. Now that their legs and lungs were warmed up, jogging back was fine. After a quick shower, they dressed for a day of exploring. The front desk clerk had information on the train schedules down the hill and return times, as well as directions on hiking to the caves. Instead of stopping at the restaurant for a big breakfast, they found the bakery and leisurely enjoyed croissants and coffee at a small table inside the shop while waiting for the next train.

In Lauderbrunnen, they learned that instead of the long hike to the caves, there was a shuttle to the caves that would leave when there were enough people. They walked the two blocks to the bus just as a group of boisterous teens were approaching from the other side, coming off the mid-morning train from Interlaken. Another retired couple was already waiting on the bus. Although not full, apparently, it was enough to make the trip to the dead-end canyon. The bus driver announced in several languages that he would wait 90 minutes before departing back to town. Anyone not there would have to walk back.

One of the teens, from Austria, had been there before, so he became the de facto leader of the group. They wandered around, taking pictures and announcing amazement at the waterfalls. Jean said she liked the tunnel that had a hole in the wall, looking down at the valley toward the town.

On the bus ride back to town, Greg announced he would buy lunch if anyone knew of a good restaurant. The group of teenagers who were staying at the youth hostel said that the pizza place was always open, but they were tired of eating pizza because it was one of the less expensive meals while travelling.   The bus driver recommended Hotel Oberhaus as having the best food in town. Greg invited him to join the group at lunch.

The restaurant staff was happy to pull several tables together. Jean and Greg sat across from the retired couple, Zoltan and Zophia Fogassy. Zoltan had been a plumber; Zophia had taught primary school before the first of their six children were born. She had been a housewife until several years ago when she had taken a part-time job with a catering company. This current trip was a result of a gift from their children, who had all pitched money together to buy them a EurRail pass. Although they still had two children at the University of Budapest, the others had already started successful careers. The bus driver sitting next to Jean was a Polish citizen who had married an English lady who was currently teaching English at the local primary school.

The teens were from a mixture of European countries, all with Eurail passes and had met on the train at various times. The group had grown from the original two to nine. They all agreed that the most difficult part of having this large group was deciding where to go next. The oldest of the group was twenty-two. She was studying software at the University of Stockholm but was taking a break. She said she had already missed a month of classes at the beginning of the semester when her father passed away. She and her mother had started the trip together, but her mother had to return home to deal with an emergency with broken water pipes in the house. They were planning to meet again in Paris at some point soon. Greg informed her of his software company and said to contact him when she graduated.

After a brief word with Greg, Jean announced to the group that if their plans included Paris, they were welcome to stay a week at their house outside of Paris and use it as a base to explore the city and surrounding area. Greg added everyone to his phone contacts, then sent each of the group a text message so they would have his as well. Greg also texted Dirk to inform the housekeeper and staff that there would be people coming to stay in the near future and that he had given everyone Dirk's number if they needed a ride from the train station. Everyone expressed their appreciation. The teen group announced that their next stops would be a theme of visiting castles in Germany, including some of the newly restored ones. Zoltan and Zophia said they had always wanted to visit the hot springs in Baden-Baden, so that was their next stop. Then they would consider Paris after that. Jean and Greg informed everyone that they were returning to the U.S. to get back to work.

***

To: OWG Original Group
From: Monique Satrat
Subject: Future Conference Plans

The next conference is planned for the end of January. Invitations went out to people living in northern climates who were accustomed to the cold weather we typically experience here in France at that time.

There are 425 countries in the world currently. If we get 50 people per conference, we will need nine conferences minimum. I recommend we plan 10 conferences for the initial round, then determine how many we need for returning people who have not been convinced in the first round. Originally, I was thinking one per month, but logistically that will be challenging. Instead, I would like to plan for alternate months, making this a two-year plan.

Since the sessions are all recorded and available on the Internet, we should host discussions over Skype on a regular basis. Or even broadcast the sessions live on the internet for the next conference and invite a broad audience from around the world to participate in post-session comments. We would need to find better conferencing software as Skype has a limited audience capability.

Thoughts?

Monique

***

To: OWG Original Group
From: Jean Moore
Subject: Re: Future Conference Plans
 Greg and I love the plans and the online ideas!

Greg made it back to his office in Arlington, Virginia, to find his two main groups full of news. The astrophysics R&D group had major improvements in the control of the Structural Cavernous Effect, or anti-gravity invention. They had, at Alex's recommendation, improved the effectiveness of the hexagon-shaped components by using another rare-earth material. They had also automated the pilot controls, almost to the point where it was self-flying, which would be ok until many more of these planes were built. They also told Greg that there was a surprise waiting for him in Wyoming.

The other group building the quantum computer had good and bad news; they had finished the prototype with one quantum chip and were done most of the way with version two, which had eight chips. The computer ran on Greg's USOS Ultra-Secure Operating System as a base, with alterations made to turn the operating system into a state machine based on linear algebra. Their biggest problem was that the error rates were too high in the qubit detection that determined a 1 or 0.

Craig said, "Since I'm not a computer hardware guy, it was explained to me that since the beginning of computers, they were based on electrons to determine bit values. Electrons behave in a steady, predictable manner so the error rate in normal computers is so low as to be almost nonexistent. The quantum world means learning a new vocabulary. Quarks, qubits, strings, anyons and more, Qubits are the bit equivalent in a quantum computer but are random beasts. Using gallium arsenide at near absolute zero temperatures, we gain as much control as possible, but the error rate is still too high. We are working with Marvin's group out in Columbus on another chemical combination that may be more stable, but it's too early to celebrate."

"I thought arsenide was very poisonous," Greg stated.

"It is. But it is the best element to stabilize the quantum state that scientists have found. Plus, we are using such a tiny amount that doesn't create a problem." Craig responded.

Craig went on to share that their second biggest problem was getting a language that would work to build applications. Craig, the head of the computer research group, had hired the project lead from the F# language group at Microsoft, thinking that many of the first rounds of problems the computer would be solving would involve number crunching. The other problem was that the computer had to run at absolute-zero temperature, making it impossible to mass produce it. On the other hand, one of these computers could do the work of a million or more regular computers, so Greg thought it was a great tradeoff. He left instructions for the team to hook his multi-terabyte disk farm containing his LIBRARY to the quantum computer.

His pilot, Tom, texted him and said, '*Meet me at 11 pm on the tennis courts at the park near your house*'.

***

Greg asked Jean at dinner whether she would like to go to meet Tom at 11 pm. She politely declined, saying that she would turn in early as she was feeling tired. With Marie in Paris at the Sorbonne and Alex at the University of Texas, where he was on a baseball scholarship, they were dining alone.

They spent the rest of the time at dinner discussing plans for their various businesses. Jean talked about some of the big projects their charity foundation was involved in. Greg informed her that his effort to create networking businesses in every country was proceeding and that in many countries, those businesses were not going to make a profit, at least not for a very long time. She said she understood and was happy to know that soon, everyone who wanted to be online would have that opportunity. At the very least, Greg explained, he was trading votes for OWG for the networking business in those countries. Was it illegal, as in bribery? Probably not provable in court, but the owners/partners of the networking companies in each country were the people who would vote or have control over the vote.

After dinner, they took their customary walk, discussing how wonderful it had been to take those five days off in Switzerland. They both agreed that another vacation soon would be nice. Jean volunteered to look online for some unique, upscale places to visit, or perhaps they would stay in one of their renovated castles. Jean also reminded him that their passports would expire the following year and that they needed to get new photos taken soon.

***

Greg was waiting at the tennis courts at the small park near their house. He assumed Tom was going to pick him up in the cloaked spaceship, so he stood looking around. At the far end of the park, there were a few teenagers hanging out at the children's playground. They were far enough away that he could barely hear their voices. At precisely 11 pm, his phone rang. "Turn around," Tom said. Greg turned around and saw a doorway light up with a man standing in the door, then went dark. Greg thought, "There was no way the large spaceship would fit in the tennis court." The light appeared again, just long enough for him to see a ramp angling down from the doorway. He opened the gate-like door to the tennis court and walked to the ramp and into the spaceship. Jax was there to greet him and hit the button to close the ramp, which doubled as the door. "Welcome to your new private spaceship!" he said.

Greg looked around. There was a full kitchen with all the latest gadgets, plus a separate area for the chef. Up a narrow, spiral staircase, there was one bathroom and a bedroom with a plush queen-sized bed. The craft would seat five. The chairs looked like upscale chairs that could be found in many living rooms around the world. Greg sat in one. It was one of the most comfortable chairs he ever sat in! Jax showed him the controls, including reclining both the back and raising the legs, the heater, the cooling control, the extensible headrest, and the vibration controls. The chairs were also movable and locked to arrange around a table that would raise and lock from the floor. "You'll have to thank your father for that design. He had called Mike earlier this year and told him that he wanted to join us in Wyoming to help design and build your private ship." Tom said. "And he's waiting for you there."

"Let's go," Greg said as he texted Jean that he was going to Wyoming for a few days.

***

The next day there was an internet video that went viral. "Suspicious man suddenly disappears!" The teens at the park had decided to film the man they saw loitering in the park. The video showed a shadowy figure near a tennis court; then, a light blinked twice. The figure walked to where the light had blinked, then disappeared.

Jean laughed when she watched it. Alex sent it to his sister to make sure she saw it. He knew exactly who it was and promised his mother that he wouldn't tell anyone.

The press picked up the thread, and the following day, this was the lead story in newspapers and blogs around the world. The story was accompanied by one frame in the video showing a rectangular doorway with a man whose silhouette was taking a step inside.

***

Greg was busy for a few days in Wyoming. The Astro team showed him different configurations of the spacecraft they were planning. There were various designs, from a five-seater like his cloaked one that picked him up to ones that would carry up to 1,000 passengers. These all had FAA-approved radar and collision detection devices. There were versions that were going to be used to mine asteroids and very large boxy ones that would pick up the minerals as they were knocked off the asteroids. There was a long rectangular version that would become their first manufacturing plant in space.

Greg appointed Tom's wife, Becky, as the mayor of Mooretown. She had gotten into the whole Western theme. No cars were allowed, only horses. The streets were not paved, just hard-packed dirt. The budget she presented Greg included pooper-scooper robots. The head of security for the manufacturing plant was the de facto sheriff, but so far, no incidents have been reported. The town stopped growing at 200 and mainly consisted of scientists, plant workers, maintenance workers and others to support the town. Becky had even opened a Starbucks instead of a saloon, for which Greg stipulated drinks would be free for anyone working at the plant or a family member of a worker. All buildings had solar panels on the roofs. She presented Greg with a list of capital improvements like a row of windmills, sewage improvements, a water treatment plant, a modern school and so on, making it as close to an ideal small community as she could get.

Becky's big question for Greg is, "What do you want to do with the missile silo?" Greg and family had toured it when they first arrived, then decided it wouldn't be useful for a manufacturing plant. "Ask the engineers for any ideas."

***

CHAPTER 20

George was livid as he opened the meeting with his staff, who had just watched the internet sensation of the disappearing man. "This is right down the street from the inventor we have been monitoring for years; why the hell didn't we know about this?"

John, the team leader on Georges's staff assigned to watch Greg, said, "Yeah, we totally missed this one, but don't worry. Our latest recruit has just been hired as a scientist on his staff at Mr. Moore's secure campus in Arlington."

***

A UFO watch group near Mt. Adams in the state of Washington had just changed shifts. The new watch crew settled into their chairs, checking the remote equipment and the monitors just as the sun was setting. One of the monitors caught movement and started tracking it. At first, it went smoothly across the sky, about the speed of an airplane. All of a sudden, it stopped, dropped down in front of one of the field cameras, then disappeared. The lead tech choked on his coffee, checked to make sure the recordings were active, then ran outside. The craft appeared again on the other side of the large field in front of another camera.

It was cold outside, but the tech didn't seem to feel it. His adrenaline was pumping as he watched the craft appear and disappear. The craft jiggled from side to side as if waving, then went straight up. It disappeared into the night sky, lost among the twinkling stars. The tech posted the video on their watch group site.

The next day, the internet blew up. Some speculated the video was a fake Hollywood production. Others took it seriously, saying it was a new military craft. Others pooh-poohed that idea, saying that the military wouldn't reveal anything that advanced. There were the usual UFO enthusiasts who claimed it was proof that UFOs were real. Experts were interviewed from NASA, the government, the military and wherever anyone credible could be talked into being in front of a camera.

Greg texted Tom and Jax. *"Do I need to take away your new toy?"*

***

Marie called her mother from Paris on Christmas morning and then asked her to put her phone on the speaker. "Mom, Dad, Alex, I have news." She wasn't in tears and seemed to be calm.

"I'm intrigued," replied Greg. "Is it good news or bad news?"

"You decide," she said. "I'm engaged!"

"Congratulations!" both Greg and Jean said at the same time. "Are you sure this is the right timing for you? You're just 21." Jean added.

"Ummm, well, the thing about timing is the other bit of news," Marie responded. "The wedding has to be soon because I'm going to have a baby."

***

CHAPTER 21

Greg and Jean looked at each other with raised eyebrows, silently looking at each other, accepting the circumstances without any hysterics. Greg nodded at Jean, who took a deep breath and responded. "You won't believe this, but I am, too." Jean replied.

Marie laughed, "OMG, Mom, I can't believe it. You're 45 years old."

"Yeah. Still, we are thrilled."

Alex sat there looking stunned for a few seconds. "Ummm, congratulations. I guess."

Marie said, "Victor and I want to get married at the Satrat Vineyards. He's visited there with me and thinks it's the perfect place."

***

"Dude, nice 'house'!!!!!" was the text Greg got from one of the teenagers when the group made it to Paris. *"LOL thought you might like it,"* Greg replied.

Jean and Greg decided to promote Dirk to Major-Domo of the Chateau as he seamlessly slid into a role other than the head of security he had been hired for. Dirk had kept the two up to date when the group of teenagers came to stay. He also mentioned that there were no major incidents from the group, other than two of them deciding a midnight ride in the McLauren sports car was a good idea. Dirk apologized for not catching them before they were able to exit the front gate and go for a joy ride. Fortunately, nothing happened besides the driver getting a ticket for speeding.

Zoltan and Zophia had arrived the other day, Dirk said in an email. Zoltan had already fixed one of the broken fountains in the garden, replaced one of the old toilets and repaired the tiles in a bathroom in the old wing of the Chateau. The couple would get up early to tour Paris and surrounding areas, then come back after lunch. Zoltan would do projects around the house, and Zophia would help the chef prepare dinner. Jean emailed back, "Offer them a job and one of the rooms."

Dirk emailed back a few days later. "They accepted the job, with a start date in one month, because they need to go home to Hungary to settle some things. I agreed that their children and grandchildren could come to visit at times, as long as no events were occurring at that time." After a quick call with Greg, who was in favor of the arrangement, Jean emailed back, "Perfect!"

***

CHAPTER 22

January 2004: Net worth $ 4.5 trillion

The next OWG conference went smoothly except for a heated debate between Monique and the representative from a central Asian country. Most of the attendees had heard of the effort, and some had watched the prior videos and read the online material. Wolfgang Schmidt updated the slides and handouts to include feedback from the first conference. Monique gave the opening remarks in French and English to establish the purpose as well as discuss the protocol for conducting the meetings. Monique and Marie were the only ones from the original group attending since the others were busy running their respective businesses.

Monique handled the debate with what she thought was grace and diplomacy as they reviewed the video recording later that evening. It showed an agitated representative waving his paddle, wanting to speak. Monique gestured to the gentlemen, who stood and began speaking. "My government would never relinquish their sovereignty."

"If you recall, "Monique replied calmly, "All countries remain sovereign with whatever form of government you wish to have. Another layer of government is being added, which will attempt to standardize educational, judicial, monetary and other systems deemed worthy of global attention."

"But the smaller, less populated countries like mine will not have enough influence to have any meaningful input into the decisions." He countered.

"The addition of a House of Representatives will establish one person per country, regardless of size or population. With more than four hundred countries in the world, this will give everyone an equal footing when it comes to passing any piece of legislation." Monique explained.

"That may work for a while." He nodded. "However, if all countries become too standardized, we are in danger of losing our cultural differences."

"It is true that national and cultural identities are strong." She spoke. "Having standards for legal and educational systems for example, should not interfere with any cultural standards or traditional ceremonies. It has been argued that standardizing certain systems can promote unity and ease of transitions for anyone wishing to move to another country."

"If you are proposing open borders, the recent influx of migrants to the United States and before that to Europe has shown that countries are not equipped to handle large movements of population."

"True. The plan current plan is starting to improve the standard of living in most countries as each area is beginning to participate in galactic trade, hopefully minimizing the urgent need to migrate elsewhere." Monique said. "However, the point is valid and improvements to current immigration systems need to happen. I like an earlier analogy made about you inviting a friend over for dinner and a thousand people appear at your doorstep."

"The risks are too great. History has shown that a centralized government often fail to address local needs effectively. Even today, there are certain segments of many countries that want to split off and form their own countries. A One World Government would be in danger of becoming a distant, unaccountable entity, disconnected from the realities of peoples lives." He said firmly.

"That is indeed a great risk." She said. "Hopefully the checks and balances that are proposed will answer those concerns. The reforms and safeguards are designed to prevent corruption and be more responsive to the needs of all people."

The result was better than expected, with an impromptu vote showing that 90% of attendees were in favor of a One World Government. Monique scheduled a post-conference call to review the outcome and discuss the next steps. She informed the group she would that a) she would hold the following conferences in March-May and the final one in July, b) the online discussions would continue, and c) she would never plan another conference in January as it was too cold to enjoy the Chateau grounds. The group laughed because they had seen that Paris was experiencing the coldest winter in 60 years due to an arctic front coming that far south.

***

Greg was shaking his head in disbelief at the enormity of the spaceship being assembled next to the airplane plant. It was easily ten times as large as any other building on the property. The engineers said it was, in volume, three times as large as the Empire State Building. It would be the only one built here on Earth because it was the foundation for the first manufacturing plant in space. In the future, even larger ones will be constructed and assembled in space. The plan was to park it near the asteroid belt between Mars and Saturn and use it to mine the asteroids, then feed the material into manufacturing and assembly machines inside this building. It would make structural components for his planned Mars colony as well as components for the next generation of larger manufacturing plants in space.

Luxury accommodations were built on one side, central control and maintenance systems in the center, farms in a third section, manufacturing in a fourth sector and a very large hanger space for the mining drones at the far end. One thousand enthusiastic people had been hired and were being trained as the final touches were being applied. Training would continue during the four-month journey past Mars, which was approaching the closest position to Earth in their elliptical journey around the sun.

Cosmologists and various scientists would be part of the crew. Their mission would be to use the new generation of powerful telescopes and radioscopes to gather and interpret data. Greg had been told that positioning the scopes outside the building would give the best information on space in the history of humanity. It would even be able to gather more information about the mysterious energy ring around our solar system. There were several five-person spacecraft in the hangar for excursions to the far reaches of the solar system.

The biggest challenge would be that it would be a weightless environment until a ring could be constructed around this rectangular container. When the ring was constructed and started spinning to create artificial gravity, humans would move their accommodations to the ring. Manufacturing for the components of the ring had already been started and was stored in the hangar alongside the mining drones. The assembly of these pieces would be the most dangerous aspect of the project.

Jillian Castor had formed a special film crew to document the project from its inception. There was a film crew onboard the spacecraft, creating episodes planned for weekly airing on Greg's new cable channel. Jillian's career had gone from being a young investigative reporter in a local Washington D.C. television station to filming Moore's first castle restoration, which led to a very popular series that had originally been aired on another cable channel. She had convinced Greg and Jean to start their own cable channel when there was enough content for several shows. Besides the very popular Castle Restoration series, there was the Moore Foundation charity series, a remake of the Lifestyles of the Rich and

Famous, one called Fantastic Inventions, and the new one called Space Race.

Fantastic inventions started as a following of Greg and Alex's inventions, then later going way back in history to talk about other inventions that moved humanity forward. The Space Race series documented everything from the first invention of the honeycomb-like structural cavernous effect material to the subsequent inventions needed to support a crew in space.

On the day of the launch of the monstrous spacecraft, Greg watched as photographers and the film crew took pictures and videos of the entire one-thousand-member crew, who looked miniscule outside the large craft, then other snaps of different teams. It took almost an hour once boarding began to get everyone situated and ready to go.

Greg had decided not to cloak the craft to make it invisible as it would delay the launch by three months. But he did not invite any public television crews to film as he wanted to make it a quiet launch. The Air Force offered to provide a fighter jet escort, but Greg decided it was unnecessary for the fifteen-minute flight to space. He had contacted General 'Ace' Venator to inform him of the launch date so that the military would not shoot down his spacecraft. To get to the final destination, the idea was to use the gravity of the moon and Mars to slingshot the craft to its desired location, supplemented by the space drives.

"So much for a quiet launch." Greg thought to himself two days after the event. Telescope teams around the world spotted the craft almost immediately and started posting pictures online. NASA was contacted, only to be told it wasn't one of theirs. The news channels around the world were going crazy, bringing on experts from various military agencies around the world, none of whom claimed responsibility. General Venator texted, *"LOL. This is fun!"*.

***

June 2004: Net worth $ 6.8 Trillion

"My back is killing me," Marie said as she waddled around the room, holding her lower back. "What I wish we had was one of Grandpa Frank's rocking chairs. Those are the most comfortable chairs and would be perfect for this last month before the baby comes."

"Let's call him and ask him to ship one over," Victor recommended.

"I'd rather visit and pick the exact one that would be best for me," Marie replied.

"A trip across the pond is not the right thing for a woman who is eight months pregnant," Victor said firmly.

"I can call my dad and ask for one of his fast planes; that way, I can be back in a few days."

After a call to her dad, she learned that her grandparents, Frank and Ginny, were still at the Chateau and had also requested a ride home to West Virginia. The grandparents had come a month earlier to see Marie graduate from the Sorbonne with a degree in Art History. She was currently working for the art restoration department at the Louve. Victor was working at the United Nations World Court, headquartered out of the Hague, but worked in the Paris branch office most of the time.

After promising Victor that she would be gone for no more than three days, she packed a small bag and called a cab to get to the Chateau. Frank and Ginny greeted her at the front door and also expressed their concern that she should not travel in this last month. She promised them that she felt fine and not to worry, she would be back in a few days.

The private plane landed in the garden near the central water feature that got so much attention from visitors. Greg had worked with governments around the world to get various spots officially declared as airports since his planes could land and take off vertically in any small area. The Chateau was one with an official declaration. The pilots still had to file a flight plan and register it with the nearest major airport, which in this case was Paris Orly Airport.

The pilots were under special instructions to use special care to take off and land with ease, which they completely understood as soon as they saw Marie waddle out to board the plane. The inertial dampeners were improved to the state where passengers rarely felt anything of the extra fast vertical take-offs and landings, but this time, the pilots promised to take extra care. Frank, Ginny and Running Bear boarded with her.

Running Bear had requested permission to have a permanent room at the Chateau and had been granted his choice of rooms by Jean and Greg the prior year. Upon learning about this short trip, he chose to accompany the group in order to see his West Virginia Shawnee family. Marie, after sinking into the comfortable chairs on the plane and reclining it to just the perfect position, remarked that maybe this was the type of chair she needed. She made a mental note to ask her father where he got them.

The group laughed amongst themselves that they had 'arrived before they left.' It had been 1 PM France time zone when they left, a three-hour flight, and a five-hour time zone difference, which made it 11 am West Virginia time. Having just had a light lunch at the Chateau before departing, nobody was hungry. Marie took a short walk out to the sheep pasture to pet the playful babies, then took her grandfather's recommendation to have a rest on the front porch when she saw him hook up the hammock. The weather was perfect. It was a warm afternoon with a slight breeze. Large, billowing clouds moved slowly across the sky as Marie fell asleep watching a dragon-shaped cloud being chased by Mickey Mouse.

The pilots left to pick up Greg and Jean from Washington D.C., where they had been residing, running their respective businesses since the last OWG conference. They had stated their interest in coming for dinner and were indeed bringing dinner, knowing that Greg's parents had just arrived after an extended leave. Marie woke, feeling very refreshed, when she heard voices inside the house. The hammock was gently rocking, creating a very pleasant atmosphere. Marie sighed and said that she didn't want to move, that for the first time in months, she felt almost weightless. She had seen her mother, also eight months pregnant, sitting in a comfortable rocking chair on the porch, with her hand on the hammock, moving in synchronicity as she rocked both of them back and forth.

"I'm taking this chair with me," Jean stated. "And the pillow, too. Frank should be selling these chairs to expecting mothers everywhere."

"And I never thought of getting a hammock either. But this is amazing." Marie stated, then laughed, "Of course, getting in here was comical. I'm glad Grandpa didn't take a video to post on the internet."

Ginny came out to announce that dinner was ready. Marie laughed again, "If I didn't have to pee, I wouldn't be moving out of this spot. I'd pretend to be a queen and have someone feed me. But I really have to go. Help me out of here, or I'll land on my butt." Frank and Greg came out to assist with extracting Marie from the Hammock. They all had to admit that it was rather comical, but Marie had them promise that no videos would be involved.

"Smells delicious," Marie announced as she entered the house and made a beeline to the bathroom.

"BBQ," said her dad. "We haven't had it in a while and thought it would be a good choice for tonight." He was referring to one of their early business ventures where they had bought a local BBQ restaurant and started a franchise that was still expanding across the nation.

Alex called on a video call to inform them that they had finished warmups and were about twenty minutes from game time. He was in San Diego on a road trip. The team was doing well, expecting to go to the College World Series again. Alex was having another good year. They wished him well and hung up. The pilots, having joined them for dinner, thought it was cool that they got to talk to a star college baseball player.

"I can't eat another bite," Marie stated as she pushed her plate away. "Those ribs are still my favorite." She got up to walk around the front room near the fireplace, where she and Alex used to sleep on foam pads with sleeping bags whenever they visited during their younger years. She had fond memories of those visits. Marie groaned and firmly rubbed the right side of her big belly. "Quit kicking."

Jean had eaten sparingly, saying she was not hungry, and joined her daughter briefly before stepping outside to the front porch. "Come on out; it's a beautiful evening." She announced. Marie joined her and agreed. They stood there for a few minutes, taking deep breaths and walking around the side of the house to get a better view of an orange sunset as the sun went down behind the hills to the west.

It wasn't much later when Jean instructed Greg and the pilots to grab the rocking chair and pillow from the front porch to load onto the plane. Both expecting mothers got a promise from Greg to contact the makers of the airplane seats to get them a version they could have at home. They learned that the chairs came from a company in Finland that had won the contest when Greg had put out a challenge to the world to create luxury accommodations for his spaceships and space mining ships.

Marie watched the departure of the airplane as the last of the rays of the sun sparkled off the side of the craft. She marveled at how quickly the plane took off and disappeared, realizing that when inside, it felt very smooth and much slower. The pilots had promised to return the day after tomorrow to pick her up for a ride back to France.

Marie told her grandparents that she was going out to the workshop where Frank made various types of furniture. She spotted two rocking chairs out in the open and a few in the corner. After trying the two available ones, thinking they had promised, she was moving some stacked kitchen-style straight-backed chairs when she got a massive pain in her lower abdomen. It didn't feel like the baby was kicking. She stood, holding onto the corner of a workbench, taking deep breaths. When the feeling passed, she took a step toward the other chairs she wanted to try. Everything seemed fine, and she checked the other two chairs. The last one was perfect, and as she sat there, she silently wished that she had brought one of her grandmother's homemade pillows with her.

The baby kicked again, but something felt weird; the kicking was at the top of her uterus, not on the side like it normally was. That could only mean one thing. Her baby was positioned to come out soon.

With a sigh, she stood up and immediately got dizzy. A strange feeling came over her, there were golden lights sparkling in the edge of her vision. She thought she heard voices and people touching her. She blinked to clear the dizziness, and when it passed, she realized she was tightly gripping the legs of an upside-down chair that had been stacked as part of a matching pair. She also realized that her legs were wet. Glancing down, the floor was wet with an inordinate amount of liquid. Marie knew instantly that her water had broken even though she didn't remember feeling anything beyond dizziness. A few steps toward the door brought another massive pain as she gripped the edge of the lathe workbench. Her legs threatened to buckle.

Frank ran in, looking worried. "I heard a scream. Is everything OK?"

"My water broke." She said, then another contraction hit, and she screamed again.

Frank eased her to the floor, then ran out, returning almost immediately with a stack of blankets. He was on the phone. "You'd better turn around and come back. Marie's baby is coming." He hung up and then asked Marie if she wanted to move into the house. She nodded, 'Yes,' but another contraction hit. Frank called the local doctor, who promised to come right away. There was a new public clinic in town, mostly built and funded by the Moore Foundation, but Frank told the doctor there was no time to transport her.

Ginny arrived, bringing a large pot of hot water and a stack of wash cloths, accompanied by Running Bear. A brief discussion ensued where Running Bear recommended an old-fashioned method of birth where Marie would lean against a wall and squat over a stack of blankets that would provide a soft landing for the baby. Running Bear told them that he had delivered many, many babies over the years, including all twelve of his original family.

Marie had removed her underwear and hiked up her dress. She was in the mental state of doing whatever it took to deliver this baby and knew it was not the time for any semblance of modesty. She told the group that there was no way she could walk to the house and was comfortable for the moment. Ginny had put a plush pillow under her hips and had given her a blanket to wrap around her shoulders. The next contraction was intense but short. It came within minutes of the prior one, so the group knew that the baby was getting close.

The baby's crown appeared at the next contraction, showing a plethora of black hair. Running Bear said it was time to move her to a squatting position. Marie bravely assumed a position that Running Bear said was the right way that the majority of babies throughout history had been born. The next contraction produced no visible progress, so Marie leaned forward with her hands on her knees to relieve some of the pressure on her back. The backside of her hips was leaning against the wall. She was straddling a folded stack of blankets. Running Bear recommended that Ginny squat next to her to help ease the baby to the floor during the final phase of the birthing.

The next contraction was very intense. Marie screamed as some of her tissue tore. The shoulders appeared. Ginny coached her that one more push should finish the birthing. The local town doctor came rushing in, carrying a travelling bag and hurriedly putting on sterile gloves. Ginny was ready when the next contraction came, and a baby girl came gushing out. The men helped Marie ease herself to a sitting position while the doctor took over the crucial part of cutting the umbilical cord and preparing for the passing of the afterbirth.

Jean and Greg stuck their heads in the door, realizing that there was no room, said their congratulations then announced that Victor was on his way. Alex called back on a video call on Greg's phone only to be told that a video call was inappropriate at this point. He laughed and said it might not be appropriate, but it would be funny and something he could tease her about later.

The rest of the night was chaotic for everyone except Marie. She felt an inner peace holding her baby. The group had helped Marie into the house, into the second bedroom. She was propped on too many pillows, almost getting lost in the excess fringe. Marie was drifting off when Victor came running in. He gently sat on the bed, gave her a kiss and moved the blanket back to get a better look at his daughter's face.

"She's beautiful!" he exclaimed.

Marie mumbled something in response and held her husband's hand. Victor made himself comfortable on the bed, while Marie shifted so the baby was resting quietly between them. Victor reached his hand around so the baby could grab his finger. They rested comfortably until dawn, when the baby stirred. Marie wanted help to go to the bathroom, so Victor held the baby and gave Marie his other arm for support as they shuffled down the hall.

Marie told Victor the baby's name was Aliya, a name he instantly liked. Victor changed the towel she had been lying on as it had become damp during the night. Back in bed, baby Aliya was fussing, moving her head back and forth. Marie assumed that meant she was searching for something to eat, so she pulled her breast out of her top and guided the nipple into the baby's mouth. A brief ripple of pain coursed through Marie as the baby pulled extra hard to start the flow of milk for the first time.

Marie awoke hours later to an empty room with pillows thrown on the floor and scattered across the bed. She had been sleeping soundly with one arm hanging off the bed and drooling on the sheet at the edge of the bed, her head facing away from the brightness of the sun streaming around the edge of the closed drapes of the window. She could hear quiet voices in the next room and tried to get up. She had no energy but didn't care. She felt at peace. She knew the baby was well taken care of. The next thing Marie knew, the sun had stopped shining through the window, and she needed the bathroom again.

As soon as she opened the door, Victor was right there, helping her shuffle down the hall. Marie came out to the kitchen moments later, seeing great-grandmother Ginny holding baby Aliya. Something delicious was simmering on the stove. Marie suddenly decided she was hungry, vaguely remembering eating BBQ the night before. She gingerly sat at the chair that her father vacated and accepted a bowl of chicken and vegetable soup from her mother.

Baby Aliya started fussing as soon as Marie said something. Ginny passed the baby to Marie, who, without a second thought, pulled out her other breast and guided the baby's mouth to the right place. Many people stopped by over the next few days, including Petr and Ilysa, who had emigrated from the country of Georgia, along with their daughter Elandra, whose thirteenth birthday was coming up. After another week of Ginny pampering her newest and only great-grandchild, Victor and Marie got a ride back to France.

Marie's baby was born just after midnight on July 1st. Victor loved Marie's proposal to name the baby Aliya, which means the exalted one. Jean went into labor the next day after they had flown back to Washington D.C. and had twin girls that they named Celina and Samantha. Marie had to stop and think. Even though the twins were born later, they would be aunts to her new daughter.

***

July 2004: Net worth $ 7 Trillion

The last conference on One World Government was interesting because all sixty attendees said they would vote in favor of a One World Government. Most of these attendees had been from smaller countries who said they felt neglected by the current structure of the

United Nations and that the proposed new structure would bring more benefit to them.

After the last attendee left, the original group had planned a meeting at the Chateau to review the final results. Jean brought the team up to date with the progress of getting the United States to agree to the U.N. becoming a one-world government. It would have to be a resolution submitted to the House, then approved by them, then discussed and approved by the Senate, then it would go to the President. On the matter of choosing the U.N. representative, which was currently a presidential appointee, it would be best to have both the House and Senate approve the U.N. representative, much like they did cabinet positions and judicial nominees. It would be a constant project to ensure enough votes were garnered to approve any resolutions and representatives. Jean's progress report was that the expensive lobby group had written a stellar resolution that was getting a lot of discussion in both the House and Senate but that it was not going to be brought to the floor for a vote because very few representatives were currently in favor.

"What do we have to do to get their vote?" Greg asked.

"Give them something they need for their district or state. We can write it into the bill, like most bills, or work behind the scenes with them to enrich their state." Jean replied.

"Well, as popular as these new airplanes are, I'm going to need more manufacturing plants," Greg stated. "I can work with the different representatives to promise to build a plant in their area in exchange for their vote."

"What about starting with the Speaker of the House and the Minority Whip?" Victor said. "They can influence the others in their parties to vote for it."

"Great idea!" Jean said. "I'll get this lobby group to set up meetings with various influencers."

"How about other things we can offer different states?" Greg said. "I don't need 50 manufacturing plants."

"Some of the states have problems with large homeless populations," Jean said. "Other states have been cited for high pollution in their rivers and lakes. Our foundation has been studying the best ways to help with those, and we can always accelerate those plans."

Dmitry chimed in, "My contacts in England have stated that a similar process will be needed to influence votes in both the House of Lords and the House of Commons. Their main concern is immigration leading to overcrowding and substandard living conditions."

Sebastien spoke next. "The same issue in France, especially in the larger cities. Immigration has been causing problems for years. There is also a problem with militant groups causing security problems."

Jean asked the group, "How do we accomplish this without being charged with corruption?"

Greg responded first, "I'd like to accomplish this without resorting to bribery."

Jean replied. "Bribery is the first form of corruption everyone thinks of. There are other forms, including influencing, access to money, networking, abuse of discretion and others. We must walk a fine line when trying to get other people to vote for our initiatives."

***

"Dad, guess what we did today," Alex asked his dad over the phone.

"Another impossible invention would be my only guess," Greg answered, thinking that it wasn't baseball season, so he turned his guess toward science.

"Yup. We passed stones through brick walls without creating a hole."

"is this one of those think-tank projects you are working on with the John Hopkins research team?"

"It's a new one. Last summer, I was reading about something called phonons, which is an excitation of atoms in solid objects, so I called the physics team I had worked with before. They did not have any current projects on this subject, but if I had time, I could stop over, and they would put together some experiments. There had been some earlier studies and papers written, but they were not aware of any major research on Phonons anywhere. I had this idea of passing one solid through another, so I stopped by, and we created a prototype machine that would vibrate stones and another one that would vibrate another physical object like a brick wall. Then we experimented with different frequencies until we got the stone to mostly pass through the wall."

"What do you mean, 'mostly'?" Greg asked.

"The stone was several milligrams lighter than when we started, and the wall was the same number of milligrams heavier."

"Hmmm, so too risky to do this to humans," Greg stated.

"For sure. But the team says it's one of their new pet projects. Anyway, we filed some patents."

"Interesting; how many patents do you have now?" Greg asked.

"Two hundred and something. I haven't been keeping track. But every project I've been involved with at John Hopkins or with your AstroX group usually ends up with more patents."

"Am I paying you now?" Greg asked.

"Yes, you've been paying me for a while now. And it's a pretty good salary, too." Alex said.

"Have you been spending it on anything cool?"

"Yes, I have a savings account and a debit card, but most of it I transfer to your stockbroker. I have my own account now, and it's making more money than my savings account. But I bought me and Sam the latest GameBoy to play on road trips to the games."

Greg jumped in, "Thanks for the tip to spin the asteroid we are mining. It makes the mining lasers sheer off the material in long strips rather than making dust particles. The strips are easier to capture with the collectors."

"What are you going to do with the material?" Alex asked.

"We're going to build manufacturing plants in space and a colony on Mars. I proposed a moon colony but the scientists say that it would constantly be out of water. Since there is no ice source on the moon nor any nearby ice asteroids, they convinced me that a Mars colony should be first. And that space engine you worked on last summer with the AstroX team, we've replaced all the original ion drives with this new one, giving us much faster acceleration while we are in space."

"Is the Mars colony your next big project, Dad?"

"That's one of them, but keep it under wraps because not many people know about it yet. Do you remember the challenge we put out to the world to build the luxury, modular homes?"

"Sure, that was to help with the homeless problems in different countries, and that company in Finland had the best design, right?" Alex replied.

"Yes. Well, I visited them recently and challenged them to secretly make a space-worthy version. I want to make it ultra-luxurious to help attract people to go to Mars. But before I forget, we need a better way to communicate with the earth. Our current technology takes too long to send and receive messages."

"Oh, yeah. I know something that should work. Do you remember a few years ago I mentioned 'strange non-local interaction'?"

"Vaguely, was that when you were reading Einstein's books and notes?"

"Yeah, he theorized at a quantum level that if you do something to a quark, there was an exact reaction to another quark in some distant location."

"Well, if you think that's the right answer, go for it. Another impossible project added to your already long list of impossible inventions is exciting. And by the way, congratulations on another winning season. I read that you are going to the College World Series." Greg said.

"Thanks, we leave tomorrow. Are you going to be able to make any of the games?"

"Wouldn't miss any. Already got tickets. I'll push my big meeting with the mayor of New York City out to July."

***

Alex and Sammy had fantastic games. The opposing pitchers had no answer to the two sophomores who had hit almost every inning in every game of the tournament. Greg, Jean and the twins had their favorite seats, five rows up on the third base side, so they had great views of Alex at third base and Sammy at shortstop. The University of Texas easily won the tournament.

It was a raucous celebration in a steak restaurant that had formerly been a bank building in downtown Omaha. The city had once been a central cattle stockyard collection point for ranchers to bring their cattle to market before being sent on one of the rail spurs out to other parts of the country. The Moore's were sitting in the former bank vault with other families of the athletes. During dinner, Jean spotted a stained-glass window with the name Kenworthy arranged in a semicircle and wondered aloud if that had been an influential name in Omaha at some point in the past. When asked, the wait staff did not know anything about it but confessed to being curious themselves.

Greg noticed that the beer was flowing freely at the athlete's table despite the drinking age being twenty-one in Nebraska. He surmised that a blind eye was turned during the baseball tournament that had become a tradition in Omaha since 1950. Alex and Sammy were laughing about something privately when Greg approached to say congratulations again. He heard something about Marie's boobs when the boys spotted him and quickly cut the conversation. He chatted with them briefly, then headed for the men's room before quietly returning to his table.

The coach stopped by during dessert, thanking Greg and Jean for picking up the check. He was the only one who knew having told others that it was an anonymous donor who paid. The Moore's had ordered several expensive bottles of Satrat wine during the lengthy meal, telling everyone that the Satrat's were their best friends and that they had been to the vineyards in France on multiple occasions. The bill was quite large, well into five figures. But the Moore's didn't mind; they were happy to share their wealth with others for a good cause.

***

July 2005: Net worth $ 9 Trillion

"I'll tell you exactly what is going to happen." The mayor of New York City said after Greg proposed building skyscrapers to help his homeless problem. "The current residents living in older, low-rent districts are going to complain that the homeless have better places than the hardworking people who have lived nearby for a long time."

"Well, how about I set a reasonable rent level and invite the longtime residents to a newer place to live? Then the homeless people can move into the older places."

"You'd have a riot on your hands from the current owners of the older buildings who will have residents that can't pay the rent."

The senator from New York was in the meeting and the two New York House of Representatives were on a video link. They all knew that Greg was doing this to garner their votes for the OWG resolution that was being planned. They had agreed to back his resolution if he could figure out a way to solve some of the problems in New York City.

Greg had hired a top architectural firm to plan skyscrapers that were as close to self-sufficient as possible. They would have a medical clinic, and the bottom floor would be various service businesses such as hair salons, nails, a small grocery store, and other businesses, all owned by tenants of the building. These store owners would be inclined to open stores in the building by giving them lower rent. The building manager and maintenance engineers would also be given lower rent. The top floor was proposed as a dining hall for the residents.

"Well, I could buy any apartment buildings from other landlords and turn them into homeless shelters." Greg proposed.

"Sure, but after a while, the city would turn into a very affordable place to live, which would attract many other people who would say they were 'homeless' just go get a cheap place to live. It's a circular problem." Said the Mayor.

"We could place a limit on how long someone could live there without paying rent. Eventually, they would have to move out or get a job and pay rent." Greg proposed.

"Yes, but a high percentage of the homeless population are not capable of holding jobs." The mayor responded.

"Good point," Greg said. "For those people, we can give them a choice to be transferred to another facility or asylum or whatever you want to call it. And if they are incapacitated enough to not be able to make that decision, I believe there is a legal process to get them diagnosed and court-ordered to go to those facilities."

"We do that quite routinely, but the state-owned facilities are already overcrowded." Said the Senator.

"As you all know, my family has a charity foundation with a rather large budget. If it would be part of the solution, I'm willing to build more capacity." Greg offered.

"That would solve part of the problem." The mayor said. "The other big problem is crime in the city. Of course, reducing the homeless population will get rid of some of the crime."

"Let's discuss crime solutions at another time." said the Senator," I'm heading for a meeting with the President."

Before they ended the meeting, the mayor agreed that Greg could purchase several condemned buildings in Queens, Haarlem and the Bronx, demolished and built as new skyscrapers. He also recommended several well-known builders who could handle the projects.

Greg called Jean and brought her up to date with the results of the meetings and told her that he would propose the same things to representatives in London, Paris and other cities where they needed OWG votes. He also mentioned that their charity foundation needed to find land to build new asylum facilities for people who could not care for themselves. His last point was that the mayor also asked for assistance in reducing crime in the city, for which he had no solutions right now other than to contribute to the police funding.

***

anuary 2006: Net worth 9 Trillion

The building projects in New York City were going well. Greg and Jean had purchased a luxury flat in the Upper East Side and enjoyed some time exploring the city and meeting new friends. The building was across, and just down the street, from the Metropolitan Museum, where they had their first luxury outing after crossing the one-million-dollar mark almost fourteen years ago. Their fifth-floor flat was on the opposite side of Central Park, but they could barely see a portion of the park from the corner bedroom window. Their main window looked down on Madison Avenue, and six blocks away, they could see water and a portion of Roosevelt Island. They didn't mind; it was an exciting new change for them. Jean remarked that they may end up spending more time in the city as they started to work with more people from the United Nations.

They didn't flaunt their wealth, but the people they met seemed to realize they were very wealthy. One of their neighbors remarked about how down-to-earth they were and not stuck-up like some of the other building residences. The Moore's hadn't met many of their neighbors and soon learned that many of the occupants were not full-time residents; rather, they lived in other countries and kept an apartment in New York City.

On one of the first days in the city, they hired a limousine with a driver who knew the city well. They essentially asked him to give them a private guided tour. It was mid-morning on a cold, windy day. Traffic was heavy in some places and almost non-existent in others. The driver kept a running dialog about the history of the city, pointing out different buildings as they drove past. He knew not only the current use of many buildings, but also the history of them. When Jean exclaimed, "What's that!" and pointed out the front window to a 3D mural on the side of a building, the driver explained, "That is from a famous local artist named Richard Haas. He has a studio here in the city, and I think he lives in Yonkers with his family. He has these murals around the United States and in many other countries. I'll point out others as we tour the city."

They specifically requested the driver include a drive by the United Nations building, wherein he remarked, "A few good people work there, but most of them are pompous asses, always putting on elite airs. And there's so much corruption involved, it's a wonder that they ever accomplish anything."

***

July 2007: Net worth $ 15 Trillion

Ailya and the twins, Celina and Samantha, celebrated their third birthday. Alex mentioned that it was nice to have all the birthdays at once; it was like having Christmas in July. Frank said it was nice to have another excuse for another family reunion. Alex, who was currently between girlfriends, was renting a nice ranch house in Colorado Springs, playing for the Sky Sox, the Triple-A team for the Colorado Rockies. He called via FaceTime and figured out a way to add Sammy and Pete to the call so they could all wish the girls a happy birthday. Sammy and Pete were living in Modesto, California, where Sammy was playing Triple-A baseball with a farm team for the Oakland Athletics. Both Alex and Sammy had played games that day for their respective teams. July was one of the busiest months, and almost every day was game day. It was a grueling 150-game season.

Alex told the adults on the call that the other wives and girlfriends on the team were constantly trying to set him up with a girlfriend, but he said that he was currently content to play the eligible bachelor role and concentrate on baseball. Greg knew he was still attending conference calls with his AstroX team, involved in whatever project they were working on at the moment. Even though the sprawling ranch house was too big for one person, Alex said he really liked the extra space as well as the views of the open plains to the east. Out the front door to the west, he had a great view of Pikes Peak whenever he left for the ballpark, which was less than a mile away.

***

"Um, hi, Aimee. This is Sammy." Stammered a nervous Sammy. For some reason, talking to Aimee by herself made him extremely nervous.

"Well, hello, Sammy," Aimee replied, laying on the sexy French accent. "Are you calling to invite me to a prom or something?" She teased. "I know you have always had a thing for me, oui?" A slight pause, then "Non?"

"N-n-now, I know you are teasing me." He stammered. "Besides, it's not me who has always had the hots for you."

"What do you mean?" she inquired.

"N-n-nothing. I've said too much. I was calling to ask if you could design a wedding dress for Pete. She's always wanted one of your dresses."

Aimee kept up the teasing. "Oh, she proposed, did she?"

"Hey, I was the one who asked." He stated firmly.

"Well, sure, you sexy beast, send me her contact information, and I will arrange measurements and fittings. When is the wedding?"

"October, after baseball season is over."

"That's not much time for a proper wedding dress, but for you, my sweet Sammy, we will make it happen."

Sammy could never tell when he was younger if she was teasing him or not, but now that she was laying it on so thick, it was easy to spot. Pete thought it was cute that it made him so nervous. Sammy sent Aimee his fiancée's contact information so they could talk directly to each other and thankfully leave him out of the loop.

"And how about you? Does your tuxedo still fit?" Aimee wanted to know.

"Yes. I'm still good. But Alex has grown again, so he may need a new jacket."

Sammy crossed that off his list. For the first time since Junior High School, he had been keeping a to-do list whenever Pete, her mom or his mom called and asked him to do something related to the wedding. The list was currently short because he was the type to get things done, but in the middle of the baseball season, there wasn't always a lot of extra time to do chores or errands. However, the list was in a constant state of flux, with three women constantly giving him instructions. Before he forgot, he texted Alex – 'don't forget to call Aimee to get a new tux jacket.' Then crossed that off his list.

***

October 2007

Sammy and Pete's wedding was a destination one in Marrakech, Morocco, a place Pete had visited during her gap year travels. The Moore's got to spend more time with Sammy's parents, who they got along with quite well. They also met Nicole's parents, the Peterson's and learned that they were fine with everyone calling their daughter 'Pete'. Greg and Jean's wedding gift to Sammy was to rent him an entire riad that would sleep thirty to forty people. A riad is a square or rectangular compound, usually built around a garden or a pool. The original plan was that everyone related to the bride and groom would stay there, but after Priya had secured an 11-hectare estate for the Moore's to rent, a new plan was established. Everyone was the age of the bride, and the groom would stay at the riad. Everyone that was Greg and Jean's age would stay at the estate. This included Sammy's current triple-A coach and his wife, his and Alex's high school coach and wife. Their coach from the University of Texas had sent regrets about not being able to make it. Priya and Mike had their own luxury apartment in the old town, inside the large ochre walls of the city.

There were a few friends from high school and a few of Sammy's teammates from over the years. A few of the guys on his current team that already had passports decided to come only when they learned it was an all-expenses paid trip, which was good because triple-A baseball players didn't earn much. Sammy had invited the whole team but there wasn't enough time for everyone to get a passport. Once pictures started getting sent back from the players who were there, there was a plethora of 'jealous' emotions and reactions.

Priya and Mike planned for guided tours of the city and surrounding areas during the days before the wedding ceremony and nightclub visits after dinner. Chefs had been hired at both the riad and the estate, or rather; chef crews had been hired because they were available all day, every day. They made local favorites, French delicacies or whatever the guest wanted.

Alajandro, the catcher from Colombia on Sammy's team, was spotted talking to Aimee the first night at dinner. It was obvious he was trying to win her favor. Sammy nudged Alex and nodded at Alajandro, who was nicknamed 'the bull' on the team. He was short and stocky, as many catchers were. They sat and watched in amusement at the conversation. Aimee was being gracious, listening and talking at appropriate times, but they could tell that Alajandro was not making any headway. After about fifteen minutes, Aimee excused herself and got up and left. Alajandro seemed perplexed, so Sammy took his plate and moved over to sit next to him.

"What's her story?" Alajandro wanted to know. "She seemed friendly then all of a sudden got up and left."

"Dude, don't you know who that is?" Sammy asked.

"No, should I?"

"That's Aimee Satrat." When no hint of recognition came from Alajandro, Sammy explained that she was a world-famous fashion designer of the "Satrat and Moore' brand and that she was one of the most eligible bachelorettes on the planet.

"All I know is that she is one of the most beautiful women I have ever seen," Alajandro said.

***

Pete led the first foray into the world-famous Souk or marketplace. The sights, scents and sounds differed as the narrow streets wound around through the old city into different squares. Each souk specialty occupied a different square between the old living quarters. The spice souk had a wonderful mix of aromas. The open-air meat market, normally a bit repulsive to Western travelers, was remarkable in its own right. The creepy smiling, skinned goat heads with flies buzzing around always garnered some comments. Some travelers rushed through, down the alley to the next souk, and some lingered to take in the various sights. The gold and silver souk took the longest to get through, with many people stopping to watch the craftsmen make various pieces, from simple bracelets to elaborate tea serving sets that sold for thousands of dollars. The largest souk offered clothing, scarves, purses, jackets, hand-stitched dresses, children's clothing, hats, shoes and a variety of general goods.

Even though the wedding party started as a group at the first souk, they finished in ones and twos. Some elected to go back to their rooms, and some found coffee and tea shops, for which there were plenty throughout the old town. Greg and Jean, having wandered hand in hand at a slower pace than the rest of the group, found themselves alone and needing a place to sit. They spotted a bakery/coffee shop with available outdoor tables and grabbed one. With a contented sigh, they lowered themselves into creaky chairs at a wobbly table, sat and watched the crowds pass by.

"A penny for your thoughts," Jean commented.

"Just thinking that it's nice to not be thinking about work for a few hours," Greg replied.

"True."

"I like this city," Greg said. "Everything seems to happen at a different pace."

A young woman, who they learned was a university student, eventually came out to take their order. Greg ordered a coffee with his croissant, and Jean ordered a Moroccan specialty, mint tea and a croissant. They learned that since Morocco had been a colony of France, then a protectorate of France, there was still a heavy French influence throughout the country. Most natives spoke French in addition to the Moroccan dialect of Arabic. French food was available in restaurants and grocery stores.

***

Dancing was lively at the club that night. The entire wedding party went just after dinner, including the parents. The DJs, noticing the age group, played a lot of Moroccan blues-style music. When a younger crowd started arriving, the music changed to electronica, hip hop and rap. The parents excused themselves and headed out to find a more sedate setting. It was a Wednesday night, and there were very few females in the club that night, so Pete, Aimee, Marie and several of Pete's bridesmaids were getting a lot of exercise dancing with different partners.

Mike had overseen security, so he contacted Rory from the security company that the Moore's used whenever they travelled.

Rory did not have an office or crew in Morocco but had the contacts to hire the best company in the area. This turned out to be a wise move for several reasons. First, when one of the dancers got too aggressive with one of the women, the undercover security team would quickly surround her and escort her back to the table. Word quickly got around that dancing was Ok, but nothing else. Young athletes have a reputation for liking to party, which as expected, included more than just dancing. A fracas broke out, which Sammy and Alex quickly joined. The Moore's later learned that several professional football (soccer) teams were housed in the Marrakesh area. Many of them had athletes on contract from foreign countries. According to the police report, one of the soccer players commented that baseball was not a real sport and a fight broke out. The security team had quickly broken up the incident, even before the club bouncers could intervene. The only damage was Alajandro getting a black eye.

The Police Commissioner came to the estate to visit the Moore's the next day to assure them that nothing would come of the incident. A tea and coffee service had been set in the garden, where they sat to resume the conversation. The Commissioner let it be known that the entire force thought the incident at the club was rather funny. When Greg asked why it warranted a visit from the Commissioner, he stated that once the names 'Satrat and Moore' were seen in the report, it went straight to his desk. Greg inquired whether it was the name of the parents or the children that garnered the extra attention. "Both." He replied. My grandfather owns the largest vineyard in this area and has some agreements with the Satrat vineyards in France. Plus, your security team sent us a courtesy note saying that you would be in the area. All my younger department members know the Satrat and Moore fashion label, so it is really both. Greg let him know that the wedding party was going to a different club that night and was surprised that the Commissioner already knew which one. "Your wife's assistant, Priya, is very efficient. She has given us an itinerary for the remainder of your visit to our fine town. I will have a few more uniformed officers in the crowd tonight."

"And one more thing, the Mayor would like to know if you could find time for a meeting with her before your visit is complete."

Greg gestured to Mike, who came over and listened to the request. "Are the Mayor and her husband available for dinner here any night next week?" The Commissioner made a short phone call, waited for a few minutes, then hung up. "Next Tuesday, Eight pm here."

"Do you know what she wants to talk about?" Greg inquired.

"I believe she has some ideas of refurbishing that old manufacturing plant you see on the way to the airport and is wondering if there is a potential partnership."

"What was manufactured at the plant?" Greg wanted to know.

"I believe the last effort was diesel truck engines."

After the Commissioner left, Mike said, "You know this estate came with a minimum rent of one month."

Greg replied, "I did not know that. But I rather like it here. How about we make it our home office for the rest of the lease? I'll let Jean know."

***

Victor and Aliya were down in the swimming pool in the courtyard of the riad, enjoying a warm, sunny afternoon. Marie checked to ensure they were ok, then made her way into Aimee's room.

"You're unusually quiet," Marie said, in French, to Aimee after she settled in. They had switched to French as their main language during their senior year of high school. Marie brought a book to read, intending to talk about whatever Aimee desired or to sit quietly and read. Aimee was sitting in her favorite position, cross-legged on a couch, sketching a new design. "More boyfriend problems?"

Aimee had gone through a string of bad boyfriends the prior year, including a short affair with a famous married man, then suddenly stopped dating about six months ago. "Sort of." She turned the sketch pad toward Marie, who couldn't quite make out what it was, so she put down her book to move over to the couch. It was a maternity outfit!

A sharp gasp from Marie. She looked into her best friend's eyes, who just nodded. "OH. Are we happy about it?" She looked up. Aimee had tears streaming down her face. Marie wrapped her arms around her best friend. The tears changed to sobs.

Marie let her friend cry for a while. When the sobs subsided, they sat in silence. "When did you find out?"

"About four months ago."

Marie thought back. Aimee had stopped dating months before then, saying she was swearing off men. It must have happened when Marie was busy at the Chateau preparing for the OWG conference. Aimee had always been tall and slender, often modeling their clothes for online videos, so it didn't appear that she was pregnant. Marie realized that Aimee had been wearing unusually baggy clothes lately; now she knew why.

Marie cleared her throat. "Who's the father?"

Aimee had lain her head on Marie's leg. She just shrugged.

"Do I know him?" Marie asked.

Again, another shrug, then another bout of uncontrollable sobs and shaking came on. Marie just held her until she quieted down, then fell asleep.

***

There were many more women at the club that night as word had gotten around that the Satrat and Moore girls were in town. Aimee and Marie took countless photos and signed numerous autographs. Social media was abuzz about what they were wearing, how their hair looked, what kind of mocktails they were drinking and every other detail that could be gleaned from a brief snap with someone famous. The same group of athletes were there, and they all got along famously. Even Alajandro, who was sporting a black eye, was having a good time partying with the same people he was in the fight with the night before. What he didn't know was that there was an agreement with the city officials and the football teams that any trouble would result in one or more game suspensions, regardless of whose fault it was.

Alajandro had not given up on Aimee, though. He kept asking her to dance, but Aimee had positioned herself in the interior of the booth, surrounded by Marie on one side and Pete on the other. Alex and Sammy provided an additional buffer. One particularly upbeat song was irresistible, and the entire table got up and danced as a group. Marie had asked Alex to stay close to Aimee without telling him why. He was glad to assist and had a huge smile on his face the entire time. Alajandro worked his way close to Aimee, as had others who had asked her to dance that evening. She gave each of them a brief moment of a dance, which was nothing more than everyone hopping up and down with their arms raised over their heads, it being too crowded for anything else. The DJs kept the beat going for almost thirty minutes, having achieved the desired mood in the club.

Aimee was wearing layers of shimmering, bright scarf-like material that flowed over her form as she moved. Marie rarely noticed the baby bump as the choice of layers worked to hide any visibility of her condition. Marie was sure nobody else would spot it. It was a tired but elated group that left the club in the middle of the night, telling each other that this was the best night of the trip so far. Alajandro kept trying to sidle next to Aimee on the trip back to the riad. She talked to him without encouragement, but he didn't get the hint that she was unavailable. She was too polite to be rude and tell him to go away, so she did the one thing that would send him a firm message – she put her arms around Alex and laid her head on his shoulder. Alejandro got the message.

Everyone slept in, which was good because the afternoon and evening were reserved for pre-wedding rehearsals, photo shoots and the rehearsal dinner. Fabulous food, plenty of great wine and excellent conversations were the norm. Jean, sitting diagonally across from Aimee, noticed that she wasn't drinking. Aimee faked a sniffle and said she may be coming down with something, so she was being cautious. The dinner was served family style, with a variety of dishes being placed on the table and everyone getting as much of their favorites as they wanted. Dessert was the same way, with choices of traditional Moroccan sweets being offered. Marie pointed to one coated in chopped pistachios, with a crunchy center and a slight honey taste, and announced that one was her favorite. Victor tried one and proclaimed that although it was good, his favorite was the miniature croissant with a creamy cinnamon-flavored center.

Jean and Marie were talking about the upcoming fashion season when Jean noticed Sammy and his dad arguing with the restaurant owner. Since French was still one of the official languages in Morocco, Jean stepped in and offered to help with any misunderstanding. The argument was over the leading figure on the handwritten bill, whether it was a one or a seven. Sammy was saying that a seven should have a crossbar and that it was a one, the restaurant owner said he wrote it like Americans were accustomed to and that it was a seven. After some back and forth, Jean solved the problem by telling the restaurant owner in French that if he would accept the lower payment from the groom's parents, she would make up the rest behind the scenes. "OK," agreed the owner and shook hands. "OK, what?" Said Sammy's father."It's a one." Replied Jean, to the obvious relief of the groom's father.

***

The wedding was beautiful, enchanting. The chapel was very old, originally built in the sixteenth century. During the pre-wedding rehearsal, the priest explained that Marrakesh had a long history of religious tolerance. Although Islam was still the predominant religion in the city and country, there had been a large Jewish quarter in the city for centuries. The Christian population was small but had been there for centuries as well. The city was famous for tourism, with destination weddings being a popular theme. When the priest announced them as man and wife, there was unexpected cheering coming from the rear choir loft. Everyone turned to see that the football team members who had been involved in the fracas at the club had snuck into the church and were now cheering. Sammy and Pete waved enthusiastically.

Once outside, the football team was invited to the reception, only to decline, saying that they had a football match that afternoon. The wedding party was invited to the match and explained that the timing wasn't right. The original reception had been planned at the church hall, but after Pete had seen the estate, she had asked if the reception could be moved to those grounds. It was the same catering company where the Moore's had hired the daily chef crew, so the change of venue did not cause any consternation.

***

Most of the guests left the next day on one of Greg's airplanes that he had arranged for the wedding party. Greg and Jean had decided to stay and run their empires from this remote location as best they could, having discovered that as long as they had a good internet connection, they could work from anywhere. Mike and Priya moved from their rented apartment in the old town to the estate so they could be closer to their respective bosses. Priya announced that she was expecting their first baby.

Dinner with the Mayor of Marrakech was interesting. Greg had done his homework and discovered that she had been reelected Mayor several times and appeared to be entrenched for a long time to come. She said she attributed it to her focus on tourism, keeping business taxes low and keeping crime low. Other than the constant problem with pickpockets that seems to be inherent with many tourists, there wasn't much crime. With the free education at the well-respected University of Marrakech, the young people were kept busy and off the streets. The nightlife was also attractive to the younger population, fueled by the low cost of tourism that brought in a younger crowd. She had increased the sports revenue in the city with four professional football teams that called Marrakech home.

When dinner was over, she got down to business. The topic was, as the police commissioner had said, an empty manufacturing plant that used to be at the edge of town but was now in the middle of the newer part of town, outside the old walls. It had indeed had a prior life supplying diesel engines for the European trucking companies. Greg had said that he didn't need any diesel engines, but if the factory could be rebuilt for other purposes, he had some ideas. The mayor was open to any suggestions, so Greg said his biggest need was to build luxury modular living spaces. He didn't say that the intended purpose was for a Mars colony. When the Mayor agreed that this could be a possibility, Greg mentioned that he was impressed with the elegant designs of the homes and riads in Marrakech and that even with the exacting specifications his design engineers had come up with for the Mars living pods, Greg was sure that the people of Marrakech would put their own unique flair to the pods. They discussed the broad strokes of a business deal, who would bring what kind of money to the effort, from the modernization costs of the current plant to the logistics of converting it to its new purpose. They discussed logistics on how these large pods would have to take over the space currently slotted for employee parking to a space dedicated to bringing in raw materials on one side and removing the finished products on the other. They decided that since there would be no space for employee parking, the mayor offered a nearby former cotton field as employee parking with constant shuttle buses running to the plant. Greg also mentioned that picking up the finished pods would be easier in one of his container ships that could hover over the factory and load the pods into one of the massive cargo holds. This would require some coordination with the local airport authorities to avoid any potential collisions. The mayor promised to get the right people together to solve that bit of logistics.

Business concluded they relaxed for a while, enjoying coffee and tea. Greg first commented on how rich the coffee was and learned that Morocco had renowned coffee plantations in the foothills of the nearby Atlas Mountains and that coffee was one of the main exports of Morocco. Greg next commented that there were a few places in the world where he felt inner peace when he visited and had decided that Marrakech was one of those places that spoke to his soul. The mayor smiled and said it was not the first time she had heard that. Greg asked about foreign ownership of property in Marrakech and Morocco, only to find out that since Morocco had become independent again, the laws were very strict about foreign ownership. However, since many of the larger estates were still in the hands of some of the original French colonial families, the transfer of ownership of those estates to other foreigners was not as strict. In addition, the mayor informed Greg that since he was now a local business owner, he could get around some of the newer laws by being considered a local if he desired. Greg further inquired about expanding his networking and cell phone business to include a branch in Morocco and learned that with the right local partners, it would be a welcome addition, especially in the rural areas that didn't have much coverage. Greg looked over at Jean, who nodded, knowing that in addition to the Chateau in France, they would soon have a nice estate in Morocco.

Once coffee had been served, Aliya and the twins had come out to say goodnight. At three years old, they were still confused that Greg and Jean were both Dad and Mom and Grandma and Grandpa. Their brains had not worked out the relationship yet. Whatever the case, Samantha, the nimbler of the three, arrived first and claimed the coveted spot on Greg's lap. Aliya crawled into her grandmother Jean's lap. Celina, the inquisitive one, stood between them and said, "I have a serious question." Once she felt she had the focus of the adults around the table, she asked, "Why do we have butt cracks." The mayor on the opposite side of the table immediately turned her head to cough to cover up her burst of laughter. Greg and Jean were stunned into silence, their minds racing for an answer. Running Bear, who had followed the girls to the table, smiled wisely, leaned down and whispered into her ear. Celina said, "Oh." Then she walked away from the table, where the adults observed her taking small steps across the lawn, then a few giant steps before skipping back to the table, satisfied that she had received the correct answer.

Greg looked at Running Bear and asked what he had told her. Running Bear smiled and said, "So we can take bigger steps." The entire table burst out laughing.

***

Greg had given his asteroid mining crew orders to start shipping material back to Earth to start making modules for a colony on Mars but changed his mind after attending a Skype conference with his AstroX team who had come up with a brilliant idea. They showed him mock-ups of a hollowed-out asteroid that would house multiple manufacturing plants that could produce a variety of materials. Jean, who was sitting across the table in the garden of the villa, choked on the herbal tea she was sipping when the scientists informed Greg that the asteroid would be slightly smaller than the island of Manhattan.

"Hey, this is space. Anything is possible, and we've learned to think big." Came the response of another scientist on the team.

Greg shook his head in amazement, wondering what he had started. The team had answers for the thousands of questions that Greg and Jean posited. Jean had put aside her work, caught up in the excitement of planning this huge facility in space. She joined Greg on that side of the table so the team could see her face on the video call, too. They learned that instead of stripping the asteroid from the outside in, they would bore a hole in the side, big enough to get the laser mining drones inside to start extracting the material inside. The result would be a hollow asteroid with walls several meters thick. The intention would be to take some of the living pods planned for the Mars colony and attach them to the interior walls, forming a town large enough to house the crew needed to man the plants.

Jean asked about oxygen. The team brought up several PowerPoint slides showing how oxygen and water for humans would be obtained from large ice asteroids that would be towed from nearby asteroid fields. Greg asked about power for the town and manufacturing plants. More PowerPoint slides were brought up, showing plans for making giant solar mirrors that would be pointed to the sun. The mirrors would be some of the first items made from materials gathered from the mining operations.

Greg approved the budget, which was not nearly as big as he would have thought. Much of the building was coming from minerals gathered from the asteroid mining operations, which Greg already owned. There was a recurring cost of bringing materials and structures from Earth that could not be gathered from space. Jean liked the fact that companies on Earth would profit from supplying the space colonization efforts.

The sun had already gone down by the time they ended the Skype call, which had originally been scheduled for one hour. The chef brought out dinner and light jackets since the temperature had dropped at sundown. "And I thought that we had big projects on earth," Jean said as she shared her thoughts.

"More impossible projects," Greg responded as he took a bite of a delicious chicken cordon-bleu.

***

Marie travelled to Paris to attend the birth of Aimee's baby. She met Sebastien in the waiting room, who escorted Marie into the private hospital room, where Monique sat in a chair beside the bed, holding her daughter's hand. Aimee smiled and held out her other hand for Marie.

The overriding question they all wanted to know was, 'Who is the father?' But Aimee was still refusing to say. Her father had talked to her privately, but she still wouldn't say. Her mother tried everything she could to get Aimee to divulge the answer, but to no avail.

After about 4 hours, the contractions were getting closer together. A nurse checked her dilation and announced she was ready. The nurse paged the doctor and then shooed everyone out of the room. She asked if the father was going to be present, only to be told that, sadly, he would not make it to the birthing. Aimee said something to the nurse, who turned to Marie and said, "She wants to know if you can stay." Marie took the chair next to the bed and took her friend's hand.

One hour went by, then two. The doctor checked, then announced that everything was ok, the baby was not breech and that this was not unusual for the first time. Aimee was in constant pain, sweating, moaning and sometimes swearing when a particularly bad contraction hit. They had given her an epidural an hour prior when she said the pain was too intense. The doctor came by when Aimee had lain back and closed her eyes between contractions. Marie, still holding her friend's hand, had also relaxed and closed her eyes.

The doctor had just walked out of the room when Aimee shrieked at the top of her lungs. Marie jumped out of the chair, startled. She felt her hand getting crushed as Aimee's hand closed on hers with a death grip. The doctor came running back in, grabbing sterile gloves from a box on the counter. He barely had time to put them on when Aimee yelled again as the baby's head crested through. A nurse came running in to assist.

A few minutes later, the doctor announced that Aimee was the proud mother of a large, healthy baby boy. The nurse quickly cleaned the baby, wrapped it in a soft blank then handed it to Aimee. The baby, still crying, snuggled his head into her neck. Aimee's parents came in a few minutes later, congratulating their daughter and saying words of pride and well-being.

The nurse let the baby snuggle for about twenty minutes, then took it for full cleaning and weighing. Aimee fell asleep as the others talked quietly. Marie compared this event to the birth of her daughter Aliya which seemed much easier in comparison. Monique mentioned that Aimee was probably somewhere in between, a prolonged delivery but relatively easy once the head started to show.

An hour later, Marie stood up and stretched her back just as the nurse brought the baby back. Seeing that Aimee had fallen asleep, she handed the baby to Monique, who was pleased to hold her first grandchild. Marie stepped closer to get a better look and burst out laughing. It was a full belly, gut-busting laugh that took her breath away and caused her legs to crumble. She collapsed on the floor, laughing hysterically, trying to speak, as Aimee woke up and mumbled something incoherent but obviously wanting to know what was going on with her best friend. Aimee's parents were looking at Marie inquiringly, wondering the same thing.

Marie recovered enough to say something, but when she looked at Aimee, the full-throated laughter returned. Tears accompanied this round. Every time Marie tried to speak, uncontrollable laughter came out. Aimee suddenly realized that Marie had figured out who the baby's father was, and her cheeks turned bright red. She nodded her head at Marie, which caused both of them to burst into laughter.

Since Marie still couldn't speak, she whipped out her phone and texted her brother. *'You need to come to Paris ASAP and pick up something extremely valuable. Bring Mom and Dad.'*

'Can't; spring training starts in 4 days.' Alex, having played Triple-A baseball the prior year had been told that he would be starting another season as a semi-professional baseball player and to report to training camp on a certain date. During the off-season, Alex had been working part-time with the AstroX team part-time with the experimental physicists team at John Hopkins in conjunction with starting his master's degrees in physics and mathematics.

'Tell Dad to bring one of his fast planes, then you can get back before practice starts.' Marie answered. She then texted her parents an equally cryptic message telling them to get to Paris ASAP and to bring Alex for a huge surprise, even if they had to tie him up and drag him onto the plane. When they asked for details, Marie responded, telling them not to ask any more questions just get here quickly. Her father relented first, only asking where they should meet. She gave the name and address of the hospital.

'is it serious?' her mother responded.

'Not deathly serious.' Marie texted back, still being somewhat cryptic. They responded that if they left immediately, they would arrive at 2 am Paris time, and perhaps they should wait until the next day. Marie concurred and then received a response that they would be at the hospital at 10 am Paris time, which was perfect because that is when visiting hours started.

Aimee's parents were dying to find out what was happening, still perplexed at Marie's hysterical outburst at seeing the baby. They thought it was a perfectly healthy, beautiful baby, although somewhat larger than normal. Monique commented that she wasn't surprised that Aimee had some difficulty with the birth. Marie only told them to make sure they were back at the hospital at 10 am sharp, and she would reveal the surprise.

Promptly at 10 am, Alex, Greg and Jean got out of a cab and entered the lobby of the hospital where Marie, Sebastien and Monique were waiting for them. Marie wrapped her arms around her parents, then turned and playfully slugged her brother on the arm before dancing out of reach before he could retaliate. "Great to see you too, sis." He said as he pretended to lunge at her. "What's the gigantic mystery?"

She shrugged, then led the group to the elevator, staying silent as they got to the floor and entered Aimee's room. She was awake and greeted everyone with a hearty 'Bonjour.' Before anyone could respond, a nurse brought the baby into the room and gently laid him in Aimee's arms. Greg and Jean took one look at the wee lad and simultaneously said, "Oh!", then looked at Alex, who was standing in the doorway looking perplexed. Sebastien and Monique were still showing quizzical looks on their faces, so Marie took the baby and held it up next to Alex's face. Their faces instantly reflected comprehension, and they both laughed as they realized the young boy looked just like Alex.

Alex, as smart as he was, still hadn't caught on. It took him several awkward seconds before he realized what everyone else already knew. His cheeks burned bright red. He tried to talk but his ability to speak had shut down. He looked around, then at Aimee who had both arms out, inviting him to a hug. Alex gratefully stepped over, leaned down and embraced Aimee in a long hug. She whispered in that sexy French accent that Alex loved, "Sorry that I didn't tell you."

Over the next few minutes, the story came out that Alex, needing a new suit jacket because he had outgrown the first one that Aimee and Marie had made him, had called Aimee. He had flown to Paris to pick up the newly designed suit that Aimee had crafted herself. During the final fitting, she had let him know that she had not been dating for a while because she seemed to only pick rotten boyfriends. Alex nervously stammered his response that he was glad because he always had a crush on her while they were growing up and had considered her out of reach because she was three years older than him, and that he felt she was way out of his league. She had looked him in the eye, realizing that he was serious, then admitted to him that after watching him grow up, she had started admiring the handsome man he had grown into. "Well, you can guess the rest," Aimee told the group.

***

CHAPTER 23

They were married six weeks later at the Satrat vineyards near Bordeau. It was intended to be a small, private wedding, but after trying to pare down the guest list, they went with a large crowd. The crème-de-la-crème of the Fashion world attended. Even though during business they were fierce competitors, they all delighted in attending the major functions of each of the principles. Besides, it was a great event to show their latest designs.

Politicians, rock stars, professional athletes, business moguls and other social elites were there. Jillian Castor was there with her best film crew, recording the event and trying to convince the Moor's and Satrats to use the wedding for her new idea, which was a modern version of *'Lifestyles of the Rich and Famous.'* She must have pitched her idea to the crowd because, after the wedding, many of the famous people approached Greg and Jean, saying that they thought it was a great idea. A day later, Jillian was given a green light after she showed them a list of people who said they would agree to participate in an episode.

Aimee and Alex agreed to postpone their honeymoon until baseball season ended. Alex offered to stop playing baseball to become a full-time dad, but nobody would hear of it. Aimee told him under no circumstances would she agree to let him stop playing. Aimee had been running the fashion business, but Marie told her to take some time with the baby and that she would run the business for a few months. The only big event on the schedule was the opening of the New York City store, which they would both participate in.

Admittedly, Aimee didn't know much about baseball, but she and baby Jean Pierre, or JP as they were calling him, dutifully sat in the stands for many of the games. Triple-A baseball was different from what Aimee pictured. The stands were often uncomfortable with metal bleachers rather than individual chairs. She sat with other wives and girlfriends, who were timid about being around a famous fashion designer, but once they learned she was a bright, funny person, they started including her in their conversations. They explained the rules as best they could.

Aimee said she was starting to understand, but before the first pitch of the next game, she started cheering and yelling, "Come on double play!" All the conversations around her stopped. The woman sitting next to her put her hand on Aimee's arm and started to correct her, then stopped when Aimee winked at her. They both started laughing and soon, it became a regular chant before the first pitch of every game. It first made the local paper, then someone got a video and posted it on the internet where it went viral.

Aimee was exhausted after going to forty games and told Alex she didn't know how he could make it through a full season of one hundred and fifty games. Alex told her the secret was to sleep a lot, eat healthy meals, drink lots of water and keep up the workouts. After a few more games, she told Alex that she was going to New York City to work in that store and that she was close enough to him that if there was a special game, she would fly over and attend. At first, she was going to live with Victor and Marie until she could find her own place in the city.

Many good things came about from attending all those games; first, she discovered that she really loved Alex; second, she enjoyed working out with him; third, she lost some of her new mom's weight by eating the same way he ate. They would do a workout or stretching routine in the morning followed by a protein shake, have a large lunch before they went off to practice or a game, and then a big salad with salmon or chicken added for dinner. Fourth, she ended up with notebooks full of new sketches.

Well, there was a fifth one if she was being honest with herself. She got to see a side of America that she would have never gotten to see if Alex had not been playing Triple-A baseball. The team played in small to medium-sized towns. They toured on a bus. Aimee recalled Alex's reaction after the first road trip game on the team's twenty-year-old bus. He spent his free time the next two days on the phone with various luxury bus companies until he found the right one and bought it for the team. The team only knew that it came from an anonymous donor. Aimee and her son would ride with other wives and girlfriends when they were available for a trip. Most had jobs themselves because semi-professional baseball players did not make much money.

Aimee spent a lot of time in the house Alex was renting when he was at practice or when she decided not to go on the road trip games. She sent an open invitation to the other players' families to hang out at their house at any time. It was a former house for the cattle ranch that used to encompass the grassy plains on the east side of Colorado Springs. Now, urban sprawl has put restaurants, grocery stores and other stores across the major road that ran north and south on the west side of the estate. Aimee didn't mind as she had everything she needed within a short distance. She especially liked Costco about a mile away. Her other favorite was a small Greek restaurant at the corner of Barnes and Powers that served the best authentic Greek food. This was a completely different lifestyle than she was accustomed to in France and New York City.

One other thing she liked was having a neighbor with horses. She had seen an old sign on the road that said riding lessons. Having never ridden a horse before, she persuaded Alex to stop by and see if they still offered lessons. It turns out they did. Aimee fell in love with horses over the summer and vowed to get her own someday.

Before the end of summer, she had an open invitation to stop by and ride on the extensive plains that undulated for miles out to the east.

As idyllic as life that summer had been, Aimee felt the pull of the fashion business calling her. The countless conference calls she had been on were just not sufficient. The fashion business was a hands-on career. It was difficult to see the finer details of a prototype unless you were there in person to see and feel every stitch. That's why she told Alex that it was imperative for her to move back for a while. He understood and said he would join her in a month when the season ended.

***

Aimee sat down with Marie that first afternoon back in New York City, and they combed through the new sketchbooks, marking the drawings with priorities and adding notes about fabrics, thoughts on accessories, pricing and groupings for the upcoming fashion shows. Marie commented that, not surprisingly, many of the sketches had a sporting theme. This would be their first foray into sports clothes and athletic wear.

There was one entire book devoted to children's wear from newborn to toddler to youth clothing. They had started the toddler line when Aliya was born. During the first few days of living with Victor and Marie, Aimee complained that she was continually tired and slept a lot. They all agreed that it had been due to the rigorous schedule of keeping up with the baseball team. However, one morning, shortly after arriving, Aimee was eating a simple bowl of mixed fruit for breakfast when she suddenly bolted for the bathroom and vomited the few bites she had managed to take that morning. Marie came in to ensure everything was ok, gave her a hug when she had finished and said, "Better call Alex."

Aimee had been calling Alex at the same time every evening because she knew most days that he was available at that time. That night, Alex answered in a sleepy voice, saying that he was tired and had already settled into bed early. He perked up when Aimee informed him that she was pregnant again. Alex lightheartedly asked how that was possible, and they shared a good laugh before he said that he was delighted. They talked about everything and nothing for a while before Aimee could tell that he was falling asleep, so she bade him 'sweet dreams' and then hung up.

***

The season for Alex had been scheduled to end September 10th, with plans for him to join her on the 11th or 12th. He called her on the night of the 10th after his last game and excitedly told her that he had been called up to play the last three weeks with the Colorado Rockies. She was delighted, of course, since it had been one of his main goals all his life. Alex saw a lot of playing time those last three weeks even though he had to play left field, a position he had not played since little league. His hitting was good, but he told Aimee one night that the pitching was so much better at this level that it took him a few games to start acclimating and seeing the ball better. As was the norm, the team left Alex with the impression that even though he was invited to spring training with the professionals, he would most likely still start the season at the Triple-A level again. Alex vowed to earn his spot at the big-league level during spring training the following year, no matter what position he had to play. Sammy said the same thing about his situation over in the American League.

***

CHAPTER 24

July 2009: Net worth $ 17 Trillion

Both Alex and Sammy earned a spot on their respective big-league teams. At the all-star break, they decided to hang out together since they were not playing. Both could afford to rent a nice place anywhere. The days of penny-pinching on a Triple-A salary were over. They chose to spend the time in Alex and Aimee's NYC apartment, although it was cramped with the four adults and the four children. Both Pete and Aimee announced that they were expecting another child next spring. Sammy mentioned that he was very happy getting a temporary spot in his coveted short-stop position due to an injury to the team's all-pro shortstop. Alex was still playing left field but there were rumors that he may get a chance to move to his beloved third base if the Rockies traded their current all-pro player at that position during the annual trade window. Both were hitting well, Alex leading his team in extra-base hits and Sammy leading his team in home runs and RBIs. Neither had an error yet during the first part of the season.

Marie and Victor were living in Paris. Victor had a job with the United Nations World Court in The Hague. Most days, he could work at home, but it did require frequent trips on the fast train to the Hague. Marie split her time running the Paris store for Satrat and Moore and working as an art restorer for the master art curator at the Louvre.

***

In their upscale apartment in New York City, Greg was pacing by the large window overlooking the city. "DAMMIT!" He shouted after learning that the OWG proposal had just been vetoed by the

U.S. president. It had passed the House and Senate after another tireless campaign by the Moore's and their rather large and outlandishly expensive lobby group.

The subdued group in the room said nothing. "That SOB promised he would not veto it! I was the largest donor to his campaign and helped quell some of the negative press against him to get him elected last year. And he's not taking my calls."

"He's probably waiting until you cool down," Jean said. "Give him a couple of days."

Greg was pacing the room, trying to think of what to do next. "This will set us back years."

***

The following week, the Moore's were at a rare family dinner. They had traveled to Pittsburg to see the Yankees play the Pirates. Alex was the starting third baseman for the Yankees and one of their power hitters. He had been traded from the Colorado Rockies. His best friend Sammy played for the Pirates, playing left field. It was a large table for ten, including a highchair for the smaller grandchild. Aimiee's oldest, Jean Pierre, or JP as they called him, was one year and four months old. Aimee was almost nine months pregnant, about ready to deliver their second child. Marie's oldest child, Aliya, was 5 years old. Jean's twins, Celina and Samantha, were the same age as Aliya.

"Not sure how to calculate our net worth if we include all the space mining and colonizing businesses," Jean said.

"Not going to include those in our tax estimates. Not giving that guy another farthing after he vetoed that bill."

"Dear, it's not good for your blood pressure to keep stressing about that," Jean replied. She had told the children about Greg having high cholesterol and high blood pressure readings after his last annual physical.

Greg sighed. "You're right, as usual. But still, there's no income coming from any of the space efforts. I mean, I could be bringing back some of the minerals and selling them on Earth, but right now, all the mining resources are going to expand the Mars colony and the asteroid mining facility."

"Have you had any visits from the golden orb guy again?" Alex asked.

"No. I imagine he's waiting until the OWG effort gets passed."

After dinner, Jean was buckling Samantha into her car seat, who had complained during dinner that her lips were hurting. Jean took a quick look and told Greg to stop at a nearby convenience store to get some ChapStick on the way to the hotel.

Greg was buckling the twins into their car seats when Celina said, "Hey, I'm five; I should drive."

Greg chuckled and said, "Hey, you made a rhyme."

They spotted a 7-Eleven on the way back. Greg was going to do a quick dash into the store, then had a thought – the girls had never had a Slurpee! He unbuckled them and escorted them into the store to show them how to work the machine. The girls both chose cherry flavors. He paid for everything and got the girls buckled in their seats before handing them their drinks. Greg had hardly settled into the driver's seat before there was a loud yell from the back seat. Greg looked at Jean, knowing that yell could only mean one thing. They both said simultaneously, "BRAIN FREEZE."

***

Greg got a text with a special ringtone. He glanced at his phone. It was from 'just the fax'. That was his dad's humor for naming the contact in his phone that Greg established for messages from the future that came via Greg's old fax machine. This text said, 'Start mining bitcoin.' That was a complete mystery, so Greg called the head of his mining company, who said he'd never heard of a mineral called bitcoin. He called his assistant Mike, who knew exactly what it was. Mike explained that it was a new type of currency and then went on to describe what he knew about the subject.

Greg sat at his desk with his head buried in his hands. His first thought was that he could not possibly take on any more projects. So, he put his feet on his desk, his hands behind his head and closed his eyes.

After ten minutes in an almost sleeplike state, he moved his keyboard to his lap with his feet still on his desk. This had become his new favorite thinking position. Knowing that he could not ignore anything the fax said, he logged into his LIBRARY and looked up Bitcoin. Before he knew it, it was dark outside. Jean had texted several hours ago to see if he would make it for dinner. He texted her back, saying he was on his way.

She had made him a mixed greens salad with spicy baked chicken, one of his new favorites, after learning that he had to start eating lighter meals. He brought her up to speed on this Bitcoin idea as well as what he learned from his LIBRARY. Apparently, cryptocurrency is eventually going to be the one world currency.

At that point, Jean got a text from an unknown number. *"Meet me at your Chateau next Monday. Isa."*

"Greg, I need a ride to the Chateau," Jean explained as she showed him the text.

"I remember meeting her at one of the OWG conferences," Greg said. "She was very interesting, and I recall that she gave very good input on how we should proceed. The most curious thing I recall is that she said she lived on a ship, but Mike could never track her to any location. Although he did mention that after his research there are a number of people who permanently live at sea and don't have an address."

***

A woman was standing at the front gates of the Chateau. Dirk took a golf cart down the winding drive to the gate to retrieve Isa after she had pressed the bell. He looked at the high-resolution video to verify it was their expected visitor. Jean was on the front steps to greet her, welcoming the warm sun on her face. Isa had her cane but didn't use it. She spryly went up the steps to greet Jean. Jean noticed her handshake was strong despite having pure white hair and a weathered face. They walked through the Chateau to the back patio, where the chefs had prepared a light lunch under massive umbrellas.

Isa asked about the grandchildren. After bringing Isa up to date on the family, they chatted about various topics before Isa finally said, "I'm sure you are wondering why I asked for this meeting."

Jean nodded, showing patience.

"You're going to have to run for President."

CHAPTER 25

"Do you mean President of the United States?" Jean asked in a higher-than-normal voice.

"Yes, it is the best way to get a resolution passed for the One World Government," Isa responded.

"But I am a complete unknown to the American People."

"Not really; you have been on the cover of Time Magazine and done numerous television interviews with the most popular shows about your charity efforts. Even your few appearances on your Castle Restoration and other cable spinoff shows mean that you are known to many people around the world."

"Most people who get elected presidents are either Senators or Governors," Jean said after a moment of thought.

"True. Perhaps the best path is to become senator first."

"Why not Greg?" Jean asked.

"It's past time for the USA to have its first female president. Plus, you are a lawyer, so you understand more about the law than your husband. Besides, his attention to other things needed to successfully join the Galactic Federation is not finished yet." Isa informed her.

"Well, our current residence of Washington D.C. does not have a Senator. But we have been spending more time in our New York City residence. I could designate that as our primary residence. New York is a blue state, so I would probably have to run as a Democrat to win. But I feel that their move to identity politics is going to cause problems for them in the future. Do you think I could win as an independent candidate?"

"That question would be best posited after you hire a campaign manager," Isa responded.

"No rest for the weary, I guess," Jean responded with a heavy sigh. She wandered around the beautiful garden the rest of the day, lost in thought. She loved this home and wouldn't mind spending more time here.

The chef had high tea ready for her and Isa. Jean invited Zophia to accompany them at tea where they had great discussions on everything from politics to the Moore Foundation projects. Zophia was surprisingly studious and well-informed in many subjects. She also filled them in on the challenges of keeping the Chateau running smoothly.

***

Jean texted Greg to call her ASAP or come to the Chateau if he could come in the next few days; otherwise meet her back in New York. Greg was in space and would eventually get her message. Next, she called Frank and Ginny who were staying in New York with her twins, to see how they were doing in school and promised to be home the day after tomorrow. She had a short conversation with Marie and Victor on a cell phone, getting caught up on their life in New York, where Victor was the U.S. representative to the United Nations. Marie had gotten a job as an art restorer at the recommendation of her former boss at the Louve, where she had been an intern art restorer while attending the Sorbonne. She loved the job because of the flexible working hours, allowing her to get Aliya off to school in the morning and then come home before school ended. Marie was also head of manufacturing for the clothing lines of Satrat and Moore, but she hired a professional for the day-to-day work and not much time was needed from her.

Jean stayed at the Chateau that night, treating herself to a quiet evening of pampering in the luxurious bath, her mind lazily floating through what needed to be done to become a senator, then president. She quietly marveled at what her life had become. Sometimes, it seemed that she was stumbling through life from simple opportunities to ever more complex ones. Other times, it seemed like she was being guided through life to a predestined outcome. Other times, it seemed as if she was always choosing the best opportunities that arose around her. She slept a long, deep, soundless sleep and awoke midmorning, her body and mind still on East Coast USA time.

Isa was also just coming down to breakfast. Jean asked her why she had asked to meet at the Chateau instead of in New York City, where they lived four blocks apart. Isa was living with Victor and Marie, as the nanny and mentor to Aliya. Victor had taken a job at the headquarters of the U.N. and had moved to the city. Isa was teaching them all IGL and IGSL, the Intergalactic Language and the Intergalactic Sign Language in the evenings. Greg and Jean also attended those lessons when they could.

"Because you needed a peaceful place to reflect on your path forward," Isa replied. "And I was already here, meeting with Running Bear, who is out walking the grounds now. "Running Bear had asked if he could establish a permanent residence at the Chateau since his story of being one of the original human inhabitants on earth had been revealed. Dirk, the majordomo of the Chateau, was fascinated by the elder gentleman, and they were often seen in conversation, either in the grand library or walking the grounds. Dirk had mentioned that he had gotten permission to write Running Bear's story. Everyone was interested in the full history of his life, having gotten little snippets from time to time.

"I'll give you a ride back to New York. It's faster than your husband's plane." Isa said, to Jean's surprise.

"I thought you lived on a ship?" Jean queried.

"I do, a spaceship!"

***

Jean called Keith Miller, the Virginia Senator she had helped get elected a few years earlier and asked for the best campaign manager. His suggestion was to call Kristopher Reinfeld, who was reported to be the best campaign manager around. Keith wanted to know more, and Jean promised to fill him in later.

Kristopher Reinfeld turned out to be a large, burley guy with a grey beard, who Jean thought would make a perfect actor playing the part of a back-woods trapper having a bear as a pet. She came away from their first meeting at lunch with the impression that he was extremely sharp and capable, perhaps a bit ruthless if needed. Kristopher, or Kris, as he was normally called, said he usually only did presidential elections, but since it was between the four-year election cycle, he was willing to take on her project. He had informed her that she was getting into the senatorial race for 2010 a bit late, as others had been at it for at least six months or more. He said it was doubtful she could raise enough funding from the right organizations in such a short period of time. He changed his mind after his initial surprise that she could be self-funded and said it would be possible to get her elected. He also said that she would still want to raise funds from normal organizations to prevent those funds from going to her competitors. His final comment both worried Jean and excited her, "Clear your schedule and get ready to sprint!"

***

And sprint they did. Over the following four months, Jean was traveling through the state of New York in a luxury bus, making speeches, signing autographs, meeting with influential people, attending meetings in rural towns and whatever else Kris had on the schedule. At night, when she had the energy, she tried to study the process of creating and voting for laws as life would be when or if she became a senator. Keith Miller became her mentor, and sometimes, instead of reading what had been supplied for her, she called him to talk. Keith's wife, Rebeccah, was as knowledgeable as her husband, so sometimes Jean would talk to her. It was from her that Jean got the real inside scoop on the other senators and congresspeople, as well as what a social calendar would look like.

***

Greg gave instructions to his quantum computer team to start mining bitcoin. The speed of the computer gives him an advantage over other silicon-based computers, and he soon discovers that he is being awarded about thirty percent of the bitcoins. One of the programmers on the quantum team told him that it cost him more in electricity than the bitcoins were worth, but he gave them instructions to continue.

Alex immediately grasped the importance of cryptocurrency and told Greg that he should start his own type of coin. Greg pondered that for a few days, then decided that although it sounded like a great idea, he was too busy to start another project.

***

July 2010

Ginny called Greg about 5 am and informed him that his father had passed away in his sleep. They talked for about one hour, with Greg promising to come home to West Virginia right away. He first phoned Jean, who was on the campaign trail in California. He convinced her to stay on the campaign until he set a date for the funeral. Alex and Marie were equally saddened by the loss of Grandpa Frank, who had been a core part of their life.

The funeral service at the church was standing room only. The side aisles and back area behind the pews were packed. There were people outside waiting to get in, trying to listen to the sounds of the sermon and eulogies as best they could. Frank had been the town's best handyman and had been to almost everyone's house at one time or another. The preacher gave a traditional sermon about the circle of life. Greg talked about growing up with a stoic, altruistic father who seemed to know a little bit about everything. Running Bear had volunteered to speak, and his message left people in deep contemplation after he finished. It was more ethereal, concentrating on the soul and a mysterious afterlife and rebirth. Frank was buried in the family plot near the grove of trees on the far side of the property.

***

November 2010

It was a tired but elated Jean Moore who stepped behind the podium in the first week of November to announce her victory as the new Democratic Senator from New York. Jean had wanted to run as an independent candidate, but Kris convinced her early on that, due to their short runway until election day, she should go with the New York norm. Still, it was a narrow victory over the current Democratic incumbent and an election where the Republican challenger got a higher-than-expected 30% of the votes.

The six-year-old twins and Marie's daughter were on the podium beside her, wearing this year's new line of Satrat and Moore children's wear. Jean was in a black Satrat and Moore suit with silver piping around the collar and down the front. It was her favorite professional outfit. She had saved this one for a special occasion and this certainly counted as one. Greg and Alex were on her left, wearing matching outfits with silver piping on their suit jackets. Marie, wearing a gorgeous print dress showing off her slim waist, was standing behind the girls.

Her six-year-old twins, normally boisterous and fidgety, were standing still in awe of the crowd of wildly cheering people. They would occasionally glance at their mother making a speech, then go back to watching the crowd. They seemed mesmerized by the whole affair, their faces lit in wonderment. Aliya, Marie's daughter, was also watching the crowd but with a studious look on her face. Greg would later comment on the difference between them after watching a replay of the speech.

That speech got brief airtime on all the news channels, but what really captured the attention of the nation was a female reporter who squatted down next to the twins and asked them how they felt about their mother becoming a senator. She first put the microphone in front of Samantha, who sweetly said, "Fine." It was Celina who grabbed the microphone and started giving her own speech about what a fine opportunity it was for this family to serve the people and do things that could make people's lives better. The reporter wrapped it up by saying to the camera, "Future President?"

***

January 2011: Greg stopped counting net worth

Jean was busier than normal after getting sworn in as the new Senator for New York. She had moved back to the old house in Washington D.C. after spending a lot of time between the New York City apartment and the Chateau in France.

Greg had surprised her by having the kitchen and master bedroom remodeled, including replacing the one drafty window in their bedroom with a bay window. It had a heated bench with plush padding covered in some type of soft velour fabric. The view wasn't great because it looked over their modest backyard and the neighbor's houses. She had a remote control where she could either darken the glass or lower the blackout shades. Greg had also upgraded the bed to one where they could control the firmness of either side. Jean preferred hers on a hard setting, Greg just slightly softer.

Jean's first few days in office were not very productive. She and her staff moved into their new offices, learned the layout of the building, and sat in on a few meetings. She had a one-on-one meeting with the Speaker of the House, who brought her up to speed on the current legislation being considered. Jean half-listened because she had already done her homework and knew what was going on. She did sit up straighter at the end of the meeting when she was told that, as a freshman senator, she was expected to vote strictly along party lines. That did not sit well with her. She nodded but didn't answer, not wanting to get into an argument. Her whole concept of being a senator was that she was supposed to represent her constituents and vote however she thought they would want her to.

Jean also had a long list of meeting requests, mostly from lobbyists representing various groups. Also on the list were groups who could not afford lobbyists. Having hired her own lobby group to push the OWG agenda, she knew how they worked. She had been coached that taking meetings from these groups was strictly up to her, but it was widely publicized who she met with. However, she had always been the type to garner different points of view while in the business world, so she thought she would be inclined to listen to opinions from opposing factions.

She asked Kris, her campaign manager, what to do with the extra money left over from the campaign contributions. "There are ways to transfer that money to use yourself, which is the most common. Otherwise, keep it in savings or in an investment account to use for your next re-election." He told her.

"But isn't it illegal to use that money for personal uses?" Jean asked him.

"Yes, but there are so many loopholes that everyone does it." It was his answer.

She instructed him to leave it in an investment account to use for her next campaign.

***

"What's new on the inventions oversight?" George asked his staff in their regular weekly review meeting.

"The usual from the big tech companies. Mostly on the software side of AI. Personal assistants are getting better, image recognition has improved, especially facial recognition and language processing are the big focus lately," was the answer from the lady who concentrated on the big tech companies.

"What about the hardware side?" George asked his other team member.

"Tesla announced another battery generation, but it's really just an incremental improvement, not the big leap forward that everyone has been waiting for." He said. "After the success of the Apple Watch, there have been a few copycats and a few patents granted around the detection of personal health indicators, but nothing that is giving us big leaps forward. Another company filed patents for improvements in solar energy collection, but again, just incremental technology steps."

"What about that Greg Moore guy? We completely missed his big invention years ago on the anti-gravity device. What's he up to now?"

"We put a new recruit on his AstroX team and have gotten a lot of information, as I've reported over the past year," John said. "It turns out that his son, Alex, is one of the main inventors in the group. His name goes on most of the patents filed by that group. They are currently working on improvements to the Mars colony. The last big invention I reported on was the replacement of the ion drives with the new style of engines that improved their space travel more than ten times faster. "

"Is that Alex Moore, the Yankee's third baseman?" asked George.

"Yeah. Same guy. Who would guess that an all-star baseball player is also one of the world's leading astrophysicists.'"

"Do we have his place bugged?" George wanted to know.

"Yes. But when he's home, he's totally playing dad. No work or anything we're watching." John replied.

"Anything else on that AstroX group?"

"Plenty. There is a sister company that has built a quantum computer that they say is faster and more powerful than an entire data center these other big tech companies are building. It's hooked to something they call THE LIBRARY that our guy says contains everything ever written or ever will be written. It is one of their secrets to building advanced stuff."

"What do you mean?"

"Let's say they need to improve the interstellar communication, which is what Alex is working on right now. He goes into THE LIBRARY, puts in certain search terms and comes up with a lot of hits. But our guy says mostly it's a waste of time because there are more wrong answers in THE LIBRARY than there are correct ones. So, it takes a lot of discussion to weed out the bad stuff. But he says it's still valuable when they are stuck on big advancements."

"The number of patents from the quantum computer group has come down a lot lately. It seems like they are not filing patent applications these days for some reason. Our guy says that he had one tour of the facility in the other building when he first started, but nothing since. He logs into that computer to do his work and tells us that problems that would normally take weeks on a regular server farm are solved in seconds. It's one of the reasons Greg Moore has been so successful in his space mining and colonization efforts where others are struggling to catch up."

George was about to conclude the meeting when John interrupted, "Oh, I almost forgot to mention that our spy says that Greg Moore is about to file a few patents for some AI software for an advanced personal assistant. It seems that has been one of his personal projects lately."

"Well, keep us up to date if anything big pops up," George said.

***

Aliya was on the playground during recess in first grade when she heard a shrill squeak. She turned in time to see one of her friends fall from the top of the iron dome and land directly on her chest and face. She bounced once, then lay completely still. A teacher immediately crawled under the bars to get inside the dome, discovered that she wasn't moving and wasn't breathing, turned and yelled for someone to call 911. No other adults were nearby. The teacher patted her pockets, realized that she didn't have her cell phone, and immediately ran into the school.

Aliya crawled through the bars, squatted next to her friend and gently touched her shoulder. The girl's body jerked. The teacher came back seconds later, on the phone with emergency services, crawled through the lower bars of the iron dome and was relieved to see that the injured girl was breathing but still unconscious.

Ten minutes later, the ambulance crew came and administered first aid, gently checking to see that the neck and spine were not damaged, then rolled her over. The girl woke up at that point and asked what was happening. They explained that she had fallen and they were going to take her to the hospital.

Aliya had been standing next to her friend. Later, she was asked to give a statement and told the police that her friend had fallen and stopped breathing for a short time. The police asked several other questions and then let Aliya go.

***

In a meeting with the quantum computer team, they gave Greg some jaw-dropping news. While researching ways to improve the pesky error rate in the gallium arsenide chips, they found that iridium arsenide worked much better, thanks to Alex's suggestion after studying the elemental chart. While testing this new chip at absolute zero temperatures, they noticed odd things occurring. Various scientific experts were brought in, but it was Alex who gave the group the theory that they may be looking at a new type of matter. Nobody believed him at first because it was too far-fetched. Once he explained that he thought it was a topological state of matter they were observing, they started doing experiments to test the theory and discovered that he was probably correct.

Greg said, with an inquisitive look on his face, "Do you mean matter as in earth, wind and fire?"

"Yes." Said one of the scientists.

Greg said, "Well, I always liked that band." As he started humming the tune to 'Shining Star.'

That got a few laughs from the older people in the meeting.

"I've heard the term topological before, but I don't understand the context here," Greg said.

"Topological state of matter refers to something that behaviorally remains the same even after being twisted or stretched or other continuous deformations." Explained another scientist.

"What can we do with it?" Greg wanted to know.

"This is getting into a branch of quantum mechanics and quantum mathematics called TQFT or Topological Quantum Field Theory. It is related to the studies of space-time manipulation. Dimensional mathematics and other topics."

Greg was silent for a few seconds, then asked. "Was it the new iridium arsenide compound that lowered the error rate in the chips?"

"Partly. Combined with the change we made in the state detection from a qubit to a thread-based detection."

"Ok, I understand state detection means determining whether a 1 or 0 has been observed. But what is thread-based detection?"

The scientists knew that Greg was fairly technical, but they still tried to keep the explanations somewhat simple. "Another quasiparticle in quantum mechanics is called an anyon, which can be combined to form a braid. We invented a way to create a pair of baseline braids then other braids are created and compared to the base. This gave us a very stable way of determining the state of the result, meaning 1 or 0."

"But wait, there's more." Said another scientist excitedly from the other side of the table. "While investigating this new topological state of matter, we may be the first to prove that a Majorana particle exists."

"That's a new term to me," Greg said.

"A Majorana particle was proposed by Ettore Majorana in 1937. He published the mathematics about a fermion that is its own antiparticle. The stability of this type of fermion is what helped us bring the error rate way down."

"Now my head is spinning. I remember you explaining a fermion to me last year, but could you define it again?" Greg said.

"Sure. Fermions are subatomic particles that have a half-integer spin. They differ from bosons, which are other subatomic particles that behave according to Bose-Einstein statistics."

"OK. Stop right there. I remember thinking the first time I tried to understand the quantum world that it has a whole new vocabulary that I would need to learn. If I had the time, I could probably learn and understand more, but for now, I'll trust that this team knows what they are doing. So, I'll repeat my earlier question from before, 'What can we do with it?'"

At this point, Alex raised his hand and unmuted his microphone. He was on the big screen at the end of the room. "Dad, how do you feel about building a super large Hadron collider in space?"

"Oh great, another impossible project. Tell me what you are thinking." Greg said.

"We'll use it to generate neutrinos, then combined with the Majorana and other quantum particles we know how to produce and control now, I think we can build an interdimensional travel device."

At that point, the whole room could see Alex's cat jump on his keyboard and disconnect him from the call. The room was stunned for a few seconds, then everyone tried to talk at once. Greg stood, holding his hands up, but was ignored. Fortunately, Alex reconnected, laughing and apologizing. The noise abated instantly while everyone waited for Alex to explain.

"There's been some breakthroughs from the large hadron colliders in different countries. Fortunately, most of the discoveries are put on the internet and there is a healthy worldwide community participating in discussions. I've been able to follow some of them when I have time. As I read and participate in these sites, I've been forming some ideas about using the newfound knowledge for practical purposes. I don't know how practical interdimensional travel is, but it is one of the ideas that popped into my head recently. According to my rough calculations, we would need to generate more neutrinos than these large hadron colliders can produce now. Therefore, we need a super large one. And outer space is better than occupying a huge amount of land on earth."

"How long would it take, and how much will it cost?" Greg asked.

Alex laughed and said, "Don't you have people to figure that out?"

***

CHAPTER 26

July 2015

"This year is not the right time to run for President," Kris told Jean. "Looks like big turmoil in the elections. Our early polling has indicated that a Democrat is likely to win, but you would not be the leading candidate."

"What about running as an independent? Or switching to Republican?" Jean asked.

"Independents can't win a national election. And the Republicans are going a nontraditional route and picking that business guy, who seems like he could win a popular vote."

"I've been a Senator for seven years, so you're saying I need to stay here for another four years before trying again?" Jean wanted to know.

"That's my advice."

"What about putting my name in the hat for the Democratic primary and seeing how well I do?" Jean wanted to know.

"That's not a bad idea. We can float your name out there saying you are considering a run for the presidency, but you're going up against the favored candidate, another female who has been secretary of state."

"Yeah, you're right, as usual," Jean replied. "Let's hold off and try again in four years.

***

Greg and Jean had tickets to a sky box as the Yankees were coming into Washington, D.C. Alex was still the all-pro third baseman for the Yankees and had been for years. The eleven-year-old twins were with them, excited to see their brother Alex play, excited to attend a game in a luxury box. Isa, who had been visiting Jean as an advisor, was with them, saying she had been an avid fan of baseball for a long time.

Jean was stopped by a reporter on their way into the stadium and dutifully gave a short interview. Alex stopped by after batting practice for a few minutes, gave the girls a big hug then told his parents that he had to head back to New York immediately after the game because they had an afternoon home game at Yankee Stadium the next day. Greg and Jean expressed delight when Alex told them Aimee was expecting their ninth child around Christmas. The Yankees won 6 to 4 due to an early inning home run by Alex and another RBI in the sixth inning when he hit a double off the center field wall to score his teammate.

In the top of the ninth inning, Celina gave a short but loud squeak and then dashed to the bathroom. The adults in the luxury box noticed it and watched her go. Isa waited a moment, then went into the bathroom to see if she could help. The adults were absorbed in the game when Celina and Isa came back into the luxury box. Jean noticed them first and asked, "Everything OK?"

"Yeah. OG says I just learned an important life lesson." Celina said, looking somewhat embarrassed.

"Who is OG?" Greg asked, getting into the conversation.

"Original Grandma, duh." Celina said.

"And what was this life lesson?" Jean wanted to know.

"Don't trust a fart!"

* * *

"Mom, Dad, did I have chicken pox when I was younger?" Alex asked his parents on a post-game phone call.

"Yes, why?"

"Aimee said not to come home for a few days unless I've had chicken pox. All the kids have it at the same time." Alex replied.

"Oh, dear, poor Aimee." Said Jean. "You'd better get home and rescue her. And call your sister in case she decides to send Aliya over to visit her cousins."

***

Victor, Marie and Aliya had been living in New York City for a few years once Victor had been named the U.S. representative to the United Nations, a post appointed by each president. Since the Moore's had been large donors to the past few presential races, Victor had been recurringly named as the representative. They lived in a flat just down the street from the United Nations building. Victor could walk to work. Marie could walk to work when she scheduled herself to work in the Satrat and Moore store on Fifth Avenue. Aimee and Alex lived closer to the store now that Alex had been traded to the Yankees several years earlier. The families often had a boisterous dinner together whenever schedules would allow. Aimee and Alex had eight children and were expecting their next. Marie and Victor had the oldest daughter by a few months, Aliya, who was eleven years old.

***

"Hey, Dad, your interstellar communicator is ready to test…" Alex told his father on a conference call.

"Do I hear a 'but'?" at the end of that?" Greg wanted to know.

"Yeah. Unfortunately, for now, you're going to need another quantum computer at both ends of the communication path."

"So, tell me about how it works."

"It's based on Einstein's 'strange nonlocal interaction' theory and math," Alex explained. "The source or sending communication device can excite an electron-positron pair and the receiving device sees another exact twin pair behave the same way. Doesn't matter how far apart these devices are."

"Why does it need to have the quantum computer at both ends?" Greg wanted to know.

"It's the only thing fast enough to excite the electron-positron pair and the only thing fast enough to detect it on the other end."

"And the communication becomes instantaneous?" Greg asked.

"Yeah. It's like talking on a cell phone today." Alex said.

"Well, congratulations, son! You've been working on this for a while."

"Indeed. The concept has been out there for a long time, but building the devices to control the electron-positron pairing had to wait until we could miniaturize certain components. Also, we needed some special materials to build the base parts because of the way the electrons work in certain rare-earth minerals."

"Was THE LIBRARY any help on this one?" Greg was curious to know.

"Not really. Either I wasn't asking it the right questions or giving it incomplete search criteria because it didn't return any useful information."

"What about that other thing? We're going to need wormhole drives to visit other galaxies."

"True. I have an idea on how to do it conceptually, but as you know, the engineering is proving to be a challenge." Alex responded. "Isa says her spaceship has one but can't tell me exactly how they function. But the important thing is that I've been on a tour of her ship, and I know the dimensions of the engine room components, so I know it's possible to build a worm drive."

"Did you ask her any specific questions?" Greg queried.

"Yes, but she says it's one of the things humans need to figure out in their own timeline. The answer can't come from anyone in the Galactic Federation."

"Did you ask her if we can buy one on the Galactic Market?" Greg asked.

"Yes. And she says that at this point, there are no humans who can even come close to affording one, so we might as well keep trying to invent our own version."

***

"Did you get all that?" one person said to another.

"Yes. We earned our paycheck tonight. The boss will be pleased after months of nothing."

The next day, John checked the overnight reports from his field agents, called a special meeting of George's group and brought them up to speed on the two things Greg and Alex were working on. George said that since they were just the watchdog group, he would pass these notes on to the appropriate groups. The first was the Presidential Science Advisor. The second was the NSA since it involved communication devices. He was never sure what those other organizations did with the information, but they probably had their ways of getting more detailed information.

***

CHAPTER 27

June 2020

"Tomorrow is your sixteenth birthday." Isa told Aliya, speaking IGL. "It's time to talk about your future."

"I've been thinking a lot about that lately," Aliya said as she did pirouettes around the ballroom.

"All this time, we've been preparing you not for greatness but for the moment you'd choose whether or not to lead Earth into the stars."

"I'm not surprised." She said, switching to Grande Jete moves. "You've been coaching me since I was very little."

School was finished for the summer, and Aliya was staying in the Chateau near Paris, living with Isa and Running Bear. Her parents were staying for a few days in their nice apartment in the heart of Paris, above the Satrat and Moore store, in the upscale shopping stores district. She was excited that her twin aunts, Celina and Samantha, were coming to visit for the summer. They were getting Eurail passes and would travel around Europe with Isa and Dirk as chaperones.

"Has my life been predetermined for me?" She asked, remembering some of the books Isa had recommended that talked about free will versus predestination.

"To some extent," Isa responded. "But only to the point that you are being put into position to possibly become the first representative. It's not guaranteed. You must earn it."

"How do I do that?"

"We are working hard behind the scenes to make sure the citizens of the world get to vote on the person who will take this position," Isa explained. "We are going to start a web page for you soon and have you create social media accounts. We'll brainstorm in a few years as you progress through college what else will be needed."

"Where will I go to college, and what will I study?" Aliya asked.

"Whatever you choose." That's part of the free will choices you can make.

"Why me?" Aliya asked.

"It was estimated before you were born that either you or one of your children would be in the position," Isa said. "As soon as you were born, Running Bear said it was you. He could tell as soon as he held you."

"But I'm not special. I'm just an ordinary girl with an empty book to write my unwritten story."

***

Jean Pierre, or JP as everyone called him, was just sitting down at the computer to do his homework for a programming class he was taking during his freshman year of high school. His little sister, Nairrin, who was three years old, came over and stood beside him and watched him. He got up and carried another chair over for her to sit in. Lately, she had been following him around like a puppy dog when he was home.

"I want the computer to talk to me." She told JP.

That was similar to the homework assignment which was to translate text to speech. The teacher had provided a link to an Application Programming Interface or API for him to download that had the subroutines to solve this assignment. He explained what he was doing to Nairrin as he proceeded to write the lines of code. The teacher had said they were using the Python language because it was the easiest to learn.

All of Alex and Aimee's children had been born with Synesthesia, a condition where the brain had excess glial cells. It could be a disability if it was severe enough because one of the side effects was that when the person was trying to read, the words often turned to colors. It was also discovered that brains with this condition could understand advanced concepts and quickly learn new topics.

JP did the first part of the assignment, which was to accept input from the keyboard and then call a subroutine to translate that text into speech. Then, the program would loop back to the top and await more input. When he thought the code was complete, he typed in 'Hello Nairrin' and press return. Nothing happened. He sat quietly then it occurred to him that maybe he had to turn up the volume. There was a row of function keys across the top of the keyboard, so he pressed the one that looked like a miniature speaker with a plus sign next to it. He typed in the greeting once again and could barely hear something come out of the built in speaker of the laptop. He raised the volume until it showed one hundred percent, then typed in the greeting again. His sister giggled and looked at JP, then excitedly said, "It talked to me!". Then she answered, "Hello, computer."

JP typed in, "How are you?"

Nairrin replied, "Good. How are you?"

JP typed in, "Very good now that I have a friend to talk to. Would you like to hear a story?"

Nairrin wriggled excitedly in her seat, "Yes."

JP leaned way over and grabbed a book from the nearby shelf. He could tell that it was one of the Dr. Seuss books because they were all organized together. A glance at the cover revealed that it was one of everyone's favorites, 'And to think that I saw it on Mulberry Street.' It was their father's favorite from when he was a child, so naturally, he had read that one to his children many times. JP opened it up and started typing.

"This computer can read books!" Nairrin exclaimed. JP didn't have the heart to correct her; he was confident that she would figure it out soon enough. She did.

That night at dinner, when it was her turn to talk about what she had learned that day, she recounted the tale of how the computer talked to her and read her a book. JP chimed in and explained about his homework assignment. The other kids were excited to take their turn 'talking' to the computer.

***

CHAPTER 28

January 2022

Aimee announced that she was pregnant again. At 40 years old, with her youngest daughter already four years old, it was unexpected. The family was delighted. The doctors urged caution with her diet, exercise routine and sleep cycles. This was her most difficult child. She never felt well. The baby always kicked when she was trying to sleep. There was a scare at about 7 months when she said she hadn't felt the baby kicking for several days, which was rare for this one, who was always active. A trip to the doctor showed a healthy heartbeat, followed by an assurance not to worry.

In the heart of New York City, nestled among concrete blocks of high rises, Alex Junior was born in September via cesarian section surgery after the doctor recommended that method of birth because of the size of the boy. He was an odd-looking child with large hands and feet and a larger-than-normal head. The oddest feature was his long arms, although only three inches longer than normal, looked strange on a newborn. Nobody called him a beautiful baby. Everybody remarked that he would have a lot of growing to do to have the rest of his body catch up with his hands and feet.

Alex Junior, or AJ as his siblings quickly labeled him, cried continuously for the first two weeks. His parents soon discovered that the doctors were wrong, he was not colicky, he was just hungry. Aimee could not produce enough breast milk, so they had to supplement with baby formula at a time when the USA was going through a shortage due to Covid related manufacturing and transportation issues. Grandpa Greg had the solution for that; he took one of his planes to several European countries that were not having shortages and bought enough to have a large pantry full of baby formula.

To Aimee's delight, the other children doted on AJ, wanting to hold him and only giving him back when he was crying again for food. The older children assisted with diaper changes and preparing food, but AJ would only eat when his parents were feeding him. Jean Pierre, or JP, was 16 years old and helped a lot in the evenings when he was home from school and sports practice.

The family was still living in New York City during the school year and living on the Colorado ranch during the summer. The children loved it because they got to ride horses. There were cats and dogs on the ranch, but they all said what they liked the most was that they all got their own bedrooms. During the Fall and Spring Breaks, Alex and Aimee let the children vote on where they wanted to go. The Chateau outside of Paris was a favorite; visiting Great Grandmother Ginny in West Virginia was another favorite, especially since most of the children got to sleep outside in a large tent because there was not enough room in the main house, which only had two bedrooms. Nairrin always voted for St. Barts in the Caribbean after the first trip. She said the beach where her mother and Aunt Marie had first met was her favorite place in the whole world.

***

CHAPTER 29

May 2026

Aliya, Celina and Samantha finished their undergraduate degree. Aliya from the Sobornne, taking her mother's alma mater. She had studied philosophy and ancient languages. Celina from Oxford, studying political science. Samantha is from Harvard with a degree in anthropology. All had expressed an interest in continuing with master's degrees and potentially PHD degrees as well. They were mostly successful at keeping their wealth hidden, but many of the school breaks were at the Mayfair flat in London. The girls had taken it over as their main party place during their university years. Travel was essentially free to them as Greg had designated one of the private five-seater planes for the family. All they had to do was to call the pilot and schedule a ride.

Aliya had already gotten her pilot's license, and the twins were taking lessons. When the pilot would pick up Aliya from Paris, he would let her fly the plane. Celina liked taking the train from Oxford to London. She said it was a way to clear her mind from her studies and get her brain into 'London mode,' as the girls called it. They knew all the best nightclubs, including the hidden bars that had started popping up almost fifteen years earlier. These bars were ones where you had to know the secret entrance door. Most were downstairs, either in a restaurant, another bar or in the lobby of some business building.

Most nights, the girls were content to come home to the Mayfair flat to be spoiled by the housekeeper, Wendy, who loved to join their conversations. Wendy was ninety-six years old and had lived in the flat for sixty-six years. Her husband, who had doubled as the butler and maintenance man, had died almost twenty years earlier, so she was happy when the girls started coming to visit. Wendy regaled them with tales of her childhood during World War II and the years since. The girls contributed stories of their varying university experiences. All the women laughed at stories the girls would tell of encounters with men who would try to pick them up.

French men, Aliya told them, were very direct and would quickly move the conversation from whatever opening line they started with to hints that they should go somewhere more intimate. She did admit they were always charming about it and never rude. Celina said that the British men would more likely ignore you if they were in a group and decided they liked you, but the fact that they would come up and talk to you privately indicated they were interested. Samantha chimed in that the American men were more unpredictable and could either be direct like the French or as patient as the British and let the girl make the first move.

The girls giddily talked about their first kiss. Celina said hers was in Junior High School in eighth grade after a play in which she played the lead role. At the after-party, she was talking with the boy who had played the lead male role when he unexpectedly leaned over and kissed her on the lips. She reported that she recoiled at first, shocked at what he did, but then quickly decided that she liked it and leaned over to kiss him back.

Samantha said her first kiss was with another girl in the locker room after a volleyball game. She liked it, but the relationship never went anywhere. Samantha went on to tell of her first kiss with a boy at the Prom dance as a senior year in high school and that she gently had to slap his hands away when they started to roam.

Wendy said her first kiss was with the boy next door when she was fourteen. Three years later, he was also her first lover. He may have become her husband, but he died in World War II shortly after joining the army and getting sent to France to fight. She was working as a secretary in the war office, where she met her husband. After the war, they married and applied for their current role as housekeeper and butler for the man who had been their commanding officer and whose semi-royal family had owned the Mayfair flat. He had been a Duke.

Aliya said her first kiss was also at the Prom dance with her date, who was a quiet, shy boy who had been in several of her classes. Aliya was amazingly beautiful, with long, straight black hair, a slender build and the same swarthy skin and high cheekbones inherited from her father. Aliya had played soccer as a youth but decided not to pursue it during high school. Her favorites were ballet and dance classes and she continued that into high school. She had also played violin in the orchestra. The Prom was the only date she had been on. Aliya had revealed that during a slow dance, her date kissed her. She liked it and responded, but after the kiss, he leaned back with a quizzical look on his face and never tried again. She thought it was odd, but she didn't mind because she didn't encounter any magical feelings. Similarly, she told the other girls other dates in college had resulted in the same thing happening. One kiss and her date would politely walk her back home and bid her adieu.

The girls tried to talk Wendy into going to the Mars colony. Wendy admitted she had never flown anywhere before. She and her husband used to vacation in Brighton or Dover at the beach, both of which were a reasonable train ride away. Wendy also told them her name had been a popular one for girls after the play Peter Pan came out in 1904. She declined the invitation, stating that she was happy with her life in Mayfair.

***

Now it was Nairrin's turn to write a program. She had a homework assignment for her computer class as a freshman in high school. The original task was to take some keyboard input, change the font and print it. She told the teacher that it was too easy and wondered if there was a more challenging project available. The teacher recommended that she find an API online that would do object recognition, then she could provide a picture of something and see if it could identify the object. The coding was easier than she thought, so it wasn't long before she provided her program with a picture she found online. She was excited when it said 'bridge' but was disappointed that it was not more specific to identify it as the 'Golden Gate Bridge.'

She thought about it for a few minutes, then called her oldest brother, JP. He had finished his PhD in quantum physics, and she knew he was a good programmer. "What you are talking about is artificial intelligence or AI." He explained. "In this case, you would need to search a database or some other source where someone had already identified that specific bridge."

"What do you mean, some other source?" she wanted to know.

"There are sites where you can post your pictures, or social media sites where people label their posts with something like 'here we are at the Golden Gate Bridge.'"

"So, if I enhance my program to connect to a picture site and scan down through all the pictures to find one that matches, I can see if someone has put a label on it. Then I could identify it as the proper bridge."

"Exactly. But it would have to be a site you could trust. Someone might label it as 'Bridge over the river Kwai,' or something like that, and your program could return the wrong answer."

Nairrin worked on the program until she had something that could identify all the pictures of whatever she downloaded, a bridge or hammer or dog, for example. It amused her that the results were mostly correct. Suddenly, she sensed someone come into the room. She turned and noticed her dad come in and look over her shoulder. She explained what she was doing and talked about the progress she had made. He said that he was impressed and also informed her that it was two in the morning, and she had to get up for school in a few hours. She was shocked, thinking that it had just gotten dark and there was no way it was two o'clock. A glance at the lower right of the computer screen confirmed it was indeed way past her normal bedtime.

"Hey, Dad, can I start attending your conference calls with the AstroX group and the other group of scientists from Johns Hopkins? I read JP's PhD thesis on Solar System and Galaxy Energy Barriers, and I understood it, even the math parts."

"Well, these calls are during your normal school hours, and that takes priority," Alex replied.

"I already talked to my math teacher, and she said since I'm already doing advanced college calculus, I can leave her class to attend a conference call. It's 9 am, and I have a free period at 1 pm, so if you can include me, it would be cool."

"Well, lately, the AstroX group has been focused on solving problems with the super hadron collider your grandfather started building in space."

"Yeah, JP has been keeping me up to date on that. He says it's almost done."

"Did you know your big brother has a few patents already, and he's only twenty."

"Yeah, and so did you at that age," Nairrin replied.

"His latest one was for a self-repairing 3D printer because it was too hard to get the parts from Earth to space. So, for the nozzle part that always causes problems and gets jammed, he had the printer keep a repository of spares and then trade it out when it had a problem. And the first thing the printer did was create a new nozzle and add it to the empty slot in the repository."

"On another subject, it's too bad grandpa's LIBRARY only contains words and not pictures," Nairrin said.

"Call him later today and tell him you want to add pictures. I'm sure he wouldn't mind."

***

"Grandpa, can I add pictures to your LIBRARY?" Nairrin asked. She then explained her project to identify pictures.

"Sure. I've been thinking about doing that for a while but have been too busy. But tell me, how much disk space would you need?"

"Oh. How would I figure that out?" she asked.

"Well, if you only had greyscale pictures at first, that would limit the size and accomplish what you need for most searches. And greyscale has 256 values with zero being white and 255 being black. And if a greyscale pixel is 8 bits, you can figure it out. How big do you think each picture should be?" Greg asked.

"I think 1,000 by 1,000 pixels would be enough. That would be one million pixels per picture times 8 bits that's 8 million bits per picture. And if there are 8 bits per byte, that's one million bytes or a megabyte." She said.

"And if we wanted every combination of possible greyscale values to represent every possible picture, how much disk space would you need?" Greg prompted.

"256 times 1 megabyte is 256 megabytes."

"Try again." He said, implying that she had not thought through the problem properly.

"Oh, it would be 256 squared to represent all possible combinations, or 65,536. So would that be 65 gigabytes?"

"Correct. Do you need help with the programming?" Greg asked.

"No. It seems rather straightforward."

"Ok," Greg replied. "I'll send you the login credentials. And congratulations, this could be the foundation for your first AI program."

Needless to say, she got an A on the assignment because she went well beyond the original requirements.

***

CHAPTER 30

The big news in the family was that Jean had announced her intention to run for President of the United States. The Democrats were desperate for a leader, but Jean was considering running as an independent as she didn't like the message the Democratic party was projecting. In a meeting with the Chairman and staff of the Democratic National Committee, she said she would only run on their ticket if they agreed to go back to the values that were the basis of the Democratic Party fifty years ago. The party agreed instantly. They were not as happy about her insisting that One World Government was also going to be a major theme of her campaign. It was a deal breaker. So, Jean said adieu and had a meeting with the Republican National Committee. They were happy to have Jean switch sides but would not concede to the OWG theme.

Alex announced his retirement from professional baseball after the Yankees got knocked out of the playoffs. He said twenty years was enough. When reporters asked what he would do next, he said he would take his eleven children to Disneyland, then to the Mars colony, which had become a popular tourist destination in the last few years. His oldest son, JP, was a sophomore at MIT. All of Alex and Aimee's children had synesthesia, some milder than the others. The youngest, Alex Jr. or AJ, as the other siblings were calling him, had the most severe case of synesthesia, which was causing a learning disability. JP and Nairrin teamed up to write an app that AJ, at five years old, could use his iPhone to scan text from a book and project audio into his earbuds.

JP had surpassed his dad's height and was six foot seven. He played basketball in high school but was not good enough to play at the college level. The coach at MIT said he would probably make the team but would ride the bench most of the season. JP opted to join the basketball recreation team instead. JP was studying quantum physics and chemistry at MIT. He frequently joined his dad on conference calls with the AstroX team, but he said that his favorite team was Greg's counterterrorism team who invented sneaky things to do to people who threatened the family. JP had taken some programming classes during high school and during his freshman year at MIT, which had been a requirement for years in all the science majors. He enjoyed conversations with his grandfather about programming projects Greg had been involved in during his career. Greg had even given him access to the source code of USOS so he could learn advanced coding techniques.

The rest of Alex and Aimee's eleven children had such a variety of interests that kept Aimee and Alex busy shuttling them around New York City or arranging drivers to take them to various practices and events. There were two sets of identical twins. They had purchased a whole floor of a building in New York City, where Alex said he was fortunate to stay with one team after being traded from the Rockies to the Yankees years earlier. The city's danger level had calmed down after the influx of homeless migrants during the early to mid-2020s had been cleaned up. Aimee and Alex still hired security people as drivers to take them and their children around.

Greg had commented one evening at a family dinner that he was the least recognizable person in the family. Jean, being a long-time senator and now presidential candidate, was instantly recognizable. Marie and Aimee, with their billon-dollar fashion business, were also well known. Alex, as a professional baseball star, was as well-known as the other two. Greg said he was happy being the behind-the-scenes influencer and would be happy being the First Husband when Jean got elected.

***

CHAPTER 31

November 2028: Net worth, something less than infinite

"And now the first female president and first independent candidate to win since George Washington, I present your newly elected president of the United States, Jean Moore!" announced the head of her campaign.

Jean stepped behind the podium as the crowd roared. She waved her hands over her head as she surveyed the crowd with a huge grin on her face. Young and old, fresh-faced teens, white-haired retirees and every age in between crowded together to celebrate the landslide win of their new president. She waited a few minutes before starting her speech.

"Let's welcome a new era of peace and prosperity around the world. I will work tirelessly to see that every citizen of every country has opportunities to succeed that we have here in the United States. George Washington warned us in his farewell speech in 1796 that partisan politics would ruin the country, and I believe that the way you voted this time, you are ready for something different. As promised in my campaign, I will back the One World Government movement that has taken hold around the planet." The crowd cheered. "As you know, we still have problems at home, and I promise to continue our efforts to fix those." The crowd cheered again. "The prior administration did us a big favor by reducing the size of the government, almost balancing the budget and starting us on the right path to reduce the federal debt to a manageable level." More cheering. After fifteen minutes of speaking, she gave the crowd a final wave and, stepped off the stage and exited.

Jean had requested ten minutes alone after the speech. Her family and campaign staff were giving speeches and kicking off the celebration party downstairs in the grand ballroom of the hotel as

Jean kicked off her shoes in the aptly named Presidential Suite. She collapsed on the couch, put her feet on the table, and leaned her head back on the soft leather. At seventy-four years old, she sometimes felt like she had the energy of her younger self, but other times felt like – well, old. A few deep breaths, in through the nose and out through the mouth, while her mind quit racing and settled into a calm, empty space.

She didn't congratulate herself; she didn't reflect on what it meant to now be the President of the United States. She emptied her mind, closing the door on the whirlwind life she had led during the campaign, forever shutting out the internet trolls and negative ads her opponents ran, even shutting out the good parts where cheering crowds met her at every town hall, every rally, every speech. It was time to move forward.

Time was meaningless. She didn't know how long the trance lasted. It could have been minutes; it could have been hours. Ever so gradually, she became aware of her surroundings again. Her hands register the soft leather of the couch. Her feet started to tingle from being stretched too far on the coffee table. Her head comfortably nestled in the groove it had created on the plush couch. Her ears now hear the sounds of boisterous conversations in the hallway. Then she remembered that Greg had volunteered to guard the door until she opened it. With a grateful smile in her mind, she got up, used the facilities, splashed cold water on her face and opened the door.

It was already past midnight. The after-party continued until dawn, at which point Greg and Jean closed the door to the elegant bedroom, changed into comfortable pajamas and, with exaggerated groans, crawled under the covers. Both wanted to say something clever or poignant, but their minds were completely exhausted.

They fell asleep holding hands despite the few remaining conversations coming from the living room.

They awoke to the soft clattering of dishes and hushed whispers coming from the other room. Kris, her campaign manager, having been through this before, had arranged for a mid-afternoon buffet for family and close friends in their private suite. Greg stuck his head out the bedroom door to wave at the hotel staff, who were trying to be quiet as they set up the tables and trays of food. He took his turn in the bathroom first as he could tell that Jean was not quite ready to escape the luxurious comfort of the bed.

Voices coming from the other room indicated their guests had started arriving. With a kiss on Jean's forehead and a playful smack on her butt, Greg got up and went to join the group, closing the bedroom door behind him. Kris was already there, making sure the buffet was arranged to his liking. Marie and Victor had just come in and were filling cups – coffee for Victor and tea for Marie. Alex was in Ohio, attending a Baseball Hall of Fame ceremony for one of his long-time coaches. He had been at the presidential victory speech last night, then left soon after.

Greg heard the ding of the elevator and a female voice unsuccessfully telling a group of children to be quiet. He glanced around the corner, noticed the double doors to the suite had been propped open and saw Aimee herding her and Alex's children into the suite. "PAPPA!" they shouted, then surrounded Greg with a group hug. Following them were another three of Aimee and Alex's eleven children, the oldest at twenty-one and the youngest at six years old.

Jean joined them a few minutes later, still wearing her pajamas. Why not, she surmised? They were Satrat and Moore originals, which had become a worldwide brand name synonymous with elegance and style. Marie and Aliya entered the room next, followed by Greg and Marie's twins, Celina and Samantha. Greg was both surprised and delighted that Samantha had decided to come, probably encouraged by Aliya, who seemed to have more influence on her than anyone else in the family. Samantha was a free spirit, living with her partner in an artist community outside of Taos, New Mexico. She had inherited Marie's artistic abilities.

Jean had visited Samantha during her campaign and had become enthralled with the Taos and Santa Fe areas. It had been meant as a private stop and not part of her official campaign, but photos and videos of her at the artist compound were used in a negative ad by her opponents trying to slur the family name. It backfired as the majority of the country seemed to accept that the presidential candidate had a daughter living her own lifestyle. And it almost certainly helped her win many votes in the LGBTQ community. Today, Samantha brought a gift for her mother, a turquoise, black and red blanket woven in the Navaho style that she had made herself under the tutelage of an elderly tribal woman.

Aliya had been living at the artist compound for about six weeks before Jean's visit, with plans to move on to another location soon. She stayed there long enough to learn a bit of Navajo, another unique language. She laughed at herself during the conversation with her mother and Aunt Samantha, saying that she was the world's wealthiest homeless person. Aliya had been offered the CEO position at any company owned by the Moore's but said she was more in tune with the charity foundation. She had tried to run the foundation for a few months after she finished her university studies but said she was not knowledgeable enough about the financial side of things to be the right person. Instead, she took Running Bear up on his idea to do a 'walkabout' as the Australians called it. Well, it was more of a drive-about as she and Running Bear drove around the world in a self-sufficient RV that had solar power, satellite communications, a water filtration system, a saltwater conversion system, and other modern technologies. For visiting remote villages that could not be reached by road, they had mountain bicycles that they locked onto the back of the RV.

Aliya had a knack for languages and non-verbal communication. She had learned English and French from her mother and Aunt Aimee. Isa had taught her IGL, or intergalactic Language and the IGSL, intergalactic sign language, at an early age. Accompanying her grandfather on numerous business trips, Aliya learned a smattering of Russian, Greek and Arabic. When they lived at the Chateau for a period of her early childhood, Zophia and Zoltan taught her Hungarian, which she came to learn was another unique language. Running Bear had taught her the Shawnee language as well as ancient Chimu, his original language.

Running Bear had been instantly recognized wherever he went due to his life story being published by Dirk Lamoureux years earlier. However, by the time they left any location, Aliya was treated as the exalted one, with people wanting to touch her one last time before she departed. They funded projects in every village and city, mostly on a common theme of improving ancient sanitation systems and repairing or rebuilding water resources. Running Bear once commented that early advancements in human technology involved 'poop' – the handling and disposal of human waste. The early tribes in all parts of the world were nomadic, mostly due to the latrines filling up. The tribe would cover a latrine, then move to another location to dig another one. All of these projects were filmed and shown on Moore's cable television channel where Aliya was a main character that the cameras followed around as she explained the goal of the project and the stages they went through.

"Dad," Aliya said after filling her plate with fruit and a croissant, "Have you ever heard of self-healing concrete? I asked Alex, and he said you had asked him the same question years ago."

Greg looked at Jean and laughed, "Yes. Where did you hear of it?"

"Running Bear and I are currently working on a project in southern Kazakhstan where there is an ancient aqueduct still delivering fresh water to the villages from the mountains. It was built during Roman times. Apparently, there was a legion of Roman soldiers and engineers that made it that far. The locals have a story that the concrete was made from algae gathered from a pond, then mixed with ground limestone and other ingredients to make a mortar. The actual ingredients and formula have been lost to time, and the locals have been unable to recreate it." Aliya explained. "They can recreate the concrete and cement using today's known formula, but it does not have the same self-healing result. They have experimented with various algae gathered from local ponds and rivers but have been unable to recreate it. Some of the young adults in the village specifically went to universities around the world to study biology and bioengineering, then returned to the village to recreate it, but no luck so far. They don't have the right equipment to discover the original bacteria."

"Do you know what equipment is needed?" Greg asked.

"They're not exactly sure. They mentioned an electron microscope, an XRF machine, which they explained could tell the exact balance of minerals involved in the mortar and possibly another machine for reasons they explained, but the science was over my head. They've called the university in Astana, which has an XRF machine, but not the others. Could any of your companies help?"

"I'll start a text with Dmitry and include you since Moscow may be the closest university to having the right equipment." Greg answered."And if you discover the right formula, start a corporation with the local village because this will become a great discovery, or rather, re-discovery."

***

"What is the plan for the Grand Reveal?" Jean asked as she glanced around the table. She was referring to the plan to reveal the presence of the Galactic Federation. The original OWG group was seated around the table with her: Greg, Victor, Marie, Dmitry, Svetlana, Sebastien and Monique. In addition, Isa and Running Bear were in attendance.

"The plan hasn't changed in several years," Monique stated. "We will start with the religious leaders of the major religions around the world. We will start a final round of OWG conferences targeted at the leaders of every country who are skeptical of joining this movement. Anyone not convinced of joining the OWG effort will be offered a ride to space. Hopefully, the Golden Orb person will make an appearance." Monique glanced at Isa and Running Bear for their input.

Running Bear glanced at Isa and said, "I will defer to Isa since she is in direct contact with the Federation. I am here to ensure that certain things happen at the right time."

"I am assured that the Federation Ambassador for this sector of the galaxy will make an appearance at that time," Isa responded.

"Should we have all the religious leaders in one meeting at the same time or meet individually?" Victor asked.

Dmitry responded, "It would be very interesting to have them all in one meeting just to observe the interaction. But it would be a risk that one or more would not attend if it was known that all would be attending."

Everyone looked at Running Bear and Isa who just shrugged. "You decide. We are trying not to be the decision-makers nor influencers." A round of discussion ensued. In the end, the group decided to attempt one meeting with all religious leaders together, at the Chateau.

They also discussed the timing and agreed that once they had most of the political leaders behind the OWG movement, they would invite the religious leaders to the Chateau. The only difference would be that the religious leaders would be shown the six-minute video from Greg's original visit from the Federation Ambassador. The meeting would then concentrate on the timing of the Grand Reveal and not on the One World Government.

To wrap up the meeting, Running Bear reminded them that the Grand Reveal could not be done until the U.N. had officially been designated as the One World Government.

***

"Greg, I don't know how much trouble I can get into by telling you this, but you have a leak in your AstroX department," Jean whispered in his ear. "My daily security briefings include a section on science advances and inventions. You are on their main watch list."

Greg sat back in stunned silence. Thoughts were swirling through his head. "OK, I'll figure out a way to fix it without any blowback to you." He whispered back.

***

Monique was busy planning the next round of OWG conferences. There would be fewer conferences needed this time because many of the countries were still in favor of the idea. Marie was busy between working with Aimee on their fashion company and running the Moore empire where she had taken over as the CEO of CEOs. Victor was still the United States Ambassador to the

United Nations and was planning on putting his hat in the ring to become the head of the U.N. in the next election cycle. Dmitry was semi-retired, grooming his son to take over his business empire.

Alex, having retired from Major League Baseball several years earlier, was a stay-at-home dad for his and Aimee's large troupe of children. They lived in New York City but spent a lot of time at the Chateau in France and at the Satrat Vinyards near Bordeau with their other grandparents. Alex still spent a lot of time on video conference calls with the AstroX scientists as well as the space engineering and mining groups, solving problems remotely. He had pestered Isa into giving him a tour of her spaceship and had gotten permission to 'invent' the improvements to their own spacecraft. Isa could not tell Alex how everything worked but could tell him what technologies the ship contained. As a result, Alex's current project was puzzling over interstellar engines and intergalactic travel. He had already figured out improved cloaking material and interstellar communication devices, even before he had gotten a tour of Isa's ship.

***

May 2029

The OWG conferences started again. They were a different format than before, with a short group presentation in the mornings, followed by a lengthy question and answer session, and then break-out sessions in the afternoons. The attendees were heads of state and had been given access to a myriad of material from previous OWG conferences, papers and speeches before they attended. This round of conferences had been shortened to two days, but several had asked to stay over a third morning to attend political and business meetings with their neighboring country leaders, mostly focused on trade.

Monique sent invitations to religious leaders around the world for a July meeting. Jean had been invited to kick off the meeting, but thought as President of the United States, it would seem like a political ploy on her part. Still, all her advisors encouraged her to go. It was Isa whose favorable nod had convinced her to make the opening remarks. Dmitry had a very large, ornate round table crafted by one of the leading woodworkers in Central America, who was known for his hardwood creations. "Don't thank me." He said he had to give credit where it was due because it had been his wife Svetlana's idea.

***

June 2029

The hopefully final political OWG conference took place with the outcome being mostly positive, with only a few cautious holdouts. All the world leaders wanted one of Greg's planes of their own, including the space-capable one. Greg was sure it was one of his leverages to obtain votes for the OWG movement but was reluctant to give them out freely.

The final conference was for the leaders of the world religions gathered at the Chateau in a separate meeting. The Moore's went to extra lengths to ensure they were treated to extreme luxury. Sebastien, who had retired as the long-time French ambassador to the United States, greeted everyone at the front as they arrived. Dirk showed them to their rooms and handed their assistants the itinerary. There were twelve who had agreed to come.

An elaborate dinner ensued promptly at eight o'clock, during which each leader was served an individually prepared dish according to the instructions given to the chef by each leader's assistant. The talk between neighboring leaders was jovial and easygoing. Most had seen the agenda for the following day but expressed curiosity at something called the Grand Reveal.

The next morning, at half past nine, all the religious leaders, their assistants and interpreters gathered in the grand ballroom. Monique, wearing a very conservative Satrat and Moore full-length dress, began the conference by welcoming everyone and explaining the agenda and the protocol for asking questions or beginning discussions. Jean gave a brief speech where she highlighted the good work the religious charities were doing around the world and pledged further commitment to assisting those projects.

Sebastien took over as the next speaker to explain what had been shown on the agenda as the Grand Reveal. He said instead of talking about it, he would show a video. With a nod to Dirk, who was acting as technical support for the conference, the six-minute video of the original space flight was shown. At the end, all the cards went up, indicating that everyone had questions.

Sebastien held up both hands and said, "I will speak for a few minutes, then answer questions." After a short pause, he continued. "The first question everyone always asks is, is this real?" He paused for effect. "We will explore both sides of the answer over the next hour. You were invited here as a courtesy to prepare your followers for the first contact on earth with otherworldly visitors, or the Grand Reveal as we are calling it."

A few cards went up, and Sebastien again encouraged patience. "To answer the 'when' question, the Grand Reveal will occur when the One World Government is approved using a modified United Nations as that governing body. The 'why' question was already answered in the video – it is because human technical capability has reached a point where we will be discovering them soon. The 'who' question is more complicated. As I understand it, many cultures have legends of ancient visitors on earth helping humans. We're assuming they are or were real. All we know at this point is that we will be meeting representatives from a variety of worlds from this galaxy and other galaxies. Now, I will take questions."

A card went up. Sebastien called on him. "And if we assume this video is not real?"

"Two choices. First, there is an open invitation to anyone in this room to take a ride in space to meet one of the galactic representatives. The second is to take the risk that this is not real and go about your normal life, then react after the Grand Reveal. I would urge you to take this seriously, prepare statements for your followers and leaders, and even prepare classes."

"Where can we go to get more information?" asked another person after he had raised his card.

"A website is being prepared that will contain all the information we receive as soon as it is given to us. Not many details are available currently."

"What is known right now?" blurted one assistant, then quickly raised his card, looking embarrassed.

"There is a wormhole near Saturn that allows travel to another place in the Milky Way galaxy that contains other wormholes to other locations. One goes to the Andromeda galaxy. There is a galactic force guarding the Saturn wormhole against forces that have been known to enslave planets rich in resources." Sebastien said.

Another card went up. "Are there any representatives living among us now?"

"Yes. There are two ambassadors in the room with us." Sebastien gestured to the back, where Running Bear and Isa stood up and waved as everyone turned around. "If you've read the book about Running Bear's Story, you can meet him at a break."

"I assumed that was a fiction book." Said an undetermined voice.

Running Bear said, "It was as real as I can remember everything. I may have gotten a few events out of order, but it is an autobiography."

Running Bear was instantly peppered with questions. He laughed and held up his hands. "I'm happy to answer any questions later. And there is a stack of books available for you in various languages to take back with you. However, let's get back to the purpose of this conference which is to help you craft messages to your constituents."

Sebastien handled the question-and-answer period until lunch was announced.

The specially crafted round table was reserved for the religious leaders while the assistants and interpreters filled their plates from a buffet and sat at two long tables. There were a variety of foods from different cultures. Much of the talk was shuffling between the food and the Grand Reveal. One assistant brought his boss a small plate of something from the buffet, who took a bite and gave a thumbs-up response.

The leaders agreed that taking the Grand Reveal seriously was in their best interest. Ideas on how to proceed floated around the table. After a short stroll around the gardens, the afternoon session started with a deeper dive into the ideas of messages to the constituents of each religion. This was followed by a very interesting question-and-answer session hosted by Sebastien.

"Do you have any knowledge of specific religious significance?" Asked one leader.

"Yes. We have been told that other worlds have a variety of religions, some based on a single deity, others based on multiple deities." Sebastien said.

"Is there a god?" asked another leader.

"Yes. All that is known right now is that there is a god pair and that they live in a dimension that we cannot get to." Sebastien said.

"Is the Christian Old Testament correct?" asked one interpreter after a question had been whispered to him.

"There were four Adam and Eve pairs that settled in different parts of the world simultaneously. The Old Testament is based on the one that chose the Caucus Mountains as their original home, then travelled to the Tigris-Euphrates area after a few years. The other pairs were settled in Asia, Africa and South America. All came from different planets in the Milky Way Galaxy and had volunteered to populate planet Earth after it was discovered and terraformed."

The conference had originally been scheduled to conclude by mid-afternoon. However, the question-and-answer period went on until almost dinner time. A ninety-minute break was announced, where everyone went to their rooms to freshen up and rest. Running Bear and Isa were invited to the round table, where they shared their stories. After dinner, the group was offered a ride home in one of Greg's planes or they could choose to stay another night. About half chose to stay until morning.

***

July 2029

Things were moving rapidly on the OWG front. The final piece of the puzzle on the political front was to get the leaders of China, Russia, the United States and Iran to agree. Jean had resubmitted the bill to the House of Representatives that would have the United States backing the movement. She was sure that there were enough votes in the House to pass the bill, but the Senate still had a few holdouts. The Moore's had funded many of the Senators in their run for re-election, both Republican and Democratic. Still, there were not quite enough votes yet to carry the Senate. The remaining holdouts were invited to take a ride to space.

The President of Russia and the Premier of China were also invited to space on a separate flight. They agreed to go on the same trip since they already knew each other. They had both seen the original six-minute video but were still skeptical. To disguise this space trip, they agreed to publicly announce a meeting in Moscow to discuss trade between the two countries, then secretly take a late-night ride in space to meet the Federation Ambassador.

Greg and Dmitry were in a special version of a spacecraft that landed in the expansive backyard of the home of the President of Russia. It would be Dmitry's third trip to space and his first one to meet the Federation Ambassador. When the two heads of state entered the craft, they stated their amazement at the luxury of the interior. They also commented on the sixteen-foot-high ceiling and one very, very large chair at the far end of the room. "That is for the Federation Ambassador," Dmitry said in English, which both presidents spoke relatively well.

The trip to leave the gravity well of Earth had dropped to about three minutes due to Alex's new improvements in the anti-gravity design. He also had to invent a method to reduce the g-force humans experienced when accelerating that fast. The result was a smooth, pleasant ride. The side walls of this craft could be switched to be completely see-through from the inside, allowing the occupants the ability to watch the entire trip. From the exterior, the craft looked like a large rectangular container with a silver coating. While not the most efficient design aeronautically while in the Earth's atmosphere, it was the best use of interior space. It was, as Alex put it, "Perfectly suitable for only going up and down."

As soon as the craft got to the right altitude above the earth, Greg pointed to the direction of Saturn. Everyone turned to watch a bright point of light rapidly approaching the craft. It grew larger and larger until a vague shape was detectable inside. When it got close enough, everyone could tell it was a human. The orb slowed when it approached the craft and then collided with the side. Nobody felt any disturbance. Instead, they watched the orb appear to vibrate and merge with the craft. They watched in amazement as the being inside the orb gradually entered the cabin of the craft, next to the giant chair. He had to stoop because the ceiling was not high enough to accommodate his full height. The being smiled at Greg as he sat down and said, "At least you got the chair right this time."

"Let me introduce myself. You know me as Apollo and other names from different countries."

Dmitry said what he was sure everyone else was thinking. "Do you mean all those tales are true?"

"Yes," Apollo replied. "Why do you think the elementary education curriculum in many countries still teaches what is known as Greek Mythology." This was accompanied by silence because nobody was expecting that answer as an opening remark. "We settled on Mount Olympus when Earth was originally discovered because the high altitude matched the oxygen levels on our planet, and it had a temperate climate most of the year, making it a most pleasant place to reside."

Greg had already had this conversation and had met Apollo when he flew to Mars to start the colony almost twelve years prior. So, he decided to continue this line of conversation for a few minutes by stating for the benefit of the others, "And Zeus is real."

"Yes," Apollo replied. "He is back as head of the Galactic Federation Council. There is a term limit equivalent to one thousand Earth years for that position. During his downtime, he is required to travel to different galaxies and live on different planets, observing the population. With the stealth technology we have, he can do it either in hidden mode or in plain sight. And to answer your next question, He has been to Earth many times. He likes it here."

Having already heard this before, Greg turned the conversation back to the present. "Let's talk about Earth joining the Federation."

"As you know, each planet joining the Federation must be governed by one ruling entity. Then, the existence of the Federation is revealed, after which education begins. This consists of the structure of the Federation, the history of all the planets and species involved, the common language of the universe and many other subjects such as protocol and cultural norms."

"What advantages does joining this Federation bring?" The President of Russia asked.

"Economic, technology, health improvements, security, and curiosity are the main reasons most planets join," Apollo explained.

"What do you mean by security? Is there danger?" The President of China wanted to know.

"Yes, there are individual planets who will not join the Federation, and there are space pirates who have been known to enslave a planet to strip all the resources. Fortunately for Earth, we control the only known travel portal in this solar system."

Dmitry asked, "What does Earth have to offer in trade?"

"Essentially, the same things that are traded among your nations today. Cotton, wool, spices, food on the natural side, gold, silver, platinum, uranium and rare-earth on the mineral side. Tourism will be a big income producer as well."

"You mentioned health improvements before," Greg mentioned, again for the benefit of the others.

Apollo reached into a satchel at his side that had been mostly hidden by the arm of his chair. He produced three identical items. "These are one-time armbands that will diagnose human health conditions and inject the proper nanobots into your body if you wish to use them. They are quite safe, live for about six months, repair anything they find, and then get passed out through your normal waste systems. Ask Mr. Moore."

They all turned to Greg, who nodded and explained that he and his wife had received their armbands about twelve years earlier. All their ailments had been corrected. He said he highly recommended doing the treatment. All three accepted and put on the armbands.

"Does this include longevity improvements?" Dmitry wanted to know.

"In a sense. These will fix your current liver and cholesterol issues, Mr. Balinov, allowing you to live longer and not die because of complications from them. But immortality DNA changes are currently illegal."

"When will you reveal yourself to the population of the Earth?" The president of Russia wanted to know, then jumped slightly and said, "Oh" as he looked down at his wrist and grabbed it. He looked around the table and noticed the others doing the same.

Apollo chuckled. "The medical examination phase is complete, followed by a quick injection of the nanobots. I should have explained before." He then resumed, answering the prior question. "The initial revelation will consist of humans who have been living among us and among you for a very long time. Myself, my family and other species will be revealed in time. The Moore's and Balinov's already know two of the representatives. They can explain on the trip home." With that, he collected the armbands and exited the craft, traveling rapidly in his golden orb toward Saturn. The pilots engaged the jets that would take the craft back to Earth. Greg started the narrative about what he had learned.

Earth was originally populated by four pairs of Adam and Eve, one each in Asia, Africa, Caucus, and what is now known as South America. All other nations and races are derivative of those. Most of the original pairs are still alive, living off the planet, or still on Earth. Only the first pairs had been granted immortality, with the exception of one daughter of the Caucus pair and one son of the Asian pair who somehow got the immortality gene passed down to them. Isa, whose original name was mostly unpronounceable, was one, and the other was currently the Supreme Judge in the Galactic Court of Law. His historic name was Confucious. The original South American Adam was currently known as Running Bear. His given name was also somewhat unpronounceable.

"We will learn about the other pairs of Adam and Eve when the history of Earth is given," Greg explained. "Which is when Earth comes under one ruling body."

"You will have our support." The Premier of China offered, with a nod from the President of Russia, who said, "And we can assist in influencing other nations who seem reluctant." During the remaining discussion on the flight back to Earth, they both agreed that their current Earthly expansion plans seemed trivial in comparison to readying their respective nations for intergalactic expansion.

***

September 2029

Dmitry called and said, "It's time."

"Time for what?" Greg replied.

"Time to take a ride to space for everyone not convinced that OWG is a good thing. I have compiled a list and have talked most of them into going. This must be a secret trip, no press. This is at the request of several country presidents who would like to be on the trip."

Greg replied that his family would like to be on the trip as well as they had let him know that his next flight to space should include them. Victor had also informed Greg that his ancestor, Running Bear, would like to go as well. Greg called Tom, and Jax gave them the list and locations of everyone to pick up and drop off at the Chateau. He said they would need a medium-sized plane that would hold 240 passengers. Mike and Priya were busy making phone calls to inform all passengers of the scheduled pick-ups.

There were no class distinctions on these planes; everything was first class. The seats were large and comfortable, and there was plenty of room between the seats. Most of the people had been picked up in their respective countries and flown to the Chateau, where they were treated to a fabulous lunch buffet with specialty foods from each region. That way, the attendees could pick what they wanted to eat. Some with the longest flights had stayed overnight. All of Greg's planes were busy, flying to different parts of the globe.

When it came time for the space flight, Greg was at the door greeting each person as they boarded. He warmly hugged Running Bear, who had been in line talking to Aimee's mother and Isa.

Greg's family had already boarded and had taken the first row. Presidents from different countries were given the window seats. Each seat had a high-resolution screen on the seat back in front of them, showing the view from the front of the craft, exactly what the pilots could see. Instructions were given that seat belts were not needed on the way up but could be used if it made each person feel more comfortable. However, they were needed on the way back to earth as it could get a bit turbulent.

Tom and Jax, the most experienced of the pilots, were instructed to take it easy, going up at half the speed of a normal flight to space. There were oohs and aahs as they exited the earth's atmosphere and watched the earth turn below them. The camera beneath the craft had been on the screens for the ride up. Tom announced over the loudspeakers that he was switching to the front view. He had oriented the craft to point to the moon, then rotated to point to Saturn, keeping a running dialog with the passengers. As the craft settled on a view of Saturn, everyone could see multiple points of light coming toward them. There were gasps and shouts of concern as the lights rapidly got closer.

As the lights got closer to the craft, the passengers could see that they were golden orbs containing human beings. Soon, each window had an orb just outside. One stopped in front of the craft and began speaking. This was the one showing on everyone's screen in front of them.

"Greetings, people of earth. This would be a more personal discussion from inside the plane. Your host, Greg Moore has consented for me to enter the craft." The audience watched in stunned silence as the orb slowly entered the plane, moved between the two pilots, and then stopped in the center of the galley. The globe slowly dimmed, and the large being was standing in front of the first row, visible to everyone.

"The reason for this visit is that Earth has advanced enough to be invited to join the Galactic Federation. There are conditions that must be met before an official invitation is offered. These conditions will be explained later. First, I must greet each person individually."

There were two seats next to each window, an aisle, four seats in the center section, another aisle and two more seats. The being went down the first aisle, greeting each person by name, holding their hands and saying something to each one. He made his way down one aisle and back up the other. When done, he got back to the front and explained the conditions of joining the federation. The main condition was to have Earth ruled by one governing body.

Once that was done, a representative would be elected by the citizens of the earth to attend the Galactic Council meetings.

With that, the being surrounded himself with the golden orb again and exited the craft. All the golden orbs gathered near the front, gave a wave to the occupants of the craft, then retreated. At once, the plane erupted with shouts and questions. Greg stood and held his hands up as Tom turned the craft toward Earth to head home. When he got silence, he addressed the people.

"This is not the first contact. Throughout history, certain leaders have been told of the conditions of joining the Galactic Federations. It has been explained to me that since there were no planet-wide communication systems before, the leaders could only imagine that global conquest was the only solution. And after World War II, certain leaders were visited, at which time the outcome was the United Nations."

Many hands were raised. Greg pointed to one in the middle of the spacecraft. "What is the advantage of joining this Galactic Federation?"

"The three main benefits are protection, economics and curiosity. There are worlds and space pirates that will conquer a planet and either exterminate the population or enslave them. The federation is very large, and trade among planets is quite profitable. The last reason, curiosity, is there for people who would like to know what other species are out there, what trade goods are available and so on."

More hands went up. Greg pointed to one on the left near the front. "And why the United Nations as the one world government?"

"Because all the other methods have failed. World conquest, British Empire, Soviet-type expansion and so forth."

Greg pointed to a hand in the back. "Is there a God?"

"There is a god pair that lives in a dimension we cannot get to."

The question-and-answer session went on while Tom returned everyone to the Chateau. Before everyone exited the craft, Greg announced that a buffet-style dinner had been arranged and that tables had been set in different rooms on the ground floor. He also announced that planes had been arranged for those wanting to return to their homes, and a few rooms were available for anyone wishing to stay overnight.

The Moore's were at the large circular table in the big ballroom. After filling their plates from tables laden with foods of the world in the long hallway, they sat at their table. Greg had invited Running Bear and Isa to join their table. He already knew Running Bear's story, so he turned his attention to Isa. "And the messenger called you 'sister' for what reason?"

"Yes." She replied. "But Isa is my title, not my name. I am an Interstellar Ambassador. I was here to be the nanny and tutor to Aliya."

"Are you one of the Eve's?" Jean wanted to know.

"I am one of Eve's daughters," she replied. "That piece of history was left out of or lost before your Old Testament was written."

"How is it that you can live so long?" Marie asked.

"The longevity DNA code was only given to my parents as a gift for them volunteering to come to earth. It was not supposed to be passed down. I am the only one of my siblings to get it. At some point, the Galactic Council calculated the rate of growth of the human population and decided to remove the longevity DNA strand so that the population of the earth did not become too great too fast."

"And we are at the point where humans have the scientific ability to introduce it back into their offspring in the next 20 to 30 years. It is one of those 'be careful what you wish for.'" Said Running Bear.

Marie started to ask another question, but Isa said to Greg, "It is probably best if you make rounds at other tables to answer any questions that you can."

***

Greg crawled into bed at 3 am, tired but elated. He was sure that the majority of the nations would now get behind a movement to make the U.N. the world government. Most nations were represented except the USA, Iran and other Middle Eastern countries who would not agree to the trip to space. However, there were wealthy individuals from each of those nations who he hoped would influence the leaders to back the movement.

Greg had answered the same questions multiple times as he went from table to table. Many questions he couldn't answer yet about where these beings came from, how many planets and galaxies were involved in the Federation and so forth. Curiosity was high among everyone.

***

November 2029

Election results were in. Headlines read: "Victor Shawnee, a native American man of 47 years old, won as the Secretary-General of the newly formed One World Government, thanks to a blitzkrieg social media campaign backed by his wife's and her family's money".

Aliya was in a remote village in Bangladesh, working on a water project funded by the Moore Foundation, when she saw the news. She texted her congratulations to her father and asked if she needed to come to any ceremony. The answer was that it would be nice if she could come to New York City for the swearing-in ceremony in January.

She checked her email and was about to delete one she thought was spam, then remembered that she had set up an account in Kazakhstan when they had created a company to make the self-healing concrete. The scientists in a lab at the University of Moscow had found a rare amoeba embedded in the samples from the ruined part of the aqueduct Aliya had been working on. A worldwide search from scientific databases returned a match from a server run by an international nautical research company. The amoeba could be found near the deep seabed on the southern side of Sicily where ancient lava flows from Mt Etna entered the Mediterranean Sea. They grew and lived near the hot hydrothermal vents linked to Mt Etna, which was still considered an active volcano. Debates had arisen on how an amoeba that deep in the ocean could be found in concrete all over the Roman Empire. The consensus was that there must have been another source because those hydrothermal vents were in water considered by today's divers to be too deep for humans to safely dive. One of the village elders remembered that there were dried, shallow ponds in southern Kazakhstan that were a mystery to the archeologists. A day trip to that area resulted in Aliya and her local team discovering these large, square indentations in the desert just outside a small village. The residents knew they were there but had no records of their use. There were no stories passed down through the generations except that the ruined building nearby had once been a Roman outpost.

Dirt samples were taken from the dried ponds and the floor of the outpost were analyzed at the university on the return trip. A normal microscope was used to detect dead husks of these amoebas, and the team created the theory that the Romans must have transported samples of water containing live amoeba with them wherever they went. Aliya called her grandfather Greg and updated him with the results. He contracted a company with an underwater research submarine to dive near Sicily to gather live samples. Aliya and her team used them to reseed those ponds and grow more. The local villagers were grateful to have established a business in their area to bring employment and income to an otherwise poor town. A separate company was created to grow the amoeba.

More research, along with trial and error, resulted in the right amount of amoeba to add to the concrete. The aqueduct repair was completed with this new concrete mixture but it would be years before any definitive result could be determined. Nevertheless, the industrious team began a clever marketing campaign to sell their unique, long lasting concrete mixture and soon they began shipping product all over the world. The ponds expanded quickly as did the concrete plant. Aliya, who was listed on the board of directors, had attended frequent meetings remotely for a few months. Her small share of the proceeds automatically went into the account in the email she had currently opened. The decision from the board of directors was to put all the profits into growing the business, but a year and a half has passed since they started. Now, some profits were being taken and Aliya was pleased to the equivalent of a few thousand dollars in her account. She didn't need it, but deep down, there was a satisfactory feeling about this being a reward for a lot of hard work.

**

Aliya was escorting a young man who had been injured while helping clear rubble from the ancient well in the remote Bangladesh village. They had just stepped into the local clinic to hear a woman sobbing in the back room. Aliya asked the young man to wait in the lobby and walked to the back. A young mother had given birth to a stillborn baby. She heard the doctor telling the parents that he had tried to revive the baby but had been unsuccessful. Aliya saw the infant lying in a bassinet in the corner of the room, wrapped in a colorful cloth. She put her hand on the baby's forehead, and the baby instantly opened his eyes and started breathing. She picked up the infant, carried it to the mother and laid it in her arms. The parents and doctor were astounded.

The doctor was a forty-year-old Swedish physician who was working in an organization called Doctors without Borders. It was a chance for doctors to donate their time and skill to areas around the world that normally did not have access to health care. His name was Tomas and he later told Aliya that after his wife died, he joined the organization and went abroad while grieving.

"What did you do to the baby?" Tomas asked.

"Nothing; I went over and brushed a lock of his hair that had fallen over his eyes. He opened his eyes and looked at me. So, I picked him up and carried him over to his mother." Aliya responded.

Tomas recounted how he had spent twenty minutes trying to get the baby to breathe on his own with no success. He also admitted that he had heard of a delayed birth response before but had never experienced it personally. It was considered a very rare occurrence.

Two days later, Aliya was supervising the digging of the new well for the village when she noticed Tomas walking up the hill from the clinic. "I thought I would come up and see what you are working on."

"We are almost down to the right depth, maybe about two more meters before we hit the water table."

They chatted for several minutes before Tomas invited her to dinner that evening. Since there was no restaurant in the small village, he confirmed her question that dinner would be at his small house that was attached to the clinic. Aliya was excited. She hadn't been on a date in years. Several men had tried to get close as she traveled around the world, only to curiously back off. When asked, they mumbled that she was not the right person for them. Running Bear had also been gone for weeks to help Victor in the last stage of his campaign.

Tomas was the perfect gentleman, making a vegetable stew with lamb-bone stock. He had tried to get mutton but the village elder said they would not be slaughtering another sheep until the following week. Aliya surprised him by bringing a bottle of very expensive Satrat burgundy wine.

"Where did you get this?" Tomas asked incredulously.

"The Satrat's are my relatives by marriage. My uncle Alex is married to Aimee Satrat. This is my last bottle."

"Well, it is one of the finest wines I have ever had," Tomas replied. "And it is a perfect accoutrement to this meager dinner." Then he thought for a minute. "Is that Aimee Satrat, the famous fashion designer?"

"Yes. And my mother is Marie Moore, the other half of the Satrat and Moore clothing brand. And my father is Victor Shawnee, who was just elected as head of the new United Nations. To top it off, my grandmother is the president of the United States." She said as they poured the last of the bottle. She was feeling tipsy, something she hadn't felt in a long while.

Tomas gave a short bow while chuckling, "I didn't know I was in the presence of royalty."

"Oh, stop. We are just regular people who put on our pants one leg at a time like everyone else." She replied, smiling.

They cleared the table and were rinsing the dishes when Aliya turned Tomas toward her and kissed him. His eyes got very wide, and he leaned back and gave her a serious look. "Who are you?" he whispered.

Aliya got tears in her eyes and said, "I get that response from men who try to get close, and I don't understand."

"When we kissed, I was moved beyond this world. I saw stars and planets and galaxies moving by very fast." He said. "I got a deep emotional feeling welling up from my toes to my head like I was surrounded by a force that I can't explain."

"I don't understand. I'm not anyone special; I'm just an ordinary girl."

He kissed her again. This time he saw time moving rapidly from the first humans living in caves to futuristic cities with flying cars and very tall towers and strange beings walking amongst humans. "You are far from ordinary. You are someone special to this world."

She shook her head, "I feel like I'm a normal girl. I don't feel extraordinary." She rested her head on his shoulder, then took him by the hand and led him into the bedroom. "Be gentle; I've never done this before."

He was more than gentle. He knew how to do things that had her soaring to heights she never thought possible. Afterward, they talked… and talked… and talked. He told her about his childhood in Malmo, Sweden, his medical school in Stockholm, and his tiring internship as a young doctor in Milwaukee, Wisconsin, before he moved back to Sweden to marry his college sweetheart. They had talked about having children soon when she was killed by an automobile while riding her bike to work. Aliya told him about her childhood, flitting between Paris, New York and occasionally West Virginia, where her great-grandparents lived. She told him about working at the Satrat and Moore retail shop in Paris as a teen, then her time at the Sorbonne, with occasional weekends to the Chateau d'Armainvillers and the long weekend trips to the Mayfair flat in London. She told him about her involvement in the Model United Nations, starting when she was in Junior High School. They both shared a laugh over playing football as youths, recounting tales of successes and failures on the field. She talked about the men she met that she was interested in dating, but they always backed off after one kiss. She confessed that she never understood their reaction and that none of them had explained anything to her until now.

"Well, I can tell you that you are definitely someone special to this world. You have an aura about you that I have never seen before." Tomas explained. "You must have a purpose that has yet to be fulfilled."

They talked until dawn, then fell asleep as the first rays of light were filling the bedroom window through the flimsy curtains. They awoke just before noon, hungry and slightly hung over from consuming the whole bottle of wine. They wandered down to the market to get something to eat because Tomas confessed that he didn't have much in store. The delivery of the baby had been over two days. He had not had a chance to go to the market to get food. The baby had been breech and had not wanted to come out even after being turned to the correct position. The labor was very painful. The baby looked normal, but there was no breathing and no pulse, no matter what Tomas tried to do. He then got very quiet, looked directly into Aliya's eyes and asked, "Are you sure you didn't have anything to do with the baby suddenly starting to breathe?"

They stopped and sat at an ancient stone bench beneath a tree at the edge of the market. "I don't think so; I don't feel that I have any special power." Then she remembered the incident in first grade with her friend falling off the playground equipment. After recounting the events of that day, Tomas said that maybe she had a hidden power. She agreed to his proposal to come by the clinic and see if the rudimentary equipment could find anything. They had a relatively new portable EKG machine.

They spent the next few days and nights together. After a visit to the clinic, the EKG machine showed nothing special, nor did a normal physical exam. Tomas recommended a cat scan whenever she got back to civilization. Aliya texted her grandmother, Jean and asked if the Moore Foundation was supporting Doctors Without Borders. A few hours later, the answer came back "Yes, quite a large donation. They are one of the better managed worldwide organizations."

Running Bear returned, having gotten a ride in Isa's cloaked spaceship. None of the villagers noticed the spaceship; to them, it was an elderly couple walking down the hill toward the village, stopping by the project in the center of town to watch the final touches of the new well being put into place. Aliya asked if they had any food available as she was tired of eating vegetable stew. Running Bear said he had gotten her message the week before saying that she was running out of supplies, so he had stocked up on all the things they liked.

Aliya helped carry boxes of food and toiletries from the spacecraft to the RV she was living in. She also informed Running Bear and Isa that dinner would be at the doctor's house that evening. Aliya texted Tomas that there would be two more guests for dinner. She then picked out several ingredients for a large meal, and they headed to the clinic, where Tomas was introduced to the two newcomers. While Tomas finished attending to his patients for the day, Aliya went through the adjoining door to the residence portion of the building and started dinner.

Tomas had never heard of Running Bear, having been in mourning when the book of his life came out. He was disbelieving at first, then accepted the tale of Running Bear having been one of the original people on earth. Of course, Running Bear explained, his original name was rather long, and it had changed at different ages when he traveled throughout South, Central and North America.

"Does Aliya have any special powers?" Thomas asked Running Bear and Isa.

Isa deferred to Running Bear, watching him as silence ensued for a moment as he gathered his thoughts. Aliya remembered that Running Bear was a special storyteller, especially when he had a private audience. "Aliya has the ability to gather the energy and consciousness around her and channel it into a single stream. It is something all humans could do if they knew the technique. It is also something that is extremely hard to learn. A few rare people in history have had this ability naturally."

"Is it something in her DNA or something about the way her brain was created?" asked Tomas.

"I never knew how this special ability works or how it is created or why some people are born with it." Running Bear responded.

"There is one entity who can tell us if he can be located," Isa told the group. "He came down to earth during a time when inhabitants of other worlds were allowed to visit the earth and interact with humans. This world knows him as The Buddha. He tried to teach the population how to do different things beyond what they could accomplish with their five senses. A few of his students were able to do some things, but not one person could do everything. With the limited success they had, these students started a school, recording his teachings and encouraging others to learn in the hopes that someone would eventually be able to learn all the techniques."

"What did you mean when you said that inhabitants of other worlds were allowed to visit Earth?" Aliya wanted to know.

"The Galactic Council granted permission for mentors from other worlds to come to Earth for a limited time. I think it was around ten generations. Some human civilizations recorded these visitors. Egypt was one that told us of Osiris and other creatures from advanced civilizations that had progressed enough to learn space travel. Humans labeled them as gods, but really, they were more like teachers." Running Bear said.

Isa continued with other examples. "India was another civilization that recorded their visitors, such as Shiva and Buddha and many others. The children of Adam and Eve that started in the Caucuses eventually spread to distant lands and had visitors like Odin and some of his children, Thor, Loki and Freya."

My civilization in what is now known as the Americas did not do so well recording their visitors. There are a few stone inscriptions of Twanaku, Inti and Virachoka." Running Bear explained. "But there were at least a dozen other visitors who taught my people different things and helped them build large structures. There was already an advanced university in what is now Mexico. These alien visitors used their spacecraft to shuttle humans from other countries in India, Africa, Europe and China to this university, where all knowledge was attempting to be recorded. Unfortunately, the Spanish Conquistadors destroyed much of that when they came over, as it was considered sacrilegious. All that is left are large stone statues carved by students in the likeness of their people."

"I'm curious when these visitors were allowed to visit Earth. If there really were only four Adam and Eve pairs like it says in your book, the history of these visitors seems like they were on earth when the population was fairly large." Asked Aliya, who had read Running Bears story written by Dirk Lameroux a few years earlier.

"Yes. My wife and I volunteered to be one of the four pairs on earth. We chose a beautiful meadow in what is now Columbia, where the weather was warm, like our home planet. The decision was that the four pairs were to be dropped on Earth with no tools, no clothes and no help from the spaceship pilot. We were allowed seven days to live in the spacecraft before it took off. To answer your question, it was at least a thousand generations before the galactic council voted to allow visitors to Earth for a limited time. By that time, the population of humans had grown enough that the different tribes had met and started to comingle and create their own civilizations."

"Is there a God?" asked Thomas, "One entity that started life in the universe?"

Isa answered this one after a moment to collect her thoughts. "There is a god pair as we understand it, a male and female. From what we know, they live in another dimension that nobody has figured out how to visit. Humans, with their understanding of the fundamentals of quantum physics, have discovered tesseracts, neutrinos, bosons, strings and other things that will eventually let them travel to a fourth dimension. Other worlds have already been able to do this for a while, but nobody has been able to travel to the dimension to meet the god pair."

"So, back to Aliya, is she supposed to be a savior for the human race?" asked Tomas.

"In a roundabout way, yes. She will hopefully be voted to be Earth's representative to the Galactic Federation." Running Bear said. "But beyond that, it is unknown what her future will bring."

Aliya was not surprised; she already knew why Running Bear and Isa had been mentoring her from an early age. They taught her the Galactic languages and had lectures on how the Galactic Council worked to tell tales of different species and their cultures from distant galaxies.

Aliya came out of her stupor to hear Running Bear continuing his dialog, "Thousands of years ago, the Galactic Council, being frustrated that the humans had not progressed fast enough, allowed these visitors to come to earth to teach humans and accelerate the progression of the races. But they had restrictions and strict guidelines on what they could teach. Humans had to figure all this out themselves." Running Bear said.

"But if you stopped travelling and started living with the Shawnee for more than 130 years, then you must have known something or been told to settle where my father would be born." Aliya surmised.

"It was more of a statistical probability and a recommendation from the galactic representative to this sector at the time. Nobody had discovered a way to predict the future until your grandfather Greg and your uncle Alex invented the device to send information from the future. As a side note, other galactic civilizations have been kicking themselves at not having invented that device before."

The clinic doorbell rang, indicating that the doctor was needed. Tomas reluctantly got up from the table to go attend to the matter. The others, noticing that they had finished dinner during the enthralling conversation, cleared the table and did the dishes.

Aliya lay awake that night in her RV, with her hands behind her head which was her favorite thinking position. Her thoughts were jumping from topic to topic, not arriving at many answers. It was more like her brain was generating a myriad of questions that would have to be answered in order for her life to turn from being a professional bum to a galactic representative.

Well, not really a bum, she told herself, because she felt that she was doing good work on her travels. But until recently, she was not bringing in any income to support herself, which she thought was supposed to be a goal of every adult human. She had wondered before whether this lifestyle would be a long-term path or if her life would take a drastic turn someday. Now she knew. Her brain jumped to the question of when. When would her life expand to a galactic role? Running Bear would have a better idea. Sigh. Another addition to her list of questions for Isa and Running Bear.

***

"Dad, I've got your new generation of batteries," Alex told his dad via text.

Greg called immediately. "That's wonderful news. How did you do it?"

"I went to Columbus, Ohio, to work with the chemists in Marvin's team. We've been inventing experiments using different chemicals and elements. Nothing worked. Then, last week, I went to sleep thinking about the problem and what we should try next and I had a dream where I visited THE LIBRARY for the first time in a very long time. When I asked THE LIBRARIAN about advanced battery technology, he brought me a book that only said 'Nicola Tessla' embedded in the page of gibberish."

"Interesting. So, this had already been invented by him?"

"Not directly, but his experiments in Colorado Springs on wireless electricity and his other experiments on pulling energy from the earth were the key. But since most of his writings have disappeared or were destroyed, it was hard to get more details. THE LIBRARIAN wouldn't come back when I asked for his writings, so I jumped on your quantum computer to access your LIBRARY and found a few things that guided me in the right direction."

"And what is the base for this new technology?"

"I called JP and he flew out to Columbus to join us since this is more his area of expertise. If you remember, he studied both quantum physics and chemistry. What we figured out for now is that if we use a traditional battery, like a car battery, as an initial source of energy, we can switch to these new batteries that draw energy from the surrounding environment. It's not perfected yet because the extraction of energy from the environment is slower than what most devices need, meaning that the output is greater than the input. It works ok if you are constantly moving, like driving a car, but for a stationary battery, it doesn't work well."

"Well, congratulations on getting this far. Sounds like it's a good start. Why don't you visit that guy that makes the electric cars and see if he's interested in using it. Maybe take JP with us since he has not been exposed to making business deals. What about that other thing you've been working on for a wormhole drive?" Greg wanted to know.

"Um. I'm embarrassed to say that I blew up the garage I was using to build the device. But nobody was hurt because I had a feeling it could be dangerous if something was wrong. And it turns out that if the device components that spin at a very high frequency are even one atom out of alignment then the whole thing crashes. Luckily, I rigged it so I could start it remotely. But Isa says I'm on the right track."

"You need a better lab. Call Marvin and have him build you a precision facility."

"That reminds me, Marvin says he is retiring again and turning things over to his son Joe," Alex said.

"Yeah, I know, this time he says it's for real. The last time he tried to retire, he heard about our Mars colony starting up and wanted to get in on the action to make things for those buildings. He's already been to Mars and loves what we've done with the place. I've offered to fly him and his family to any of our castles or resorts for his eightieth birthday, and it looks like he's going to pick one in Greece." Greg said.

"I told Aimee about that, and she said Greece will be our next vacation spot. She browsed the properties online and really liked what she saw. Oh, and before I forget, can I get about 100 million dollars?"

"Ahhh, I have to decide whether you are joking or if you have a huge project in mind or what," Greg responded.

"Aimee found that the largest ranch in Colorado is for sale. It's about 170,000 acres at about $1,000 per acre. We can safely kick in about 70 mil but will need another 100 to complete the sale. It's called the Trinchera ranch, named after the Trinchera Peak, which is about 13,500 feet in altitude." Alex said, then continued with, "Let me read from the online description. It is in Costilla County, between Walsenburg and Alamosa, in the southeast corner of Colorado. It is part of an original Sangre de Cristo land grant of 1843. The main water source is Mountain Home Reservoir with many snow-based rivers feeding it. There are three 14,000-foot peaks, Blanca, Little Bear and Mount Lindsey, on the northwest border. The total ranch is 250 square miles off Highway 160. The main ranch house is at 8k ft altitude. It is a working cattle ranch with a portion used for growing hay and wheat." Alex said. "As you know, Aimee fell in love with horseback riding during the brief time she lived in Colorado Springs, and she said this would make a good birthday present."

"What do the kids think?" Greg said, knowing that they still had a bunch of their children at home.

"They love the idea on the one hand but said they would hate to leave their friends and teams and other groups."

"Well, let me know what you decide. I'd be happy to be partners with you in any venture you choose."

***

January 2030

Victor was sworn in as Secretary General of the United Nations. In his acceptance speech, broadcast to the world on every available television station and online streaming service, he promised to reveal to the world the reason why there had been a major push to get the U.N. to become a one-world government. That statement, midway through the speech, overshadowed the opening statement, promising a new era of peace and prosperity, a phrase he had borrowed from his mother-in-law's presidential acceptance speech.

Everyone had their own theory of why, at this point in history, the U.N. was being morphed into the new structure. World peace was the first reason leading the headlines. Improved economics is the second. The third was the possibility of people easily moving anywhere in the world where jobs existed. Aliens came in as a distant reason, way down the list. Most people dismissed these pundits as kooks. However, when private polls were taken, a great many people had a desire or curiosity to know if it really was aliens.

The idea of people moving to where the jobs were quickly became the number one reason. Everyone was sure Victor was going to announce worldwide open-border policies. With the improvement in robotics, 3D printers and the advancements in artificial intelligence, jobs were scarce and getting scarcer. The outlook was not good. The new generation of 3D printers was even producing electric cars. For the past several years, there has been a population boom as young couples have been staying at home more than ever. Socialist countries were becoming bankrupt because they were not bringing in enough tax revenue due to the lack of jobs. Economists were privately telling world leaders the trends were not favorable.

***

Victor had worked with Isa to make the date of May 1, 2030, as the Grand Reveal. She had been in contact with the leaders of the Portal Guardians as they had stated they preferred to be called. They had one main capital ship and could bring in as many as the Earth wanted to canvas the world for all to see. After many heated discussions about having one large ship or many spread around the world, Victor decided that one was the right number to avoid a panic that might occur if the world population thought it was being attacked. That sparked another round of heated debate as each country wanted to be the host. Victor proposed a solution that was soon adopted: China, Russia and The U.S. would each supply an aircraft carrier that would meet in the Pacific Ocean for the visiting spacecraft to visit.

The Admirals from each country were nervous as each aircraft carrier headed toward the coordinates accompanied by the normal escorts of destroyers, cruisers and submarines. This much firepower in one area made everybody nervous. The captains of all ships were under strict orders to keep their weapons locked down.

Each carrier had large guest contingents of reporters from a variety of countries. There were two other carriers, one supplied by the U.S. and one supplied by Russia, that had been due to be retired. Anyone could buy a berth on those two ships for a high price. The available slots had quickly filled.

By mid-April, word had gotten out about the plan, and the number one reason for the Grand Reveal had switched to aliens. Otherwise, the news agencies and online influencers surmised, why would the middle of the Pacific be the chosen spot? The actual coordinates were kept secret as long as possible for safety reasons. If a huge flotilla of private ships accumulated in one area, there were bound to be accidents. Private yachts had professional captains who were bound to abide by known safety rules. But too many smaller ships piloted by non-professionals were the big worry.

There was an area of the Pacific that was known to be mostly calm and rarely had storms. Isa had told the planning committee that the very large spaceship could disperse any storm clouds that might happen to gather at the event. Another reason this location was picked is that it was also near the extremely large plastic and trash flotilla.

Most people had heard of this 'plastic island,' but the world leaders agreed that videos and live reports would be more effective if the world saw the extent of their waste. The Moore's and other charity foundations had permanent cleanup ships scooping the trash, cleaning it, and then converting it to reusable material. There was a machine that created bricks and wood-like planks, which were then used as building material. Another machine created material used by 3D printers.

* * *

Aliya and Running Bear had moved the RV to Africa to do projects in remote villages. Greg had loaned them a container spacecraft to fly the RV from Bangladesh. They had tried to get visas for China and Mongolia, but even with her grandmother recently having been elected president of the United States, they could only get short-term visitor visas. Running Bear recommended Africa and had already contacted the U.S. State Department to get the proper visas for all the African countries. He looked at a map on his phone and, chose Chad in central Africa and told Aliya that they would travel in a zig-zag pattern throughout the continent.

Water improvement projects were occasionally needed in the remote villages. When interviewed, the inhabitants said reliable electricity was the main need. Most village elders agreed that solar was the right solution. In each village Aliya visited, she would order a container spaceship to drop off the solar panels and control systems. Running Bear insisted that Aliya shake hands and greet as many people as possible, just as she had done throughout their travels. The first project took about three weeks. Subsequent projects took approximately one week since villagers from other nearby settlements came to visit and learned how to set up a new system.

Aliya was interested to learn that almost all adults had cell phones, mostly due to her grandfather's networking business expanding around the world. Their challenge was keeping the phones charged because the electricity was not reliable. A few villages needed water access improvements or sewage improvements, so Aliya hired the right experts, usually from the capital of whatever country they were in and paid their salary through the Moore Foundation for the duration of the projects. She and Running Bear worked until late April, when she caught a ride on one of her grandfather's airplanes to attend the Grand Reveal.

***

May 1, 2030

The five aircraft carriers formed a circle. At dawn on the first day of May, all hands were on deck. It was very windy, so the captains had the crew erect as many windscreens as possible. The sunset the night before had been spectacular, which gave promise for great weather the following day, at least according to the ancient saying, 'Red sky at night, sailor's delight; red sky in the morning, sailor's take warning.' The sunrise that morning was boring.

The camera crews had multiple devices aimed at the sky. The reporters were chattering away even though it was still hours before the spacecraft was due to arrive. Many of the reporters switched to segments detailing the scenes of the nearby plastic island and the previous day's tour of the processing plants aboard the large recycling ships. The captain of the Moore Foundation recycling ship had arranged a pickup of a container of the reclaimed material, telling reporters that prior to the invention of the anti-gravity device, large ships would come out to do a ship-to-ship container transfer, which was costly and dangerous. Now, the large boxy aircraft would hover over the ship, pick up a full container, and then move over to the other ships owned by other foundations to pick up more containers. The cleanup effort was estimated to last at least twenty more years.

News organizations broadcast scenes from around the world of people gathered in public places to watch the event, from large cities to remote villages. Almost every person on earth had the opportunity to view the event. Many people travelled from remote areas to the viewing sites as word spread around the globe.

As time for the Grand Reveal drew near, the production crews switched back to the live reporters. The weather was sunny and very windy. The impromptu windscreens helped somewhat but reporters still had background wind noise coming through the microphones. Victor was on the U.S.S. Enterprise aircraft carrier, giving a live speech about the reason for the United Nations, stating that it was indeed beings from outer space who would only reveal themselves once the earth had organized under one governmental body. He ignored questions in order to continue the remainder of the short speech. He timed his speech to end shortly before noon.

Every screen had a countdown timer showing. With one minute to go, a hush drew over the crowds. The reporters even spoke in quieter tones. Precisely at noon, an extremely large shape descended from the clouds, circled the flotilla and stopped in the center of the circle of aircraft carriers.

The ship was massive, easily twenty kilometers in circumference. At first sighting, reporters' voices rose to an excited pitch, akin to the last-minute winning goal at a World Cup football match. This high level of excitement lasted almost ten minutes as the crowds around the world took in the meaning of meeting beings from outer space. Some online antagonists were saying this was just various governments having hidden high-tech spaceships from the world, playing tricks on everyone.

A large gasp came from the people on the aircraft carriers, in crowds around the world and from the reporters with microphones as portals opened on the bottom of the ship. Golden orbs with various forms of beings inside emerged and descended toward the three main aircraft carriers to land on or hover above the podiums reserved for these visitors. Everyone had cell phones recording the event, even the Navy sailors stationed on the carriers.

Victor had a short 'welcome to earth' speech, promising peace and collaboration with the visitors. One of the human figures, a black man and woman with sub-Saharan African features, stepped to the microphone. "Hello, Earth. We are one of four pairs of Adam's and Eve's who originally populated Earth. The others are standing here with me."

Questions were immediately shouted by the reporters. Adam held up a hand to signal for quiet but was ignored. He gave a wry smile pressed a button on a device on his wrist, and the crowd was muted. Cameras still showed reporters raising their hands and speaking, but no sound was heard from the podium microphone.

"Questions will be answered in due time." He spoke. "This introductory meeting has a sole purpose: to welcome Earth to the Galactic Federation of planets. You will soon learn the true history of Earth and the history of other planets. Some of the species you will meet are here with me." Adam gestured with his hand to some of the hovering orbs containing different species. One looked like a cross between a giant praying mantis and a tarantula spider. Another had a vague similarity to a koala bear but with almost human-like hands. A third was the classic depiction of an alien called the Greys – a short humanoid body with a big oval head, large black eyes and a greyish, almost purplish shade of skin.

Eve stepped to the microphone to continue where Adam left off. "You will be able to travel and meet species from other planets once you have chosen the right Galactic Representative. Guides will remain on earth to assist you in this process. With that, we bid you farewell." Golden orbs surrounded most of the beings except Running Bear and Isa, then rose into the open portals, which closed behind them. The massive spacecraft then winked out of existence.

THE END OF BOOK 2

EXCERPT FROM UNLIMITED BOOK 3. BRINGING ORDER FROM CHAOS.

Chapter 1: New Horizons

"Five, Four, Three, Two, One. Portal entry initiated." Jax Lunders said. He was the pilot of the first human-built spacecraft to travel through the galactic portal that had been discovered near Saturn. The passengers were Greg Moore, Aliya Shawnee, his granddaughter, Celina Moore, Greg's daughter, Running Bear and dozens of scientists with different specialties from various countries. To the passengers inside, the interior of the spacecraft seemed to waver as if the craft had filled with water and someone dropped a pebble that created a series of expanding ripples. Jax turned on the option that made the walls of the spacecraft transparent. The passengers were treated to a spectacular light show with all colors of the rainbow shimmering, dancing and sparkling as far as the eye could see.

The trip would only take a few minutes through the wormhole. It had been explained to the people of Earth that the portal was a wormhole through space that led to the planet Proxima B in the Alpha Centauri solar system in the Milky Way galaxy. One scientist came up with a diagram that was the most popular due to its simplicity, even though it was not as accurate as other diagrams. It showed an hourglass shape lying on its side, with a label for Earth on one side, the wormhole as the narrow center and Proxima B on the other side.

Proxima b was not inhabited by a sentient species. There was water and amoeba in the water, but nobody had claimed the planet due to an abnormally high concentration of nitrogen in the air and water. Several species from other galaxies had explored the planet for possible mining, but nothing had been created yet. There was a portal guardian station closer to the weakest of the three suns in the solar system. It would take about two hours to transverse from the Proxima portal to the guardian station. The second portal jump was longer than the first because the other side put them in the Andromeda Galaxy, which was about 2.5 million light-years from Earth.

A decision had been made to stop at the portal guardian station. The standard docking dimensions had been shared with Greg Moore's AstroX team, as he called the group that designed and built his spacecraft. This was a private company, fully funded by the Moore family, not sponsored by any government on earth, which was a highly controversial decision on earth.

Jax slowly guided the craft to the docking station and allowed the computers to take over for the final connection. The circular docking door had been outfitted with a ring of lights, showing red, yellow or green. The passengers watched as red changed to yellow to green. Greg stood up from his seat nearest the door and pressed a button. The doors slid open, similar to a sliding glass door on a house on earth. A few seconds later, a door to the space station opened. One human and one Veyltharian stood waiting to greet them.

End of preview for Unlimited Book 3.

AUTHORS NOTES FOR BOOK 2

Ever since childhood I wondered why we were taught Greek Mythology and why it was still in the curriculum when my children were growing up. During the writing of this book, I posted the question on LinkedIn to my colleagues around the world and discovered that Greek and Roman mythology is still taught in every European country and some Middle Eastern countries. So, I just had to invent a way to weave that into the story. Hope you enjoyed that part.

THE LIBRARY is real and can be found at http://libraryofbabel.info. It is incomplete as it does not have the article stitching algorithm that Greg Moore had to invent in this book, Unlimited Book 2. And even he admits after creating an imperfect version, there is no way to tell what the true version of the subject is you are searching for. Years ago, one journalist, Jerry Adler, said of the library, "It just may be the most fascinatingly worthless invention in history." In my opinion, it added to the mystery, suspense and excitement of this book. Go ahead and search for any phrase up to 3200 characters long on that site; it is mostly a 'Complete Waste of Time' (as Monty Python called its software released in 1994).

***

ACKNOWLEDGEMENTS:

Thanks again to my wife for allowing me time to write this book. She actually encouraged me more this time after reading the first book, saying she was anxious to read the next one. She listened enthusiastically as I would ramble on, usually during meals, and gave great feedback. She is my muse.

A special thanks goes to my seven siblings, their spouses and numerous children who were the first to read book one. Your feedback was instrumental in making this second book higher quality. I learned a lot from writing the first book. Hopefully, you will notice improvements in this book.

Celena and Samantha, the General Manager and front desk clerk at the hotel in Colorado Springs where my wife and I stay when we visit our grandchildren, thanks for taking good care of us. I told you that I would find a way to fit you into this book! I love the layout of your lobby with the numerous power plugs and USB connections. The energetic atmosphere at breakfast makes it easy to sit and write a few chapters.

***

Kevin Cox